The King's Letter

by
Tony Berry

First published in Great Britain by Silver Books 2000
(23 NN36JF)
ISBN 9780953961535
Printed by First Call Direct, Brixworth Northampton

Second Edition (revised) Published through Amazon and Silver Books Northampton 2020
ISBN 9780953961535

For Sheila

Prologue

Like a black cloak, the rooks rose from the crumbling tower of the derelict church. Disturbed they gave vent to their annoyance with shrill cries of complaint that echoed in the crisp December air. The young man looked at them without emotion, dismounted and stroked the muzzle of his nervous mare, whispering softly in her ear to keep her quiet.

His breath smoked white, the crystal drops mingling with hers and mirroring the frost of the hard earth. It was numbingly cold and most creatures were at home; that was why he had come today. He needed time for his search, and he must not be seen or disturbed. As sentries, the rooks had done their work. To those that understood, they had announced his presence, but on a day when the cold gripped the bone, no one, he thought, would be interested in discovering what had disturbed the chief inhabitants of this lonely place. Sharp senses and quick reflexes, he knew, would service him best here. He had neither his sword nor flintlock for defence. A small knife and a fast horse would have to suffice if matters went wrong. For two months he had evaded Parliament's troopers, and he retained the confidence of youth. He approached the roofless church cautiously, placing each foot where it made no noise. For reassurance he pressed the small, but heavy, gold pendant suspended under his jerkin. The twin was around his father's neck. It was a bond between them and they both felt that it brought them together and brought them luck. The frost echoed every sound, and he listened with great care as he slowly approached the pile of stones that had once been an entrance to the house of God. Despite the cold, he began to perspire, not from fear for himself, but from fear of what he might find.

He was more than a year late for this meeting, and yet he hoped his search would not be settled here. The man, the father he sought, had vanished; here was the spot where they were to have met eighteen months ago, after the battle had been won. But the battle had been lost, and father and son had gone their separate ways, fleeing for their lives. Perhaps his father had come here anyway: perhaps this was the start of a trail, and not its end. He could not shake off a feeling of foreboding as he surveyed the ruins.

It was over a hundred years since the church had been desecrated and closed. Tudor rule had not been a good time for those of the old faith. Over these years, slowly and gradually nature had reclaimed this spot for herself. The roof had long since collapsed, leaving some timber and slate to be seen amongst the rough grasses on the floor. Most of the walls were no higher than a man, and bushes and trees grew in the corners. Only the tower retained an entrance and provided shelter from the four winds. Grim-faced, he picked his way into the square of bare earth that was once the bottom room of the tower. There was no staircase, and only the sky for a roof. In each of the far corners lay heaps of rubble, mainly wood and stone, and one was covered with undergrowth and the bare branches of a hawthorn bush that bespoke the years of neglect and decay. He looked around him intently at the walls and the floor. A near corner held the black ashes of a fire, but they were not recent. He shivered in the cold.

"There is nothing here; there is no one here. "

He retraced his steps out of the tower and began searching for some sign, some clue, within the curtilage of the church. Something was at the back of his mind, there was a sign but he could not see it. A picture half-formed nagged at him. He could not grasp it. Wearily, he walked from the ruined church and began to explore the old graveyard that flanked its eastern side. It was a depressing place. Thick undergrowth shrouded those gravestones that were still standing and those that had fallen were covered with moss and lichen. The young man let his mind relax as his eyes wandered over the fallen gravestones. Some names he could, and with great difficulty, read - "James ...Alfred...Elizabeth...".He could see his own name, scraped clean free of the green mould covering.

Suddenly his mind snapped alert with an image of a pile of rubble, also free of moss and grass and shrubs.

"*Why so clean?*" he thought.

"*No long-standing growth!*" came back the answer.

He turned and ran back to the tower. Fear drew him with a mad urgency to the corner free from undergrowth, to tear at the stones and wood and dirt. His gloved hands raked the pile in frenzy. Suddenly, he found some scraps of cloth. Finally, with great care, he uncovered the mortal remains of Sir Roger Desborough, of Holcot in Northamptonshire.

He felt empty. For some time, he sat and looked at the body without moving. To have his worst fears confirmed in this way provided a cold certainty which left him without any will. His father was dead, and he could see he had died badly, for the remains of a noose were around the broken neck. The smell of death was strong, and the young man lurched to his feet, retching, as he staggered to the doorway of the tower. Gradually, he regained control of himself, and a savage wish for revenge entered his soul. He, Ralph Desborough, his father's heir - even if dispossessed by law - would find whoever had committed this act. Kneeling, he searched what remained of his father. He noted grimly that all the pockets of his jerkin and hose were empty. His rings and his neck chain were gone, as was his sword. Ralph knew he had a trail to follow, places to search - and a murderer to find.

But first he had a more pressing and urgent task to perform. Once more he searched the body and its surroundings, but there was no sign of that which his father had carried, that could also cost a life; a life that was, perhaps, even more important than his father's. For an hour he maintained his search until the failing December light made it impossible to see. He would return again tomorrow with friends and family to accord his father a decent burial and to continue the search. With one last look, he returned to his grazing mare and mounted, then turned away from the church and, under the darkening December sky, left his sad discovery behind him.

Chapter 1

Twenty troopers of horse in double line, headed by their officer, breasted the hill, and halted to rest their horses before descending the winding road that was the last two miles to the town of Northampton. Tired, hot and dusty, they yet made a brave show in the June sunshine, and amply demonstrated the power that had broken the King's line, and his heart, at the battle at Naseby nearly two years previously. Cavalrymen were the best-paid soldiers and the pick of the New Model Army; to a man, they carried themselves confidently in the saddle, with heads up and shoulders square. They rode lightly, for their swords, helmets and breastplates were stowed away in the wagon that followed behind. Only the officer rode fully dressed and armed, proud of his men, his rank and his army. Each man, however, wore the regulation two pistols in his belt for, although what was to be called the first English Civil War had ended and Charles the First was a prisoner, the countryside was still dangerous and travellers could still meet desperate Royalist groups, or unpaid Parliamentary mutineers who had quickly degenerated into gangs of cut-throats.

England was a sorry place in 1647, riven by five years of civil war, with commerce and industry disrupted, and mistrust and suspicion a fundamental means of avoiding trouble. The wounds of civil war had gone deep between communities and between individuals. One protagonist, the King, Charles Stuart, was a prisoner of Parliament in the great country house of Holdenby some five miles from Northampton. Although he was a prisoner, the restrictions placed upon the King were light and did not prevent him from corresponding with his "friends". He had lost the war, but still had cards to play, which could enable him to win the peace.

Already Parliament and the army were in bitter opposition. Parliament had tried to disband the army and send what was left to Ireland, ignoring all claims for back pay and reneging on responsibilities to army widows and orphans. The men who had won Parliament's war would not meekly submit to such treatment and in May 1647, "agitators" elected from the ranks were taking control of regiments and demanding redress for their grievances. Army commanders like Fairfax and Cromwell tried to mediate between the army and Parliament but the breach was too severe and now they were being pressed to choose their side, army or Parliament.

Although they made their brave sight on the Northampton road, every Trooper there knew well of the treachery of Parliament, the dissembling of the nearby King and the uncertainties of their commanders. They also knew that both Parliament and the Army Council were besieged with requests from war-weary communities for help in restoring stability and normality and that this troop was the response by the Army Council to the ancient borough of Northampton's request, for Parliament had not replied.

Trooper Ketch headed the right line of horsemen, which had the advantage that the only dust and dirt thrown up at him was from the Cornet's horse - and as Cornet Marlowe tended to break off from the troop to shepherd them along, and to talk to other travellers, such dust and dirt was bearable. The disadvantage of such a prominent position was that Ketch was at hand for the various tasks that officers required Troopers to perform: scouting ahead, moving people and objects blocking the road, and a thousand and one other duties. Ketch was a good Trooper, both effective and efficient at his job and Cornet Marlowe in the last three days had grown to rely on him, without fully realising it. Ketch found that he was usually trusted by his officers, but he was always careful not to court this. Cornet Marlowe, his new officer, was known to be a brave and honest man, strong for the army and a devout Christian. He was liked by his men and his brother officers, and much of this liking was because he kept his strongly held beliefs to himself.

A Cornet of Horse was the most junior officer rank in the new model army, but Cornet Marlowe was an experienced soldier. At twenty-five years of age he had enlisted as a Trooper at the very outbreak of war and had worked his way up through the ranks. He was the army's oldest Cornet, but also probably its most effective.

Although they had known each other for only a short time a mutual respect had grown up between Cornet Marlowe and Trooper Ketch. Riding comfortably side by side just an hour ago, their conversation had touched on affairs of the moment. Marlowe had leaned from his saddle and spoken softly.

"I know you are not an agitator, Ketch, even though you have got the education for it. Now we are hard by Charles Stuart, I do not want politicking. I want the men kept steady."

Ketch had nodded assent to the Cornet's words and there had been a long moment of silence before he replied.

"But the men described as agitators speak of matters that must be resolved, and I agree with many of their arguments, as does every man in this troop, most of the army and, I suspect, generals Fairfax and Cromwell themselves".

Again, there were a few moments of silence before Ketch picked up the threads of his thoughts.

"We all have our own conscience, Cornet, and, having humbled a King, no Parliament of self-seekers is going to give us an unworthy discharge that will leave us on the Poor Rate. It is the army that has delivered us from our civil strife and we should have as much a say on the future as those that sit in the Parliament."

Ketch's forthright reply had brought a long silence from Cornet Marlowe. He agreed with everything Ketch had said, but he wanted men who would obey orders, not argue the point each time. Yet he felt strangely comforted by Ketch's reply, and his confidence in the loyalty and good sense of at least this member of his troop had heartened him. He felt he could rely on Ketch and he knew that this ordinary Trooper was held in similar regard by the rest of the troop.

As the short rest period came to an end Marlowe cast his eye over the resting Troopers. Some remained on horseback, relaxed and at their ease, others had dismounted and were moving gently to stretch aching limbs, some were sitting on the grassy slopes and chatted or sat silent as the mood took them. He saw them as a collection of hard and dangerous men, but each was an individual.

"Not one saint," he mused,

"But plenty of sinners."

By now he knew the ones to watch - the idle, the mean, the thieves and the cheats; he also knew the better ones - the quiet, the pious, the family men. And then there was Ketch - able, clever, well educated sometimes frighteningly self-composed, and above all, his own man. The Cornet moved away from the Trooper who had been the end point of his musings and mingled amongst his men, chiding some and encouraging others. Ketch, in turn, faced to look down upon the destination of their journey, the town of Northampton.

The town lay before them in the shallow wide valley of the river Nene. It remained a compact medieval town, little changed since the time when Henry VI and his adversary, Warwick the Kingmaker, had shed blood beneath its walls. The roofs of the town were a sea of irregular yet pleasing dark shapes, but two massive military features, the walls and the castle dominated the homes of the citizenry. The great walls of Northampton, constructed by a succession of medieval monarchs, were high and wide enough to take six men in line abreast. The castle, the seat of Parliaments, the resting place of monarchs and Thomas a Beckett's prison, provided a fortress of military strength that had in all its history only been taken through treachery. Situated half way between Oxford and Cambridge, the town's pivotal position in the war with Charles Stuart had resulted in those walls being fully repaired and strengthened and the castle returned to its garrison role. Despite being but forty miles from the King's military headquarters, not once was it the subject of a siege. Throughout the war it had stood foursquare as a bastion that could not be taken - Parliament's rock in the very heart of England.

"Ketch!" said Cornet Marlowe, taking his Trooper from gazing,

"I want you to ride ahead of the troop to the Northampton Council House and inform both a Major Blake and the Council Clerk that we will be in Northampton within the hour. Then find our quarters, tell them we are coming, and await our arrival."

"Yes, Cornet!" replied Ketch, and, spurring his horse to the canter, he headed towards the South Bridge that led, as he well knew, to the Town Gate.

Ketch himself was twenty-five years old; a six-foot, broad-shouldered man who, like many Troopers, kept his nut-brown hair short. His slightly hooked nose was placed firmly between two dark brown eyes that emphasised his most distinctive feature - an inordinately pale face. Throughout his life Ketch had suffered an unsought prominence because of this face.

Schoolmasters, employers, officers and women picked him out for attention because of his drawn visage. Only five years a soldier, he had in that time acquired considerable experience of life, and he had learned quickly from his experiences. Learning came easily to Ketch, for he had been educated by his own father to become, in his turn, a schoolmaster and to take his place in the new school endowed by the mercers of Bedford. But, prepared for the schoolroom, Ketch had become a soldier.

This change of career had been precipitated by the death of both parents in the Plague of 1638. Disputes with authority had led to Ketch being forced to leave the school. He had, at first, gone to live with an elderly aunt in Huntingdon. But for a young man of seventeen, Huntingdon and an elderly aunt were insufficient excitement, and within six months he had borrowed twenty pounds from her to fund his wish to see something more of the world. The twenty pounds had not lasted long, but he had travelled for four years, mainly in the Lowlands, but also in France and Germany. Returning to Huntingdon in the summer of 1642, he discovered that his aunt had died four months previously. Without legacy and penniless, he had been easily recruited by the Deputy Sheriff of Cambridgeshire into Lord Manchester's Regiment in the service of Parliament against the wayward King Ketch savoured the moments of freedom that the

Cornet's orders offered and he gently eased his horse to walk down the wide path that sloped towards the town of Northampton some half mile away. He knew the town well and was looking forward to a pleasant stay in what had been a staunch stronghold for Parliament. The people he had always found hospitable and, as the town had remained unstormed throughout the troubles, he relished the prospect of something approaching the normality of life that existed before King and Parliament had fallen out. Ketch pondered why his troop was going to Northampton. In the midst of considerable turmoil, when half the army were preparing to storm London and some regiments were refusing to obey orders, this small troop had been detailed under Cornet Marlowe to ride to Northampton. In a way, Ketch was relieved to be part of such a commission. He had not enjoyed the break up of regimental discipline, even though the men's demands were just. He preferred action and the certainty of a job to do.

The bright sun of a June afternoon, the drowsy colours of the oaks that flanked the path all engendered a feeling of considerable well-being in Ketch as he set out to perform his Cornet's orders. He reined his horse to a halt and for a moment gazed solemnly at one of the distinctive sights of Northampton. Before him was the memorial cross. It had been decreed for Eleanor of Castile by Edward I, one of a series of monuments erected wherever her coffin rested overnight on the funeral cortege's journey to London. Base, plinth, alcoves, statues and the cross itself were of a grey, hard stone, quite unlike the warm brown stone of Northamptonshire. Ketch mused on life and death, and on the balance and harmony of medieval construction. The width of the memorial was one-third its height; there were three faces on the memorial, with three small statues, and three-times-three steps led up to it. Wherever possible, height and depth were proportions of each other to the power of three, the Trinity.

Ketch reflected that such medieval harmony was not a characteristic of England in 1647. Like thousands of his honest countrymen he felt the route to a fair and lasting peace was unclear. The King could not be trusted; Parliament itself was divided between Presbyterians and Independents and had turned viciously against the army. Like many in the army's regiments, he had discussed the new political ideas. Although he was not an "agitator" he was attracted by the ideas of toleration and a people's government. The many serious and godly Troopers who had called for a new commonwealth based on justice and equality had moved Ketch. Whilst some had shown the impatient certainty of the fanatic, many others had a quiet tolerance towards those that opposed their views. Such tolerance commanded a greater respect in the men that heard them. Only the army seemed to enjoy a strong element of men who were genuinely for the nation and not for interest. "*It might be time for the army to manage affairs*" he thought to himself.

Ketch's reflections ended as he turned his horse away from the memorial and continued his journey down the hill towards the South Bridge, the one Southern entrance into the town of Northampton. The bridge spanned the slow-moving River Nene and led directly to a gatehouse. During the day travellers passed unhindered into and out of the town, but at night the great gates of the arch were closed and the entrance manned by a night watchman. Being mid-afternoon, Ketch crossed the bridge without hindrance. He clattered through the gatehouse, his horse's hooves echoing on the cobblestones. For a moment, he reined in his horse and sat forward in the saddle as he appraised the town.

Ketch was no stranger to Northampton for, as a boy, he had lived in Bedford, a distance of some seventeen miles away, and on two or three occasions he had visited the town in the company of his father. He much admired the town that proudly wore its medieval past; in particular, he enjoyed the old castle, brooding over the town, its high stone walls holding its secrets. Clustered around and below the castle, the medieval and Tudor houses complemented each other, and a bold street pattern seemed to draw both residents and visitors to the Market Square, the largest in England. Just beyond the town gate and leading up to the Market Square was Bridge Street, a hill some two hundred yards long flanked by multifarious houses but also a few shops; bakers, butchers, drapers and cobblers. Trade for these was clearly slow, as there were few customers in the street and a number of owners were at their shop fronts taking the air and chattering with their neighbours.

Ketch, wishing to assure himself of his destination, stopped his horse outside a shop fronted by trestle tables and benches with above them a large boot hanging in a frame like an inn sign. A stout, ruddy faced man dressed in plain jerkin and hose and wearing a leather apron was sitting at a table working an awl into leather.

"Good day to you, cobbler" said Ketch.

"Is the Council House where it always was? Can you direct me to it?"

"I can, and what is more, I will" said the cobbler, putting down his work and rising to his feet slowly and with deliberation.

"Have you come far?" he asked in return as he wiped his hands on the large leather apron that covered his ample girth. Ketch realised that the habits of barter were deeply ingrained and that, if he wanted information, he would have to trade some in return.

"Today from Woburn, before that I cannot tell; but I'm followed hard by a Cornet and Troopers."

It was not Ketch's habit to give out any military information, but he knew that soon enough this news would be commonplace.

"Now then" he continued, "Where is your Council House?"

"Top of the hill, and turn to the right by the church of All Saints," said the cobbler, "and it's facing you".

Before Ketch could ride on the cobbler was able to get in yet another question.

"You would not be from the Northampton garrison, then - you are not part of Colonel Fell's regiment?"

"No," replied Ketch, "Cornet Marlowe is my officer".

At this news a broad smile covered the cobbler's face. "Well!" he said. "That's fine news! How many are you?"

Ketch was not to be drawn into answering any more questions. He gave the cobbler a salute of thanks and spurred his horse to the top of the hill. Here he faced two of the most attractive buildings in Central England; in front of him was the town church of All Saints, a beautiful structure that, despite the attention of the local iconoclasts, retained a dignity and grace born of the symmetry and line of its construction. Beyond the church was the council house, the largest structure in the town, apart from the castle. It was built of local Northamptonshire stone and sported many an interesting gable and turret. It was the focal point for civic affairs, for not only was it the meeting place for the Common Council, but justices of the peace and exchequer agents were frequently to be found conducting their affairs within its rooms. The two buildings provided a civic counterpoint that challenged the military dominance of the castle.

Ketch dismounted at the Council House and secured his mount to one of the metal rings set into a water trough by the side of the building. Before entering the council house, he enjoyed a moment to stretch his muscles and to look about him. The area in front of him was some sixty yards square and now he could see the rear elevation of the church, with its large windows and graceful tower surmounted by a gilded cross. To his right was Northampton's commercial centre and the source of prosperity, the market square. It contained the largest alehouse in the county, the Peacock Inn, and a place often alive with activity. Today its wide space looked somewhat empty, although there were a number of stalls set out, and a growing crowd of citizens looking to do business. Although not a market day a number of stallholders still thought it worth their while to cry out the value of their wares. Both buying and selling seemed to be actively pursued by town and country people. To Ketch, it seemed that little had changed since he had come to Northampton as a boy.

He turned and entered the council house through the large wooden double doors that were left open during the day, and found himself in a small antechamber. Seated at a desk, writing carefully and deliberately, was an elderly, white-haired man of some sixty years, wearing the plain black of a clerk.

"Good day to you, Sir," said Ketch.

"I ride ahead of Cornet Marlowe and twenty troopers, and I seek a Major Blake and your Council Clerk. Can you direct me to them?"

"The Clerk you have found," replied the scribe, placing his pen with care in its holder.

"James Hedlow is my name, and Major Blake has an appointment to see me at this very hour. You are most welcome with your news; both the Council and the town have been waiting."

Ketch was surprised at the Clerk's enthusiasm for a troop of Ironsides, but he continued.

"My orders are to inform you of the troop's imminent arrival and of our need for lodgings."

The Clerk's face broke into a smile.

"All is ready," he said.

"The Town Council has prepared and paid for your lodgings.

"Sit!" he said, gesturing Ketch to a chair, "and await the arrival of Major Blake."

He rang a small bell and, to the young man who appeared at this summons, he said,

"Tell Botterill of the Peacock Inn that the Troopers are here."

Ketch found all this baffling.

"A troop of the New Model Army is to have its lodgings paid for, and these lodgings are to be at an inn in the centre of town."

In his time, Ketch had forcibly impounded lodgings, paid for lodgings himself, or had them paid for by his officer; never before had he been quartered in an inn, for townsfolk usually preferred soldiers to be out of town, away from taverns - and well away from their wives and daughters.

"I see all this finds favour with you" said Hedlow.

Ketch was momentarily annoyed that his pleasure had been so obvious.

"It is a little unusual, Sir," he said.

Before he could say more, through the same inner door as had been used by the servant came a tall dark-haired man, clean-shaven and dressed in the uniform of a cavalry officer with a short sword at his waist. About thirty years of age, his hair was short, in the Puritan fashion. His face was handsome and had an openness about it that engendered trust. The sword, however, betrayed his profession.

"Major Blake!" said Hedlow, and Ketch leaped to his feet.

Major Blake greeted Hedlow with a handshake, and turned to Ketch. "Report, Trooper," he said, in a low, quiet voice that impelled an answer.

"Cornet Marlowe and twenty horse are within sight of the town, Major, and Master Hedlow has us billeted at the Peacock Inn, the place of Master Botterill."

Hedlow nodded approvingly at Ketch's fluent, and accurate, account. Major Blake, however, chuckled.

"Hedlow, when did a town council last pay for troopers to be billeted in an inn?"

Hedlow did not answer, but turned to Ketch:

"Inform Cornet Marlowe of lodgings provided and ask him to wait on us and the Common Council this evening at six."

Ketch turned to go.

"Hold, one moment" said Major Blake.

"What is your name, Trooper, and what regiment?"

"Ketch, Sir, of Colonel Butler's Regiment."

Major Blake nodded and, there being no sign of further conversation, Ketch turned and walked outside into the mellow heat of a late summer's afternoon.

The square facing the Council House was now rather busier with the noise and clatter of people going about their business. A cluster of men was debating matters of commerce; there were one or two groups of women gossiping, some of them with young children in their arms or dragging at their hands. A large dray was being loaded with barrels, and two dogs were barking at the men struggling to finish their task. Carts were being trundled through the square by hand and by horse. Northampton, thought Ketch, was a lively, bustling commercial centre; but amongst all this bustle and normality, Ketch could sense something else, an uncertainty, a lack of ease, almost a fear. It was an atmosphere not unknown to Ketch. He had met it many times before. It was the feel of a township living under an uninvited and unwelcome military rule. He sensed it in the lowered voices of the women and the troubled faces of the men. Somewhere close by were soldiers who were to be feared because of their power and arbitrary violence. Ketch wondered about this Colonel Fell, whose regiment clearly made its mark on the town. "But," he sighed to himself, "there had been many such Colonel Fells throughout the civil war, men who could terrorise a whole community, and no doubt there would be many others in the future."

As Ketch moved to remount his horse he noticed in the far corner of the square, up against the fine old church, that a group of some dozen men and women were clustering around a tall, gaunt figure wearing a full-length black coat with a dark waistcoat and breeches. The grubby whiteness of his collar clearly stood out as the only lightness about him. He was a man of some thirty years, generally unkempt, and with lank black hair. But there was passion in his face as, with eyes raised upward to the sky, he clutched a bible in both hands.

Before he spoke a word, Ketch guessed that this was an itinerant preacher. Many such "Independents" were to be found in the Midland towns. Fierce in religious conviction and radical in political view, they often wandered from town to town preaching their fiery gospel to anyone who would listen to them. Generally, city fathers tried to move them on, for wherever they settled they tended to foment trouble and community dissension. Ketch could just hear his opening words. In a quiet and deliberate voice, the preacher warned –

"Brothers and sisters, people of Northampton, the Devil is amongst us. The Devil is amongst us - look to your souls, pray hard for salvation, come pray with me now!"

He repeated his words, this time a little louder, and then once again, but in a stronger voice, and more urgently, and the crowd joined in on the "Amen!"

Once more he cried out, and the "Amen!" came back loud and strong from his audience. Now speaker and audience were becoming one, and he told them of the Devil's grasp, and the loss of God's glory. His audience was now swollen in number as people came to see what was happening. The preacher's voice rose and fell in a rhythmic cadence that held his audience in thrall. Their eyes never left his face, and his every gesture of hand and arm brought forth a responding movement from them.

"God's strength must be used to purge sin and to destroy the idolatry and fornication that is all around us!" He cried.

Ketch was always surprised at how easily honest; straightforward citizens could be turned into an unthinking mob. Men and women who spent their daily lives in raising families and dealing straight with their neighbours could, in a matter of minutes, be incited to the point where they would attack those selfsame neighbours both verbally and physically. Now, before his eyes, such a transformation was happening.

Just as the preacher hit the peak of his emotional address, a prettily dressed young girl, escorted by two young men, turned into the Square. Talking animatedly, they were oblivious to anyone but themselves, and the laughter in their voices bounced around the Square. She was a comely girl, happily enjoying the flirtation and the attention of her escorts.

Ketch, from his vantage point, could foresee the inevitable clash between puritan fervour and the energy and life of youth. He had himself, suffered the excesses of the former, and still enjoyed the latter, so it was with concern - especially for the girl - that he observed events.

"There is Jezebel!" cried the preacher.

"The Scarlet Whore of Babylon, flaunting the Devil's works before us!"

He pointed his finger accusingly at the young group, and his audience turned with him. Their eyes glittered with a hardness that horrified, as they identified scapegoats.

"Take them! Cast them out and cleanse this town!" urged the preacher.

First a few men and then the crowd as a whole responded with a rush that was a release of pent-up emotion, and surged towards its victims. The three young people stopped in their tracks, only now aware of their peril. The two young men, both white-faced and searching for their courage, stood protectively in front of the girl.

Ketch's concern grew. This sort of confrontation was not unusual. Fiery public preachers often accused passers-by of sin; it was part of their repertoire. Up and down the country, he had witnessed similar scenes, but nowhere had he felt such venom in the speaker's words, or seen such relish in a crowd for a victim. Hungry to hurt someone, the crowd surged towards the small group. Elsewhere, Ketch had seen young men toss back the speaker's words, and stand up for themselves, defying their accusers with the strength and vitality of youth. But here, the young men were silent, and the girl cowered behind them, as if admitting her sin.

The mob, now apparently confident of willing victims, surrounded the three figures, engulfing them. Blows rained upon them; the young men raised their arms over their heads, and the girl fell at their feet. The preacher continued to urge the crowd on and, devoid of humanity and exultant in their power, they beat the young men to the ground. Ketch expected this to end matters but, from within the crowd, staves appeared, and their wielder approached the three figures prone on the ground Blood was now flowing from the young girl's head, and Ketch could see that murder was about to be done. A figure touched Ketch on the arm. It was the uniformed Major.

"Come on, man!" he said, "Help me!"

He plunged into the crowd, snatching a stave from a large, burly fellow and dealing him a blow on the head. After but a moment's hesitation, Ketch leapt after the Major, laying about him with arms and fists and feet. The mob did not welcome this intrusion and the attempt to frustrate them, but they would not be pushed back and they did not withdraw. Urged on by the cries of the preacher, now on his knees in exaltation, the mob subjected the two interlopers to a hail of blows about the head and shoulders. Whilst defending themselves and giving stout blows in return, Ketch and Major Blake could only hope to protect the young people by standing over them.

Ketch felt the Major fall against him, and heard his gasp of pain. Then Ketch saw the flash of a knife; forgetting all other blows, he concentrated on following the knife that was stabbing at him. He had to find the hand, and grasp it tight - for he was now in mortal danger.

Incredibly, suddenly the knife disappeared, the rain of blows stopped and the press of the mob eased. A thrown stave dusted Ketch's shoulders, but the Major was able to regain his balance and stand firmly beside him. Their assailants began to edge away and become recognisable as individuals again. Then Ketch heard the clatter of hooves and, spinning round, he saw the troop headed by Cornet Marlowe, in line abreast, walking their horses towards the crowd. Two of the horses reared up; the Troopers knew how to control civilians with their horses, and were using their skills of horsemanship to clear the mob from its intended victims.

"Ketch!" barked Cornet Marlowe, sitting firmly astride his chestnut mare.

"What riot is this? Report, man!"

Before Ketch could say a single word in reply to his officer's command, the preacher, elbowing his way through his own religious troops, strode forward to confront Cornet Marlowe.

"Does the army now support sin?" he asked.

"The cleansing of God's people can not be stopped by sword and iron; repent your folly before you, too, face the wrath of God."

The preacher pointed an arm towards heaven and with the other thrust one of his bibles up towards the quiet, sitting figure.

"You take upon yourself the sin of those you protect."

Marlowe kicked his heels and his horse edged forward towards the preacher. The preacher stumbled back in alarm and, keeping up his arm to protect himself, fell with a thud to the ground. He quickly sat upright but religious fervour was difficult to sustain when looking ridiculous. Cornet Marlowe's face darkened. He was himself a religious man, regular in re-dedicating himself to God, but he was also a soldier, and knew both a mob and a rabble-rouser when he saw them.

"The Lord God does not welcome murder, preacher" he said,

"And the army protects all subjects and keeps the peace. Get ye gone, and be gentler in your speech, or my Troopers will have the last word with you. Among those you are so happy to batter is one of their comrades."

Raising his voice to direct the crowd to move and go home, he motioned his Troopers to clear the square. Faced with resolution and mounted men, the crowd fled from the square leaving hats, staves, barrows and bags. The preacher, surrounded by his immediate acolytes, threw a glare of pure hatred at Marlowe, and shook his fist at Ketch and the Major, but said no more, and stumbled from the square.

Cornet Marlowe sat on his horse, his eyes shepherding the preacher away. When he was gone, he turned abruptly to Ketch.

"Well, Ketch. Report." said Cornet Marlowe.

But, again, before Ketch could say a word, Major Blake stepped forward, nursing a bruised shoulder and with a thin trickle of blood running from his scalp.

"Cornet Marlowe" he said,

"My name is Major Blake, of my Lord Essex's regiment, on special duties for the Army Council. Your Trooper has been in support of my actions and was acting on my orders to prevent, as you have rightly said, civil disorder and possible murder."

Cornet Marlowe instinctively stiffened in his saddle in the presence of a senior officer.

"Major Blake, Sir!" he said. "My orders are to report to you and the Clerk of Common Council and place myself and my men fully at your disposal."

Turning and looking carefully at Ketch, he continued. "I am pleased that one of my men has been able to make himself immediately useful to you."

"And stoutly so," said Major Blake, and with a rueful smile he looked about him.

"But for his support, I doubt that I could have held out in time for you and your men; so, he has my thanks. Here is my hand, Trooper Ketch. You are a credit to your troop."

Cornet Marlowe struggled with his feeling of gratification that one of his men had performed well, mixed with a concern at the open and free way that a Major was shaking hands with a Trooper. Ketch shook the proffered hand, saluted the Major, and then turned at attention to Cornet Marlowe.

"Trooper Ketch reporting, Sir! Mr Hedlow, Clerk to the Council, has arranged lodgings for you and the troop at the Peacock Inn, and requests that you join him and Major Blake in the Council House to meet members of the Common Council at six-o-clock."

The delivery of this formal report re-established military positions, and Cornet Marlowe was able to reply with good heart.

"Thank you, Ketch. Retrieve your horse and take the Troopers to their lodgings. I shall speak further with Major Blake, and look for a more detailed account from you later."

Having dealt with his troops, the Cornet turned to the Major.

"If that has your approval, Sir, I would welcome some further words with you."

"Of course, Cornet" said Major Blake. "Come and meet Clerk Hedlow. We have much to discuss with you."

In the square, the two young men had risen shakily to their feet and were attending to the girl. Major Blake turned and exclaimed,

"I am forgetting that this young lady and her companions are grievously hurt. Perhaps, Marlowe, you will help me to assist them to the Council House, and Clerk Hedlow can send for the apothecary."

"Thank you, Sir" said the elder of the youths.

"May name is John Capstick, and this is my brother James. We are cousins to this lady, Mary Desborough."

The aforesaid young lady was lying in James Capstick's arms. Her low moans spoke of hurt, but also of life.

"Carry her carefully!" ordered Major Blake.

All was done as the Major ordered, and Mary Desborough and her two cousins were tended in the Council House. Fortunately, no bones were broken, but shock and exhaustion had taken a powerful toll of all three. As the apothecary performed his tasks,

Cornet Marlowe requested quietly of the Clerk if he knew them.

"Oh, yes" replied Hedlow. "The girl is a pretty young thing, no more than eighteen years. She is the daughter of the late Sir Roger Desborough, killed at Naseby, but whose body was recovered only some months ago. All his estates, of course, were sequestered by Parliament, and she lives with her sister in a small house in Northampton, property of her mother's family. It is the Capstick family that took the women in. They have an estate at Ecton, some five miles from Northampton, and they also own other properties in Northampton and Bedford. John and James vie for her favours, and either would be a splendid match for her. They frequently come to town to see her. There is another sister" continued Hedlow.

"Martha Desborough, some three years older; but she is the quiet, plain member of the family." Hedlow sighed.

"There is also a brother - Roger Desborough. But, like his father, a cavalier, and supporter of the King. He is known to be in France - "

His speech was interrupted by the arrival of Martha Desborough at the Council House. Where her sister Mary was young, comely and with golden curls, Martha Desborough was a tall gaunt woman with prematurely greying hair and a face that was lined and weary. Dressed in dark clothes, her appearance and her manner proclaimed to the world the unhappiness of her life. Her arrival provided the room with the hint of lavender associated with the elder spinster.

Sending John and James Capstick on their way home to Ecton, she scolded them for endangering their cousin. But her actions belied her harsh words, for she saw that each of them had been properly tended, and gently examined their limbs and heads. Only when satisfied that any injury was minor did her tongue have a bite.

"Back to your father, and tell him your tale. No doubt he will beat you himself for the problems you have caused."

Although she was but two or three years their senior, the Capsticks meekly took their verbal medicine. Chastened and still mixing apologies and farewells, they left for home

Martha turned to her sister,

"I will take her home now" she informed the company.

"Not yet, and not without an escort" said Major Blake.

"Let her rest for a few moments more."

Whilst this tending of Mary Desborough was taking place in the Council Room, Ketch had assembled the troop and, with each man walking his horse, he led them the hundred yards along the square to the Peacock Inn. Botterill, the innkeeper, was waiting for them.

"Welcome to the Peacock Inn" he addressed Ketch.

"I have stables for your horses, with lofts above for the Troopers; and you shall all take food in turns in the kitchens."

A stable lad was given the task of looking after them. Having been led to the yard at the back and shown their quarters, the troop duly sorted itself out into a comfortable billet. Soldiers everywhere do not find it difficult to make themselves comfortable and such was the case with these "Ironsides." All experienced veterans, they soon had a fire going and, horses duly tended, they relaxed in the stable yard, boots off and jackets and shirts loosened.

The Peacock Inn was a rambling old wooden building, two storeys high at the front. The yard at the rear was surrounded on three sides by stables and barns, which, in turn led on to other low buildings. Flanking the main building were the kitchens with their larders, storehouses and cellars. Ketch found himself a snug part of the loft above the main stables and, ensuring that it was free from draughts, he set about making himself comfortable. He had just finished arranging a straw bed when Troopers Tull and Holditch clattered up the ladder into the loft.

Tull and Holditch as troopers formed a complementary pair, and had both attached themselves to Ketch. Like him, they had signed up in Cambridge into Lord Manchester's regiment in 1642 and had grown into professional soldiers. Many were the times that Tull had pulled Holditch out of a difficult scrape, which service Holditch had often reciprocated. The two had stuck together through five difficult years. They had been separated from Ketch when the Model Army was established, but they had been reunited long before this Northampton duty.

Soldiering was a dangerous business and the three had formed a deep friendship born of mutual self help and sticking together. Everyone in their regiment knew that if you took on one you took on all three. Many a skirmish with friend or foe they had survived because they were three rather than one.

"What happened to you in the square?" asked Tull.

He was tall and dark and thin and spoke with the burr of the West Country, where he had spent his childhood. Tull was some forty years old and was a taciturn man who kept himself to himself. He had once been a family man, but had lost his wife and three children when a town fire had destroyed a large part of Bridgewater some months after Naseby. Like the many others that had suffered a similar loss, Tull had found some basis for life, but he now lived it in a day to day fashion, neither mentioning the past nor caring about the future. Ketch and Holditch were his only companions; everyone else, whether man or woman, he treated politely but avoided any real social contact. Tull was also quietly prone to religion in the way of many an Ironside, not broadcasting a certain faith but struggling deep inside to find one. Tull was a reliable soldier and a firm and honest friend and when he did speak, Ketch always listened.

"An officer decides to rescue a young lady from a puritan mob; and, of course, he requires a Trooper to help him." replied Ketch.

There was a slight lilt in his voice on saying this, for Ketch knew that officers were not favourites of either of his two friends.

"Typical," grunted Holditch, shorter and bulkier than his companion, with a round, almost chubby face.

"They play the gallant, and it's ordinary Troopers who end up doing the job."

Sometimes in life opposites attract and such was the case with Tull and Holditch. Where Tull was slow, quiet and taciturn, Holditch was all energy and ebullience. Constantly chattering, Holditch, was a continuing source of humour and good cheer. Liked by almost everyone, nevertheless his banter and open-handed manner had often drawn him into confrontations, which had required supportive interventions from Ketch and Tull. His rare, but inevitably enthusiastic, involvement with women had from time to time caused them all unnecessary trouble. There was, in addition, one other talent that made Holditch a vital part of the three. He was a born merchant. The skills of buying and selling at a profit came to him quite naturally. For Holditch any collection of people constituted a market in which he could exercise such skills, and it was in no small measure thanks to him that the three Troopers had all their military equipment intact and had rarely gone cold or hungry through lack of food or clothing. Holditch's foraging around the regiments had sustained them.

Before hearing any of the details of Ketch's tale, Holditch, with Tull occasionally nodding in agreement, treated Ketch to a diatribe he had heard many times before on the iniquities of ranking officers; their effete life-styles, the purity of the common soldier, and his sterling honesty. What always amused Ketch was that Tull and Holditch were the most loyal of Troopers, always obeyed orders, and were always in the thick of action; in fact, in their daily lives, they did everything to support the authority of officers. Eventually their muttering subsided, and Ketch was able to give his companions an outline of events.

"Who is this Major Blake?" asked Tull.

"And what is he doing here in Northampton on his own?"

"Spying" said Holditch.

"That's what it will be, and something to do with us being here, I shouldn't wonder."

"Why are we here, Ketch?" asked the tall West Countryman.

"I don't know" Ketch replied.

"But I fancy you are right about Major Blake. He is a quiet man-of-action who keeps himself to himself; and he must have a good reason for being here in Northampton."

Tull went off to reconnoitre the kitchens whilst Holditch brought their gear into the loft. As he clambered up and down the rickety ladder carrying leather bags, saddles and tack, he chattered away to Ketch.

"That was a real dustup Ketcjh. Something to do with that face of yours, no doubt! You should wear a sack, Ketch; protect the public and stop Troopers having to rescue you."

His somewhat portly frame quivered with amusement at his own good humour.

"I thought Cornet Marlowe was going to have a fit when he saw it was you at the bottom of that pile. And when that preacher started spouting religion - well, I'm not surprised he nudged him with his horse. He's a preacher himself, the Cornet. Of course, it might have been some sort of professional jealousy."

Ketch smiled as his companion chattered and fussed.

"Holditch" he said,

"You are getting matronly in your ways."

Dodging the bag hurled at him, Ketch settled down for a quiet nap. He wondered for the hundredth time why they were in Northampton and what special task had been given to Cornet Marlowe; and now, how far was the mysterious Major Blake involved?

It seemed no time at all before Ketch found himself rudely woken "Message from Cornet Marlowe: Ketch and small party to escort ladies to their home'" exclaimed an excited Hilditch.

"Holditch has volunteered to help you in this task," said Tull, "and I doubt whether much good will come of it."

Before Holditch could respond, Ketch intervened.

"Very well. To secure a straightforward task, you will both come with me - but I want no nonsense from you, Holditch. I am tired. I have had a full day's ride and a dusting in the street; I have no energy for your excesses."

Ketch and his comrades walked the short distance from the Peacock Inn to the Council House to obtain more detailed orders. Entering through the double doors into the Council ante-chamber, Ketch saw Major Blake in quiet conversation with Cornet Marlowe, whilst Clerk Hedlow kept his eyes discreetly lowered to his desk as the apothecary tended the wounds of the girl from the square. Kneeling beside her was an older woman, whom Ketch guessed to be her sister.

Major Blake left it to Cornet Marlowe to issue Ketch and the others with their orders.

"Ketch, this lady, the one you protected in the square, is Mistress Mary Desborough, who was cruelly the victim of violence this day, and her sister, Mistress Martha. The apothecary says that Mary may walk home slowly and carefully, and that Mistress Martha may look after her. Fortunately, her wounds are slight, thanks to the intervention of yourself and Major Blake. They live by St Sepulchre's Church in the northern part of town; make certain they are returned there safely."

Looking carefully at Tull and Holditch, Cornet Marlowe added "and return immediately to your lodgings. I want no gallantry or offers to assist these ladies once they are safely home!"

After thanking all those present for their assistance, a pale-faced Martha put an arm around the still-trembling Mary, and turned to go. The three Troopers fell into position and, with respectful courtesy, escorted them from the Council House.

Ketch, occasionally directed by Martha, led the party through the streets of Northampton. Tull remained silent, but Holditch's chattering had its effect and, by the time they had reached the front door of the Desborough home, Mary had regained a little of her youthful verve, and Martha had smiled, briefly. Even as they thanked Ketch, he sensed a tension in Martha and an apprehension as she opened the door and ushered Mary rapidly into the small house.

"Right!" said Ketch, "Straight back to lodgings."

And the three Troopers set off at a smart pace back towards the Peacock Inn and the Market Square, enjoying the sound of their marching feet on the cobbled streets. However, Ketch could not keep from his mind the atmosphere that brooded over Northampton, making it an unhappy, even fearful, place. His thoughts were quickly snapped back to reality as a Trooper, in disarray and riding bareback, hurtled towards them.

"Ketch! Thank God I've found you! There has been an accident. It's Cornet Marlowe!

Chapter 2

Ketch slewed his mount, borrowed from the messenger, into the yard of the Inn. He slid to the ground, threw the reins to a lad, and pushed his way through the crowd milling about the doorway. Inside the large public room, he found a swarm of people around the prone figure of Cornet Marlowe. Botterill, the innkeeper, looked flustered and flapped his hands in distress.

"Oh, my! Oh, dear Heaven! What a terrible accident!" he wailed.

"We will look after you for as long as you like."

These last words were addressed to Cornet Marlowe, whose face was set and hard. He was obviously in pain. The same apothecary who had earlier attended Mary Desborough was engaged in setting a broken leg.

Major Blake was kneeling next to the Cornet, who gripped hard on his arm.

"Gently, gently!" hissed Blake to the healer.

"This man is important to the army."

The apothecary rose to his feet.

"I have done all I can." he said.

"Rest and nature must now do their work."

Looking hard at Marlowe, he added,

"You must lie still for at least five weeks. Do this, and you will ride and walk and run as now. Ignore my words and your leg will forever hinder you, and it will finish your army life."

Cornet Marlowe was a Christian, a very strong religious man, but he could not help himself.

"God damn me!" he swore. "Five weeks! By God, Blake, I'm no good to you now. An invalid kept to his bed cannot do your work."

In his exasperation, he moved his leg, and his head jerked back in pain.

"Steady now, Marlowe." soothed Blake.

"Your men will still do what you say, whether your orders are given from your bed or not. It's not your legs I want, it's your brain - and your men."

Turning to Botterill, he ordered.

"Put this officer in your best room and mind him well. I shall visit him personally every day to see that all is goes well with him."

The normally open, kind face presented to the world by Major Richard Blake was set firm, and his eyes warned that his will would be done.

"Apothecary, I thank you for your work. All will be as you advise; we will keep him still."

Courteously, he showed the apothecary to the door.

Major Blake, seeing Ketch, beckoned him over.

"Dismiss those Troopers, and come with me."

He led Ketch into a side room where Botterill and two servants were gently lowering a now pale-faced Cornet Marlowe onto a large bed." "Everyone is to leave" ordered Major Blake.

Then lowering his voice, "Ketch, stay,

"We must have a council of war."

"I am sorry to put this to you now, Marlowe" went on the Major.

The three of them were now alone.

"You need rest and peace, but I can not wait. You were to see the Common Council this evening, and now you are not able. Pointing his finger at Ketch, he continued.

"Is this man as good as he appears? Can he be trusted? Has he his wits?"

Marlowe turned on his bed desperately trying to find a position that would ease the pain.

"Ketch is a good soldier," he said.

"But they all are in Colonel Butler's regiment."

" Yes, yes" said Blake, just a little testily.

"He will have to do."

"No" said Marlowe.

"No, I am wrong. Ketch is loyal, brave," he paused, and deep. He will suit your purposes, whatever they are, very well."

"Good" said Major Blake.

"Both of you must listen carefully to what I have to say."

Turning to Marlowe, he continued.

"Your troop from Colonel Butler's regiment has been sent to Northampton with the public purpose of supporting the Common Council in its wish to bring peace, normality and order to the town. I say 'public purpose', because that is what the Common Council thinks, and why it is paying for twenty troopers to be at the Peacock Inn. There is, however, a more private reason why you are here; one, which led me to suggest to the Army Council that it, is in its interest to accede to the Northampton request. There are, after all, many councils and many towns seeking such help from Parliament. But I am in Northampton on a purpose where I need troopers as well."

"So, Ketch" he continued,

"If Marlowe agrees, yours will be the hand whereby he controls his troop, and you will appear with me before the Council. You will be the instrument of meeting the Council's demands, and the means of supporting my mission for the army".

"My orders" interrupted Cornet Marlowe,

"Were to report to both you and the Council. Now you are saying that your orders are paramount, and those of the Council immaterial! Well, whilst you are a senior officer, my own direct orders can not so easily be over-ruled".

"You are, of course, right" said Major Blake, and he took from within his coat a small letter with a red seal, which Ketch could see was broken. "Read this, Marlowe," said Blake.

"Observe the signature of the Secretary to the Army Council and that of General Cromwell".

Cornet Marlowe read the letter carefully and returned it to Major Blake.

"Ketch! Follow Major Blake's orders as if he were Cromwell himself" Then with a groan, he relaxed and lay limp on the bed.

"Come, Ketch," said Major Blake.

"This Cornet needs rest, and we tire him. Sleep well, my friend," he added, placing his hand briefly on Marlowe's shoulder. Then, quietly, he and Ketch left the room.

With only a brief detour to give Botterill clear instructions on the care of the Cornet, Major Blake led Ketch across the courtyard to the troop's main billet.

"I had better speak to your men Ketch", he said.

Ketch hastily mustered the troopers in the courtyard of the Peacock Inn where Major Blake explained that, although Cornet Marlowe was confined to his bed, he was still their officer and in command. All his future orders, however, would now be passed through Trooper Ketch, who would be given the temporary rank of Corporal. He, Major Blake, would not be available for anything other than advice, as he had other duties to perform. Whilst it was clear that this was a considerable surprise to the troopers, it came as no shock to Ketch. He had half suspected that Major Blake would not take over the troop and, in his heart, he was resigned to having the responsibility thrust upon him, so there was no surprise in Ketch's pale face at the announcement, and he was both internally and externally calm before the troop.

Having delivered his instructions, Major Blake dismissed the Troopers and, turning to the new Corporal, added.

"Ketch, I shall need some time with you before we meet the Common Council. See that these Troopers stay here and do not wander. I want them fully set and ready for my order, at any time. We meet the Council at six; come to my rooms in Abington Street at five, and be on time!"

Ketch escorted his officer out of the yard and turned to meet nineteen pairs of eyes, some bright with good humour, some dull with disinterest, a few sharp with hostility. He sighed inwardly to himself, now he had a job he had never wanted. How was he to get nineteen individual troopers to not only follow his orders, but to do so willingly. These were hard men, rough fighters, and survivors, any of which, individually, was capable of giving Ketch trouble and, collectively, ignoring his orders and even threatening his person. Bullying, stealing, disobedience and desertion were commonplace events, especially now that the king's authority, Parliament's authority and even the army commanders' authority were questioned and challenged by the common soldier. He had to make certain none of those things were to break out in this troop. Sergeants and Corporals never had the title, and rarely the money, to secure obedience. Ketch knew he had to hold each man to himself by friendship or fear. Thankfully, he could rely on Tull and Holditch. For the rest, they would be a test of his wits and his experience.

"Right" he said and placing both thumbs in the top of his belt, he braced himself to stand tall, feet apart, head up, every inch a cavalryman. If his first orders went unchallenged, he had a secure future as a Corporal. If those orders were ignored or challenged, his life and position would be intolerable. Now was the time to present himself as the troop's new master.

"Cornet Marlowe has broken his leg and lies in the inn. I do not know what this Major has up his sleeve for us, nor this Common Council that is paying for you and me to stay here. What I am sure about is that

I am in charge. So that means, Tunstall, you start bringing in the feed for the horses".

At this point Ketch turned and fixed his eyes upon his chosen starting point. Tunstall was not the best of troopers; neither was he the worst. He was one of a group of four who generally ate, slept, stole and fought together. Tunstall opened his mouth to make a retort but, seeing the cold look in Ketch's eyes, thought better of it and with a grunt turned away and walked towards the stables.

"Larkin! You can help him" snapped Ketch.

Larkin was an easy target. He was the oldest of the troopers and always obeyed orders. Ketch then turned to Trooper Mutch. Mutch was over six-foot tall, bulky and strong. He also had a fierce temper and had once killed a fellow trooper in a soldier's fight. Mutch had sat himself down on the ground, arms set out behind him and feet splayed out in front.

"Mutch," said Ketch,

"You will start a fire going for hot water."

This was the real test of Ketch's future as a Corporal. If Mutch obeyed then Ketch's authority was secure. If Mutch did not obey him then Ketch knew that he would have to fight him. Mutch turned his head and looked up at Ketch, an inquiring look upon his face. Ketch stepped forward and stood over the sitting figure. Mutch sprang to his feet in front of Ketch and the two men confronted each other. For

Ketch the tension was palpable. The rest of the men were absorbed in the test of wills.

"Well, Mutch?" said Ketch very slowly and very quietly. There was a long silence. For Mutch, this was now the moment to make his move. For some seconds he stood motionless looking full into Ketch's face. Then he spoke:

"Yes, Corporal," he conceded.

He glanced round the troop, suspicious of any sniggers, and turned away to set about his required task. The tension immediately evaporated and, inside, Ketch was elated. He had seen it through, put himself at risk before the most dangerous of men. He knew he would now determine the life of the troop. Relaxed now, he issued a number of further orders before dismissing the rest of the troop. The men broke away to go about their individual tasks.

"I reckon that's two pence a day more for you" said Tull .

"When the Cornet's up and about, we will have some ale from you Ketch!"

"As a Corporal," said Holditch, giving a deep throaty laugh.

"Your first order was to confine the troop to an inn. That is a fine tale for the rest of the army."

Ketch groaned. That was all he needed, to be the toast of the common soldier as the Corporal who confined his men to an alehouse! Slightly weak from his recent test, Ketch allowed himself a secret smile as he strolled to his quarters.

Tull and Holditch watched with some relief as their friend, with firm orders and clear directions, took over the troop. They, in their turn, sought to help by creating a state of stable, normal activity, polishing their belts and boots and the horse harness, supporting and legitimising Ketch's new position. The period of industrious activity was interrupted by Larkin and Tunstall passing by, carrying leather buckets heavy with water. They were grumbling, their voices deliberately raised in order to be heard by Tull and Holditch, and thus to provoke them.

"Damn my eyes," snorted Tunstall.

"A jumped-up, pastry-faced Corporal in charge, there'll be trouble with this!"

"Is he man enough?" worried Larkin..

"I hear he was a schoolteacher's lad; plenty of learning but no heart in him."

"No heart!" exclaimed Holditch, rising to the bait.

"Let me tell you, Trooper Larkin, that if there is one man between you and a troop of Prince Rupert's fancy boys, pray to God it's Ketch! You should be down on your knees, Larkin, and you Tunstall! He's the finest trooper in this New Model Army of ours. He has saved Tull here from certain death twice to my knowledge, and I've had a few kindnesses from him, myself."

Tull, the taciturn West Country man, snorted at the excited chatter of his friend.

"Whilst my good friend, Trooper Holditch, is right" he said in his soft drawl

"He sometimes misses the nub of the matter. Ketch is clever, lots of book learning. But he also has heart, and he's tough. And if he had religion," at this point Tull sighed a personal reflection.

"He would be another Cromwell."

He now had all their attention, and launched into the story of his first meeting with Ketch.

"1642 'twas, that hard winter. I'd joined up with Lord Manchester's regiment - part of the Cambridgeshire Association, and we were all new boys, raw as beets and untrained."

Tull paused to settle himself on a grainsack, and leaned back against the stable wall. Liking a tale, the others drew closer as he continued.

"A group of us were camped outside Cambridge, on common land by the river. The wind that whistled over that flat land! Cold, we were, and thick snow on the ground. You had to keep moving to stop from freezing to death. Well, late on one afternoon I wandered down to the river. 'Twas frozen solid, and had been for some days. I had a grand time, slipping and sliding like a youngling on that ice, and it fair warmed me, too."

The others smiled in happy recognition of boyhood larks.

"Well, then came trouble. There was a thin patch of ice over weed, and it gave way from under me, and down I went into that black, icy water. Took all the breath from out of me, that cold did. And there was a current, pulling at me under the ice, and I was trying to hang on the edges that just kept crumbling away. I thought that was it for me, getting dark, nobody about, and that current pulling me under."

Tull took from his pocket an empty pipe and started tapping the bowl on his hand. Holditch, recognising the sign, handed Tull his own tobacco pouch. Tull extracted a large wad, returned the pouch with a nod, and started to fill the bowl of his pipe.

"Well, I'm praying, and shouting as best I can, more of a croak, really - but my legs have stiffened up, and I'm about ready to go. Then, out of nowhere, there is this man. He whips of his belt, dumps his sword, then he's on his stomach on that ice, wriggling his way towards me. He throws me the loop of his belt as the ice starts to crack, and I manage to hook my wrist through it. I'm that frozen I couldn't have held on. And he pulls, and the ice is going, but he drags me out and backs off onto the firm ice. Then he picks me up and hoists me onto the bank. That was Ketch who saved me, but that's not all."

At this point, Tull felt it appropriate to stand, go over to the communal fire and take a small brand to light his pipe. His audience did not move.

"Ketch stripped me like a baby," Tull continued, settled once more in his place.

"And then he stripped himself, and put his dry clothes on me, shirt, trousers, socks, boots, the lot. Then he takes up my wet clothes, drags me to my feet and says "Run lad, run for your life", and the pair of us set of like a couple of stags for the nearest campfire. Him naked and me exhausted, we run into camp and straight to the warmest spot. I tell you; we got some jeers and comments! But I also tell you, Ketch that night saved my life. I had no ague afterwards, no coughing fit. He stripped naked and ran me through the snow, so don't you talk about spunk to me, Larkin."

He pointed his pipe at the offender.

"And, by the way, Trooper Mutch thinks Ketch will do fine as a Corporal - do you wish to take it up with him?"

Tunstall and Larkin were beaten, and they knew it. With sober nods, they agreed that Ketch would make a powerful good Corporal.

It was precisely five o'clock when Ketch knocked on the door of the first-floor lodgings taken by Major Blake. They had been easy to find, and a rather plain daughter of the landlord had shown Ketch up the stairs to the very door itself.

Major Blake opened the door. His demeanour was apparently more relaxed than at the inn. He had changed into black hose with comfortable black trousers set at the knee and dark green waisted jerkin buttoned up to his throat, where there was a military style silver broach. He every inch resembled a prosperous military man welcoming a friend into his home. His face was smiling but, despite the affability, Ketch was on guard, for he knew that this was to be an important interview. Major Blake had things to explain.

The room into which Ketch was invited was small but welcoming. A large window looked out onto the street below, and it provided a flood of light onto the dark oak table and two chairs that occupied the centre of the room. An old dusty dresser and a bed in the corner with a trunk stowed beneath it constituted the remaining furniture. The hearth was the focal point of the room and, even though it was early evening in June, a small fire brightly sparked out its warmth and sent a trail of wood-smoke up the chimney.

"Sit down, Ketch" said Major Blake.

"Take a seat and sit by the fire. I have things to tell you that are of national importance and I want no set answers, no old soldier 'Yessirs' and 'Nosirs'. I want you to relax and listen and, above all, think."

He stood foursquare in front of Ketch, and looked him full in the eye.

"You probably consider that I am some sort of government spy," he continued.

He gave a laugh.

"And you would be right! We live in dangerous times, Ketch. The people fight the King, the people win. Who then governs?"

He left his question unanswered, paused as if giving Ketch the opportunity to say something. But Ketch, his pale face showing the light of the fire, thought and said nothing.

Until this point in his tale, Major Blake had been standing, but he now took the second chair and, setting it the other side of the hearth, sat opposite Ketch and turned the gaze of his dark eyes searchingly upon the trooper's pale face.

"Ketch, I want you and your troopers to help me finish a mission that is vital to the army's cause. Cornet Marlowe was to have been my man, but he is out of this game, and I want you. But I don't want a soldier who will do as he is told. I want a partner, an associate, someone who will think, make suggestions, get involved. Someone who will really help. Marlowe thought you could do this. I don't know your politics, but as a soldier you have sworn to obey orders, but can you do more?Before I go any further, I must know if you are the man for this job."

Ketch sat solidly in his seat and swallowed hard. He recognised that this was an important moment in his life. He was being asked to make a crucial choice. Was he with the Major? Could he *not* be with the Major? Would the stiff answers, the non- committal answers of the stupid soldier get him out of this problem? Ketch thought the Major was a man of distinction, no ordinary officer; to be asked to help such a man, to be his confidant was flattering.

"What do I want to do?" he considered,

"Am I to be a simple trooper all my life, or become involved in a secret world of spying for the army?"

Ketch's reply surprised him. He had considered his thoughts carefully, but something inside him rushed out and provided the answer.

"Major Blake, I was educated to be a schoolmaster. I can read and write I know something of history, philosophy, law and the classics. That quiet, useful life was denied me, and I became a soldier. Not because I believed in Parliament or hated the King. I joined Lord Manchester's regiment in '42 because there was no other work and in part, I decided that if forced to choose I was for the people, and wanted to be of service. A vague, unsatisfactory reason, I know, but that was it."

Ketch leaned forward and he looked the Major full in the face.

"These last five years have taught me that the ordinary soldier can be cruel, merciless, drunk and faithless, but he can also be loyal, trustworthy and intelligent. And I have learned that the ordinary man can control his own life, he does not need masters. He can choose a life for himself. I'll help you, Major Blake. I'll work with you, because with this Parliament, there is now no hope for the common man."

Ketch paused for breath at this point. He found that putting his thoughts together in this way was itself exciting and, having thus been encouraged by this Major, he determined to finish what he had to say. "Parliament has betrayed the common man and the common soldier; and as for Charles Stuart, if he is put back in all his power, he will have too many old scores to settle. So, I am with you, Major. I'll give you both my sword and my wits, to do whatever tasks you require."

"That answer pleases me." smiled Major Blake.

He continued more seriously.

"But I must warn you, Ketch, that ours is a twilight world."

He turned to gaze at the fire and for a moment his face gave evidence of memory.

"We must often do unsavoury and unpleasant things that would upset ordinary, honest men. And whilst pursuing dark purposes, we must smile and lead an apparently normal life."

The Major was now speaking slowly and stressing his words, urging Ketch to fully understand what was being said.

"It is important that we do not stand out in any way at all. We must observe, but not be seen. No flamboyance for us, no gaudy colours; we are always grey men or women."

"Do women do this work?" asked Ketch.

"Oh yes" replied Major Blake, "and they are the best at it, they seem to have the temperament for it!"

The Major smiled at Ketch's look of surprise, but continued with his words of caution.

"There is one other matter Ketch that it is important for you to understand.Inevitably, for us, duplicity and a double life become part of our nature. It is our profession, 'though it is sad to think of it."

He leaned back in his chair and looked carefully at Ketch.

"At the moment, you are a good man, Ketch. You should know that this work will change you. Slowly, the lies, the deceits, will become second nature to you. You will become practised in the arts of dissembling. You may not like what you become. So, you may ask, why do we take such a risk with our souls? Why do we follow this life?"

The questions seemed to galvanise the Major. He rose from his chair and began to pace the small room. Although the light was bright outside, the room was darkening, and it seemed a small place to Ketch. He listened carefully to the Major, whose every word was soft and clear, and purposefully stated.

"You struck a chord within me, Ketch, with your answer. I, also, seek to serve, to help build an England for all our people. I agree, we seem to have a limited choice of masters, scheming members of parliament, or arrogant courtiers. Now the army must be the best hope for us all, it has asked many fine men to die. We must make sure that this has not all been wasted."

He paused and then chuckled softly to himself, and his features softened a little, as some internal tension was broken.

"These words are over-serious!" he said.

"Come, Ketch, what is your baptised name? In this world of spying there are no Majors and Troopers, we are all brothers in a dangerous game; my name is Richard."

So, saying, he held out his hand for the second time that day to the still seated Ketch.

"My name is John," said Ketch, rising to his feet.

"I shall be your brother in your dark games, and we will work well together for the army and people."

Major Blake moved to the dresser and, from the lower cupboard, brought out a bottle and two glasses.

"We will drink one bottle of Madeira wine whilst I tell you why I am here, "he said.

The bottle was placed on the table, and with full glasses, the two men seated themselves opposite each other across the hearth.

"I know you were at Naseby, John, with Colonel Butler's regiment; and the story I must tell you starts with that battle, and strangely the girl that you and I, together with Cornet Marlowe, saved from the mob earlier today. Outside Northampton, by some four miles, is the parish of Holcot, and within this parish lie the home and estates of Sir Roger Desborough. The family owed their prosperity to the Stuart Kings and in our recent struggle, Sir Roger and his family fought for Charles Stuart. Sir Roger himself was a widower, but had a son, Ralph - who now must be some twenty-four, twenty-five years old, perhaps your own age - together with two daughters, Martha and Mary, of whom you have now met. Sir Roger, by all accounts, was a good man, liked by his tenants, a magistrate and a benefactor to local charities. His son, Ralph, took after the father, if occasionally wild in the manner of young men with means and too much time on their hands. When the King raised his standard at Nottingham, the Desboroughs were among the first to join him. Of course, they lost everything by this act. Northampton has been for Parliament from the outset of this war and, at the beginning of the conflict, welcomed my Lord Essex's army from London. The Desborough estates were confiscated. The daughters, Martha and Mary, first lived with their cousins, the Capsticks, before moving into their mother's property by St Sepulchre's. Although objects of suspicion, the town tolerates them. There was much in the town's tolerance, for the Desborough's father and son have served Charles well, especially in the support of his cousin, Prince Rupert. Their reputations as soldiers even gained grudging recognition locally."

Ketch had listened intently to the Major's tale and had not touched his wine. Before continuing the Major pushed Ketch's glass towards him encouraging him to drink. Ketch took a long sip of the sweet red wine.

"As we know," Blake went on.

"Naseby was effectively to decide the war between King and Parliament, and Sir Robert and Ralph were both at Naseby. Ralph, we know, was with Rupert, and took part in the crazy charge that gave us such a shock. But he is of little consequence! I am here, we are here - because of Sir Roger who, throughout the battle, was kept close to the person of the King. We have the testimony of royalists captured after the battle who were also close to the King, and we captured the great majority of the King's papers. The testimony and the papers not only confirm the presence of Sir Roger, but tell of a final despairing letter written in Charles Stuart's own hand and entrusted to the care of Sir Roger Desborough to deliver to the King of France and his chief minister Cardinal Mazarin."

The Major sipped his own wine, before carrying on.

"It is not fully known what was in that letter, but it is suggested that, in his despair, Charles offered not only Catholic toleration but an established Catholic Church for England, in return for a French army that would restore him to his throne."

Here Blake paused in his narrative, and Ketch could not restrain himself, and leapt to his feet.

"Good God!" he burst out. "Of all the things about Charles Stuart, I had thought him a confirmed Protestant. With that letter, he breaks his coronation oath to preserve the Protestant religion and betrays every Englishman to a French army!"

"You are quite correct.," said Blake.

"Oh, it is rumoured that he regretted his desperate act even on the battlefield, and tried to recall Sir Roger. But it was too late. Having despatched Sir Roger, he had no time to recall him, for, in the final moments of the battle, we know that Charles was dragged and bundled away from Naseby almost against his will."

"So" said Ketch, "Sir Roger was riding to the French King with information which, if discovered, would turn every Englishman against Charles Stuart and make every one of them call for his immediate death. I can see why Parliament wants that letter, Major. Whosoever has that letter has the King within their power!"

Ketch shook his head, as though the enormity of the information had dealt him a physical blow. He sank back into his chair. "So, then, what has happened to Sir Roger, and what, in the name of Heaven, has become of that accursed letter?" he asked.

Major Blake sighed, and then took up his narrative. "After the battle, which you remember was in June two years ago, Sir Roger and the letter completely disappeared. It was, of course, a time of chaos and uncertainty; fugitives, the wounded, camp-followers and those just out for loot were all mixed up and skirmishing with each other. And there was no reason to be especially interested in the fate of one royalist gentleman. By the autumn, however, we had some idea of the importance of Sir Roger, and our contacts in France and the Low Countries were ordered to find both him and the letter."

"The importance of that letter was now paramount in our minds. With that letter Parliament can have the King's life without one Englishman dissenting, or, if they choose, bend him to agree to any settlement they may care to impose. However, despite the efforts of our best agents, many of them close to the King's sons and daughters, nothing could be found. Except that there were those on the Royalist side similarly searching for the same quarry, none more so that Ralph Desborough, who had managed to escape to France. He was frantic to find his father and to save the family honour. In a sense, it was a race between Parliament's agents and those of the Royalists, to find Sir Roger and that letter."

The Major stooped to place a large log on the fire; it had the temporary effect of cooling the area around the hearth. Ketch's legs had grown used to the warmth of the fire; he actually shivered. In response, he rubbed his hands.

"Go on, Major." he said. "This is still but half a tale. You are not in Northampton by chance. What scent brought you here?"

Blake smiled grimly as he resettled himself into his chair. "Last December, just after Christmas, news came to London that the body of Sir Roger Desborough had been discovered, and buried in the family vault at Holcot, just north of the town. That was when I received my commission to come to Northampton. The Army Council, in particular, wants Charles's letter!"

"What?" interrupted Ketch. "I can understand Parliament wanting the letter, but why should the army bother with such a thing?"

The Major leaned back in his chair and paused to gaze up at the low ceiling. After a short silence he returned his eyes to Ketch.

"Politics, Ketch." he said.

"Perhaps the most important product of our century. The army council led by Fairfax and Cromwell have now lost all faith with Parliament and will soon move against it, but these same men still trust the good faith of Charles Stuart and will not move against him. They still hope that if Parliament is a lost hope then they can still make an accommodation with him."

His own speech impassioned the Major and he slammed his hand flat onto the table shaking bottle, glasses and Ketch.

"If treacherous Parliament and King come together, Ketch, and, by God, if Parliament's agents find that letter it could happen, then any plans the army council have will be for nothing. We must find that letter, Ketch, to convince our own generals to go it alone, to trust neither Parliament nor King."

"So where is the letter?" insisted Ketch.

"Patience!" admonished the Major.

"Hear the full tale. Desborough's daughters say that they found the body, by chance, in a ditch deep in the woods to the east of the village. Hedlow, the Clerk of the Council, whom you have met, also saw the body, and verifies that it was Sir Roger, but God knows how! In eighteen months, a body looks pretty nasty! Hedlow and the daughters were certain, however."

"Are you sure that Hedlow and the daughters are not in some conspiracy?" inquired Ketch.

"To put you off the scent, perhaps? It could have been the corpse of some other soldier. They could have Sir Roger hidden somewhere."

"Yes," said the Major, nodding agreement.

"That is possible but, their grief appears genuine, and Hedlow has the reputation of an honest man; he was a major influence in keeping Northampton in the cause of Parliament. I do not really see what they would have to gain from such a charade, for the main point is that no letter has been discovered."

Ketch looked to the Major with his now empty glass and, on receiving a nod, he refilled it from the bottle, and poured more for the Major. Thus fortified, he ventured a further question.

"How can you be sure that the daughters did not search the body, find the letter, and destroy it?"

"Because," Major Blake snapped his reply,

"Now, six months later, Royalist agents are still searching for it. I did not believe the daughters when they showed me the supposed site where they found their father; they had no decent explanation as to why they were in those woods. I think they found him elsewhere: a secret place, which they return to from time to time to continue their search for the letter."

"And before you ask," he continued.

"The letter was not buried with him. One dark night, with a lantern - and not a little courage - I verified that myself!"

"So, John" he said.

"That is how matters stand. The letter is still unfound. It may be lost forever; but for too many people, the risk, or chance, of it being found forces them to continue to search for it. The best hope lies in the two daughters, Mary and Martha, who know the real place where he died. That is why I keep my eye on them, and why I rushed to Mary Desborough's rescue. It is not a habit in our profession to perform conspicuous acts of gallantry, but I need those ladies unharmed to lead me to that which we seek."

"What about the troopers?" said Ketch.

"You and your troop are here to protect and help me, Ketch, no other reason. Remember, both royalist agents and those of Parliament seek the letter as anxiously as I, and they are dangerous and ruthless; and what is worse. "

At this point the Major cast half-glances about the room. "We are in Northampton, the very heart of Parliament's strength. Northampton is controlled by Lord Le Vaughn, the army's bitterest foe and probably the most important man in Parliament. One who has ambition, money and power. He has his own regiment here, garrisoned in the castle, to do his will. We are all very vulnerable, Ketch, you, me, and your little troop". With that warning the Major rose to his feet.

"Come, Ketch," he said"

"We must now meet the burghers of Northampton. But remember! This conversation has not taken place. It must be hidden deep within you. You now revert to Corporal Ketch, and I, given a moment, will don my full uniform and once more become Major Blake, with our normal army relationship. You will become more stupid and slow, and I will become pleasant, honest and straightforward - but our eyes and ears are always alert to serve our purpose!"

"Yes, Sir!" said Ketch, at attention.

He could not mistake the strength of that warning. Both men drained their glasses, set them on the table, and within a few minutes Major Blake was ready and together they left the room. Major Blake paused a moment to lock the door carefully behind them, and Ketch stood aside dutifully to allow his superior officer to pass.

And it was a Major of the Cavalry, followed by a Trooper, who stepped out into the evening sunshine of Abington Street.

Chapter 3

Mary Desborough was not badly hurt, she was bruised and the cut on her forehead was still open, but it was clean and had long stopped bleeding. She lay asleep on a couch in the downstairs front room of the house she shared with her sister. It was a small room, but it was well lit and the furniture was solid and respectable. Cut wild flowers were in small pots on both the central table and the old dark dresser, and crochet work provided mats. The couch, the table and the dresser, together with three straight-backed chairs, were all the furnishings apart from a tall clock case. It was a room for gentlefolk, very fitting for the disinherited daughters of a Stuart follower.

Martha Desborough entered from the only other room on the ground floor, a kitchen and washing room that gave onto the small rear garden that flanked the cemetery of St Sepulchres.

Seeing that her sister was asleep, Martha approached the couch quietly. She was anxious about Mary, and wished to see if her sleep was that of peace and rest rather than of dreams and nightmares. She was reassured by what she saw, for the rise and fall of her sister's chest was regular and steady and her face, surrounded by golden hair, was quiet and serene. Martha's face-hardened at the sight of the cut on her sister's forehead, and she thought bitterly of the hard times both she and Mary had experienced. The shock of war had been frightening, but to have been virtually abandoned by father and brother had been particularly hard, especially for Mary.

Martha remembered her sister being dragged from the hall at Holcot when it was sequestered by Parliament and her humiliation at being thrown into a cart and driven away to temporary imprisonment. The two sisters had suffered many indignities, and she knew that they had each reacted differently to them. Now they were virtually penniless and Mary now concerned herself only with the moment: she never thought of the past or future, only the present. It was as if the horror of remembrance drove her to enjoy to the full every day she was given.

Martha knew that she, too, had changed, but in a subtler way she had lost her naiveté, her innocence of life. Now she was cautious, calculating and careful; she planned well ahead, and could dissemble, lie and even cheat if she had no other recourse. Martha was unhappy with herself, unhappy with Mary and a little bitter about her brother.

"It was the war that brought us down. The war, and the stupid loyalty of the Desboroughs. So-called 'family honour' has lost us our home, our estates, crippled us as people, and caused the murder of our father."

That same family honour had also brought their dear brother, Ralph, back to the very heart of his enemies. Martha fiercely hated the concept of 'honour' that had broken father, sister and herself; and now, her beloved brother - tall, strong Ralph, was at terrible risk.

Backward and forward Martha's mind travelled between the two men she had loved - the dead father, and her living brother. The thoughts of her father, she knew, were slowly growing softer. The great rage she had felt when he had abandoned both her and Mary for the King's cause was being tempered gradually by happier memories of other times. The fear and worry at his disappearance after Naseby, the dreadful anxiety of Ralph's sudden appearance and his continued searching, had finally ended that December evening when he had returned, grey and cold, with the news of their father's murder. Finding the body, bringing it to Northampton and its burial at Holcot had been grief-ridden task, but they had finally left Martha free of torment and concern. She could do no more for her father: Sir Roger Desborough of Holcot in the County of Northamptonshire was dead. She would now fondly remember him, but she would no longer carry him as a burden.

Her brother, Ralph, however, was constantly in her mind, filling it with apprehension and concern. His activities, his firmness of purpose, his determination to take risks, were burdens that kept her awake at night and jostled her consciousness throughout the day. Ralph had followed his father to the side of Charles Stuart, and for that she had once hated him. This emotion was but a small fire that was quickly put out by the floods of concern she had felt for him; and besides, he had only followed his father, who was the one really responsible for their abandonment.

It was news of Ralph that had quickened her heart, and the sickening silence from him after Naseby had only finally ended with a smuggled letter four weeks later, saying that he was safe in France. But Ralph had not stayed safe - he had foolishly returned in secret to England to search for his missing father.

She would never forget that day in early December when, invited to Uncle Martin's farm at Earls Barton, they had entered the low, thatched farmhouse - to be embraced by Ralph. That had been a wonderful moment; the family, at least in part reunited, had sat around the blazing hearth listening to Ralph's account of his adventures, and Uncle Martin's recapturing of old times and telling of old stories. The laughter had not remained long, she remembered. Ralph was determined to find his father and was convinced that he was somewhere in the county, hurt, wounded or in hiding. She had never understood the urgency and the passion of Ralph's search for his father. Every day he left the farm, sometimes on foot, sometimes on horse, to scour the countryside. Every day, for hours he would search. It was a powerful passion for his father's welfare which was bitterly broken when the awful discovery was made.

Mary stirred, and opened her eyes, which gradually realised that it was her sister in the room with her.

"How are you, my dear?" said Martha, seating herself on the edge of the couch, and smoothing her sister's hair with tenderness.

"The apothecary said you must rest and grow strong again."

"I'm well enough," said Mary, raising herself to a sitting position against the head of the couch. She caught at her sister's hand.

"It was horrible, Martha. Those people, the terrible things that the preacher said - poor John and James - and the fighting!"

The words tumbled out from her. Martha let her speak, seeing some release in her need to talk.

"What will happen to us now, Martha? Is everyone against the Desborough family, even us two poor women? Oh, it is not right that we have lost everything and still they seek to hurt us."

Lowering her voice, she turned confidentially to Martha.

"We should go back to live with Uncle Martin. It was a mistake to come and live once more in town. Let us sell this house, Martha, and go away! Why does Ralph want to stay in Northampton? He has found father; he has done his duty. Why does he continue to roam the streets of Northampton at night? Why does he visit alehouses? Why does he always wear father's clothes and rings and sword? Why does he pretend to be father at night?"

"I don't know" sighed Martha. She held her sister's hand in both of hers.

"I am your sister Mary, and I love you very much. And we both love Ralph very much. All our lives have been destroyed by the King and his war. We have lost home, father, position - and our friends are few. We must all be together if we are to survive. Sisters and brother must help each other. Uncle Martin and James and John at Earls Barton may be our final refuge, and one-day we may have to flee there. But now we are in Northampton, and we have a brother who is in great danger and whom we must love and protect. I do not know why he goes out at night, and who or what he is searching for. I can only guess that he is trying to surprise or startle someone into giving up some secret about father. I only know that he is our brother."

Dropping Mary's hand and standing up, she continued in a brisker voice.

"He is even now expecting our visit with food and news!"

"Oh, Martha," sighed Mary.

"I hear what you say, and your words are truth, but I am frightened. I do not have your strength of purpose. I do want to help Ralph, but what will happen to us if we are discovered? I am sure there are people who watch this house, who watch us!"

Mary did not cry, but her shoulders slumped, and she lay back on the couch. Like a small animal, exhausted by pursuit, she wanted an end to it all.

"It is too much for me, Martha."

Martha rose to her feet.

"Come, Mary. Be strong! I will look after you, and Ralph is expecting us both. and two are needed to take the food and drink he expects of us."

Martha did not scold Mary, for she too felt strongly the very fear of which her sister spoke.

"We can manage together," she said and, with a wry smile, continued, "Perhaps two frightened sisters may make one passable brave one."

Mary took some heart from this, and rose from the couch, shaking her skirts into order.

"Yes, I am ready Martha. I am sorry to be so fragile a spirit."

The two sisters began to gather together the necessaries for their daily visit to their brother. In the kitchen, Martha wrapped bread and cheese in a clean linen cloth, and put a few early strawberries into a small pot. She filled a flask with cool water from an earthenware jar, and pressed home the stopper firmly. Mary brought down from their bedroom two light woollen shawls. As they made their preparations, Martha was thoughtful.

"I think you are right about us being watched. Don't be frightened, it is not all the time. I think that from time to time I have caught a glimpse of that Major Blake, more than is usual."

"I hate that man," said Mary, her face hardening.

"He looks fair, and speaks softly, but always there were questions. Questions about father: where he was found; how we found him; what we were doing in Holcot Wood. I am glad you told me clearly what to say, Martha. I am sure that otherwise I would have got it all wrong and spoken of Ralph and where he really found father."

"You did very well, my dear," encouraged Martha.

"Major Blake is indeed a clever man, and vigorous and careful in his questions. But you see, we did it - two sisters bested a full Major!"

In her mind's eye, Martha saw an image of Major Blake. Tall, courteous, civilised, even cultured. Not a typical soldier, she thought. He was, she knew, a single man and, in a quiet way, attractive.... But Martha knew him as her personal adversary. She was what lay between him and her beloved brother and Major Blake should not have him!

The two sisters left their small house by the front door, closing it carefully behind them. They paused a moment, and seemed to decide that it was too warm still to put on their shawls, carrying them casually (but taking good care of the food hidden within) they set off demurely to walk the short distance to the church.

It was a journey they had made many times, for, although Ralph spent some time away at their Uncle's farm, much of his time was spent in Northampton. But his sisters' house being small - and suspect - the church was his most frequent hiding place. Church, churchyard, garden, houses - this was the territory around which Ralph Desborough moved to keep himself hidden and safe.

The Church of St Sepulchre was built by Simon de Senlis in 1110 and took the general form of a crusader tent; it was, thus, one of only seven round churches to be found in all England. The oldest church in the town of Northampton, it had witnessed many great occasions. Kings and queens had prayed within it, and Edward I and one hundred of his knights had pledged themselves at its altar to go on a crusade. It was a much-used church, and one that had enjoyed the generosity of the Desborough family. Martha knew that Ralph would be hidden somewhere within the church, for Troopers at the house would have made unsafe any other part of his domain.

The church was not empty as the two sisters walked down the central aisle and moved across to take a side pew. As they lowered themselves onto the solid oak bench of their pew, they knew that they dare stay only so long, and if necessary, food and drink had to be left hidden. As they lowered their heads in prayer, the peace and calm of the church seemed to seep into their souls and calm their minds. The tranquillity was somewhat broken by the rustling and whisperings of the two elderly ladies, who, evening devotions completed, discovered that their joints had stiffened as they rose to leave the church. As the great door creaked shut behind the dames, evening shadows filled the darkening church. Now the two sisters were alone.

From the shadows a darker shadow moved, and the lithe figure of their brother slid into the haven of the great pew beside them.

"Are you well?" he enquired; his face anxious.

"I saw soldiers at the house, bringing you home what has happened?"Then, with a start,

"Mary, your head!"

"Hush, Ralph," soothed Martha.

"Mary is well. She and your cousins, John and James, fell foul of Preacher Hyack's mob. Soldiers intervened and escorted us home."

"Yes" interrupted Mary.

"Major Blake and a Trooper called Ketch came to our rescue. But we know that Major and his interest in us!"

Again, Martha calmed her.

"Do not fear, Ralph. We keep ourselves away from public gaze, and 'though the Major shadows us, you are safe."

She turned to her sister.

"Mary, I have words to say to Ralph. Go stand watch by the door so that we are not disturbed. I will tell you all later."

Mary was reluctant, but a look from her brother, now the head of the family, stopped any rebellion, and she went meekly to do as she was bid.

Martha turned urgently to her brother.

"How long must this go on?" she burst out.

"Ralph, why do you stay here? You have found father, he has long been buried, but you still insist on coming into the town and wandering its streets at night. Why do you put us all - Mary, Uncle Martin, John and James - in such danger? Oh, I am so worried about Mary - the trouble this afternoon has her at a pitch where she will, against all her wishes, give us away. But it is you who are responsible, Ralph. If you go away, we shall be safe!"

Martha's hands were tight in her lap, and the tension of her fingers seemed to fuel the flow of words.

"I have not said this before, but Ralph I know there is some other urgency for you, something else to do with father. But we can stand this no longer. Please! Please! go away!"

Martha fell in tears against her brother's shoulder.

"Oh, Martha, Martha," he sighed, as his arm encircled her shoulders. "Please do not abandon me. There is something that must be found, and destroyed! It was in father's possession, and now nobody knows where it is. I must keep searching. In this matter, my safety is not important -even my sisters must be put at risk - but I can do this no other way. It is a despairing chance that someone on seeing who they think is father may say something about his death. It is all I can think to do."

"But Ralph" interrupted Martha urgently.

"Not only is there Major Blake, who is, you say, your adversary in this matter, but he has been joined by his own soldiers He now has twenty horse Troopers, led by a Cornet Marlowe, to help him."

"Thank you for that news, Martha. That makes the urgency of my task even greater."

His face set into determined lines.

"We must face this danger together. Go now, thank you for the victuals. Take Mary, try to play a normal part, and tomorrow I shall return to the house early."

As her eyes searched his face for any sign of relenting, he pressed her hand and smiled encouragingly.

"Please, Martha?"

She managed a small smile in return; her appeal had had no effect on him - he was resolute. She kissed his cheek, and rose and went into the aisle to collect Mary, waiting at the door. She turned back to him, but there was no brother seated in the pew, only dark and darker shadows closing in. She squared her shoulders as the church doors closed behind them. There was no change. Ralph was determined to see his task out. His own life was clearly of little importance - and their lives also were to be risked. Martha felt cold: a brother's love had its limits.

Chapter 4

Clerk Hedlow sat at his table in the great hall of the Council House and let his eyes roam the rafters and dark stained oak benches that gave the chamber its sombre mood, a mood that was evident even on a June evening. It was dark in the chamber and he had given orders for the lamps to be lit, and they in turn cast their light over the six figures that occupied the front bench of the chamber. Hedlow turned his attention to his companions, his masters, really. These six men represented the Common Council of Northampton and were beyond doubt the six most important persons of the town. All were men of substance, men of commerce, who had survived and even prospered during the terrible time of civil war. No landed gentry here, no idle aristocrat with time on their hands. These were tough-minded free men who had fought and clawed their way to a position of pre-eminence in the town. They were all non-conformist in religion, generally Presbyterian, but Hedlow suspected a few of being Independents. Whatever their religion might say, they were well dressed, well fed and prosperous.

"Where are they, then, Hedlow?" demanded a round-faced, fleshy, middle-aged man.

"They will be here on time, Councilman Trussel," replied Hedlow. "We said six o'clock."

"I still think we are making a terrible mistake" piped a thin-faced, crouching figure.

"It is not too late to send them away, Trussel."

"Nathanial Parfitt, it is far too late!" boomed Trussel.

"We six persuaded the Council to write to Parliament and the army council asking for Troopers, and now they are here."

"But what will the Garrison Commander, Fell, say?" bleated Parfitt."And what will the County Committee say?"

"We have discussed all that" replied Trussel, testily. "You voted with us, Parfitt, and now you will stand by us. Unless," and his voice went soft and cold, so that even Hedlow shivered, "unless you want to leave now, as you are free to do."

"No! Oh, no...." replied Parfitt, hastily.

"I am with you....er.... I am with us. Its just that, well, sometime I become a little.... concerned - at what others may say and do.And remember, the officer has now broken his leg."

"Gentlemen!" interrupted Hedlow.

"All six of you, together with the other members of the Council instructed me to inform firstly Parliament and secondly the army council of our need for disciplined Troopers from the New Army; I followed your instructions. From Parliament I heard nothing. The army council, however, have sent us twenty Ironsides. Colonel Fell at the Garrison may, as Councillor Parfitt suggests, feel slighted that we have not informed him. He may wonder why his own troops have not been seen fit..."

" Not those cut-throats" spluttered Parfitt.

"Lord Le Vaughan" continued Hedlow.

"And the Northamptonshire County Committee will, no doubt, be informed by Colonel Fell that we have gone behind their backs and appealed directly to Parliament and the army. All this has happened, and we must now grasp the opportunity to bring some order to our town."

"Colonel Fell is no more than a black-hearted villain" snorted Trussel. "He uses soldiers paid for by the Northamptonshire levy for his own purposes."

"We pay four hundred pounds a week, for him and his band to bully and threaten us."

This was from Brompton, a man who disliked spending money, whether his own or others.

"But he is still only a small part of the Le Vaughn faction" said Trussel. "Le Vaughn is his master."

"All this is true," said Hedlow. "But perhaps we speak too loudly and too strongly. Ah, I hear the arrival of our visitors!"

Major Blake and Ketch entered the great chamber and, moving into the pool of light shed by the lamps, bowed to the Council Members.

"Welcome to you both," said Hedlow, rising to his feet.

"Come, I have arranged seating for you."

He guided Blake and Ketch to a bench that faced the Councilmen but would allow them, by a slight turn, to address him also. Remaining by them, Hedlow continued

"Let me first introduce to the Council Major Blake and Corporal Ketch, both of the New Army. Corporal Ketch has some twenty red Troopers with him and is here, under the command of a Cornet Marlowe, in response to our appeal to the Army Council. Major Blake is here on other duties and is in attendance at this meeting because Cornet Marlowe has suffered a most unfortunate accident of a broken leg. You are both welcome, gentlemen. Now, if I may turn to the members of our Common Council - you understand, we have asked only the senior members for this first meeting." Hedlow at this point returned to his seat, before continuing, formally, "We have Councilman Trussel, and Councilmen Brompton, Frayne, Sheep, Lugg and Parfitt."

Each Councilman gave a nod of the head at his name, and Ketch and Blake gave a brief bow in response to the introduction before seating themselves. All the faces were strange, bar one. Ketch recognised in Councilman Lugg the cobbler who had guided him earlier in the day. Lugg and Ketch simultaneously gave a nod of recognition to each other, followed by a quick smile at their common courtesy.

"This is a private meeting" commenced Hedlow.

"And there will, therefore, be no official record."

He carefully placed his pen and papers well away from him. "Perhaps, Councilman Trussel, you will explain, particularly to Corporal Ketch, the Council's purpose in seeking additional troops from the New Army."

"Thank you, Hedlow" said Trussel, and for a few seconds he remained still and thoughtful, gathering himself, and then he began.

"You may not know much of Northampton, Ketch. It is an ancient borough; we received our first Charter from King Richard the First and, indeed we were much patronised by his brother, King John. Over the years the town has had mixed fortunes and remained small but generally we prospered. We are a serious, perhaps, a pious county, certainly not a county to respect an over-mighty King and his fawning bishops."

"And therefore," interrupted Lugg, the cobbler.

"We have stood steadfast for Parliament throughout the troubles. No other county has been such a bulwark for the Parliamentary cause."

"All right, Lugg!" admonished Trussel.

"Let me tell this tale."

Lugg nodded in agreement, but mumbled something about being a bit sharp about it then.

"The King's capital and headquarters from the beginning of the war has been at Oxford, but forty miles away; but we have held this part of England for Parliament. You will know that it is not twelve months since Oxford, Worcester and Litchfield still held for the King..."

"What he is saying" interrupted Lugg, undeterred.

"Is that we have been active in the front of things since Lord Essex first brought the army of Parliament to Northampton five years ago..."

"The battles of Edgehill, Cropredy Bridge, and, of course, Naseby - have all been fought in and around Northampton" interjected Councilman Sheep.

"Northampton raised over one thousand pounds in one week for Parliament three years ago" agonised Councilman Brampton.

"And we have always supported Lord Grey and the County Committee..." from Councilman Frayne.

" Small thanks for that" sniffed Parfitt.

"Gentlemen! Gentlemen!" rapped Hedlow.

"Let us all keep silent and listen to Councilman Trussell."

"What I am saying, gentlemen" continued Trussel, rallying his dignity, "Is that we have been loyal to the Parliamentary cause, and now that we need help, we thought Parliament would support us."

He paused, and this time no one interrupted him.

"Things have been bad in Northampton this last year, or even eighteen months. It has been hard enough being a garrison town; soldiers in town fight get drunk, loot and murder our citizens and we get scant recompense from the officers in charge - especially Colonel Fell. But, besides these problems, there are bands of deserters - royalist and parliamentarian, who roam the county, robbing, burning, and murdering our people."

"If I can add to your tale" offered Lugg.

"Not only have we been fighting the King, suffering a garrison, and fighting murderous bands of cut-throat deserters, but also Parliament's own soldiers. Wellingborough, a town not ten miles away, loyal to Parliament's cause, was ransacked and looted by Parliament's soldiers."

"After Naseby" added Council Frayne.

"There was such a general pillaging of the countryside that it was as if the town and Parliament had lost the battle!"

"All this," Trussell continued,

“Has taken its toll of trade; journeymen pressed into service, apprentices running off to join the army, merchants unable to move goods. All this is bad enough, but for the town it has become worse. In a sense, all this is but background to our concerns, for these last twelve months strange and unhappy events continue to take place and to add more terror to our fears. Lord Le Vaughn is now the power on the County Committee, and Colonel Fell takes orders only from him. Garrison troops continue to harass and bully citizens - especially those that speak against Le Vaughn's party. Le Vaughn sees himself as some sort of new leader and he encourages all sorts of strange pastors and preachers to order our lives and work. They have followers who stamp on any opposition, beating people, smashing property; in particular, the shops of traders who will not pay the dues, or tithes, as they call them, that they levy unlawfully."

Clerk Hedlow intervened at this point.

"Thus, gentlemen, you can see that such directed soldiers and preachers terrorise our townspeople, but there are other strange and terrible occasions. Sir Roger Desborough, a Royalist but still a well-respected county man, was found cruelly murdered. There are still Royalists who walk the streets at night and confront townsmen; and sorriest of all are the women camp-followers, not all of them harlots but simple good wives, caring for their soldier husbands, who were disgracefully treated after Naseby, whipped and shorn and scarred. They are still to be seen about, shunned by all."

The Council Chamber fell quiet. The pity of war was the destruction it brought to ordinary lives.

"Sirs," Ketch broke the silence.

"The army council has sent you twenty Troopers. I can help keep order. But I cannot fight the Garrison of Northampton. A Colonel and a full regiment will be too much, even for my twenty Ironsides. As for your county politics, that is not a matter for me. I cannot remove your complaints, but I shall try to ease them. But you must understand" he continued.

"I shall have to pay a courtesy attendance upon the Garrison Commander, your Colonel Fell. My orders are clear in placing me under your command - and that of Major Blake - but such a visit will be expected, and I must give an explanation for my presence."

"I would expect nothing less," said a cold, thin voice behind Ketch.

All heads turned at the unexpected interruption. A broad-shouldered, heavy man of about forty years of age, in the full uniform of a Colonel of Infantry, stepped out from the shadows that curtained the door to the chamber.

"Good evening, Members of the Council" he continued.

"Good evening, Hedlow," and made a slight mocking bow of his head.

"Colonel Fell" replied Hedlow.

"What brings you to our meeting?"

"I hear that the Council and Major Blake have brought some New Army Troopers into Northampton, and I have some questions to ask."So, speaking, Colonel Fell walked slowly to stand behind Ketch and Major Blake. Appearing out of the darkness behind him, pikemen, dressed and armed, fanned out around the walls of the Council Chamber until they ringed all the occupants.

"Have a care, Fell!" cried Trussel.

"We are a chartered corporation, and well-loved by Parliament."

The six Councilmen had risen to their feet and, instinctively, had clustered together close to Clerk Hadlow's table.

Colonel Fell had a dark olive skin, betraying possibly some Spanish ancestry, but what always held the attention of his listeners were his large, bulbous eyes. Almost fish-like, they now searched the room and examined the inhabitants. "The only person not known to me is a common Trooper; and yet, this common Trooper sits before the wealth of Northampton!"

Ketch was by now standing to attention as, at this point, Major Blake stepped forward.

"Colonel Fell" Blake greeted him cordially.

"This is all very excessive. What need is there for armed troops in a council chamber? This Trooper, on behalf of his injured officer, is following army council instructions and reporting to the Common Council of Northampton, who have successfully petitioned for Troopers to help sustain law and order in this town."

"Yes" boldly intervened Councilman Lugg.

"We have had enough of your bully-boys. Your soldiers not only fail to protect us from gangs of cutthroats and loyalists, but take their place. We have had a dire time of late!"

Colonel Fell turned his eyes on Councilman Lugg.

"I know you, Lugg. You are someone who is strangely prosperous in a time when many good men of commerce have been ruined. What is the source of your prosperity, Lugg? Have you been in the pay of Royalists? I have no doubt that I could easily root out men who will swear to having delivered Royalist gold to Councilman Lugg."

Lugg was not to be browbeaten, however.

"In your torture rooms, Cromwell himself would claim to be a Royalist!"

"Enough!" snapped Fell.

"I will not bandy words with conspirators. Net them all up, and to the Castle with them - Councilmen, Clerk, Majors and all. I am the master in Northampton, and I will have this matter out."

"One moment, Colonel!"

Major Blake stepped forward, took the Colonel's elbow and propelled him a few steps away so that they were separate from all present.

"If I could but have an instant of your time in private, it will be to your special advantage."

The Major had acted with such speed and his voice carried such a degree of authority that the Colonel had followed him before having had the chance to consider the request. To Ketch's eyes, Blake seemed to pull something from an inside coat pocket - a piece of paper -, which he showed to the Colonel.

"So," thought Ketch, "the same paper he showed Cornet Marlowe - will it have the same effect?"

He watched as Colonel Fell took the paper from Major Blake and looked hard at it for some seconds, then dropped it back into the Major's hand. Fell turned to his pikemen:

"Leave us!" he commanded.

"I have matters to discuss."

He waited as, with much stamping of boots and scraping of walls, the soldiers left the building.

"Councilmen" Fell continued.

"Major Blake has convinced me that all is well, and that these Troopers are yours to dispose of as you will. that is, until I, and the Major," and he turned his eyes full on Major Blake,

"Have discussed this matter fully with Lord Le Vaughn. I bid you goodnight."Bowing curtly, and with a face set in stone, he turned and left the chamber.

The break in tension sent the six Councilmen to fall upon each other, shaking hands and slapping backs.

"Ah-ha!" cried Trussel.

"we saw him off! We saw him off - Ketch and his Troopers are ours!"

"A glorious victory" cried Lugg.

"You were extremely fortunate" sniggered Parfitt. "I thought you were due for the dungeons, for sure, Lugg. You certainly showed spirit!"

Clerk Hedlow, with soothing words, calmed the mild hysteria of relief felt by his Councilmen.

"Let us close this meeting. Will the Council be happy if I give orders to Corporal Ketch on his duties, and we will meet again next week to review matters?"

"Aye!" came the reply, in unison.

"Come Sheep, come Lugg and Parfitt, and all. You are welcome at my home. What a night! What a victory!" exulted Trussel as he shepherded his colleagues towards the door.

"Thank you, Trussel" replied Hedlow,

"But I have invited Major Blake and the Corporal to sup with me tonight, and they have accepted."

"Sup ye well, then" cried Trussel.

"We have all earned our evening repast with this night's work."

The six Councilmen, laughing and chattering, left the Council Room where Hedlow, the Major and Ketch were silent for a moment.

"I apologise for the subterfuge of my dinner invitation and your acceptance. I have not had the opportunity to issue my invitation, but I hope you will accept and come with me now to my house in the Derngate, where I can offer you a fine leg of pork."

Ketch looked at Major Blake and said.

"I think, Major, that Master Hedlow has much to tell that will help the both of us in our efforts for the army and Northampton."

"I am offering pork, ale, wine - and information tonight.," said Hedlow. His papers collected up, the lamps snuffed, he led his guests out of the Council Room, carefully locking the great doors behind him.

"You have both had a long and tiring day" he sympathised.

"Now, for a time, you can relax."

He led them in the cool, darkening evening the short distance to his home, close by the South-eastern entrance to the town.

It was a good, solid but modest house, near to the spot where once had stood the "Dern" gate of Northampton. However, neglect and domestic building needs over the years had led to the gate's ruin and demolition. The most famed feature of this part of the town was Thomas a Beckett's Well, reputedly the spot where the Archbishop had stopped to refresh himself before escaping to France. Whether fact or fiction, what was undeniable was that the water still ran clear and sweet, and remained a major source for the townsfolk of that area.

The house they entered had a warm, welcoming air to it. Hedlow led his guests into a fine room where the panelled walls were adorned with pictures and small tapestries. Locked away in a cabinet were gleaming, heavy silver dishes, and the centre of the room was graced by a large, lovingly polished square oak table surrounded by four matching chairs.

"You are indeed comfortable here, Master Hedlow" approved Major Blake.

"Yes, that is very true." acknowledged Hedlow, contentedly.

"Aye, very true. I never married, but the life of a lawyer has provided me with a sufficiency that allows me to employ both a manservant and a housekeeper ...Ah, Robert!"

He greeted the man who now entered the room. He was followed by a tall, graceful figure of a woman,

"Bring us some wine, and then you and Anne can serve the supper."

Robert, a grey-haired, stooping man with a walnut-wrinkled face, went immediately to the sideboard to take out decanter and glasses. As the woman turned to leave the room, a lamp flared bright in a current of air, illuminating a face of startling beauty framed by heavy wings of rich, dark hair. Ketch caught his breath in horror as the left side of the face came into view, a cruel, livid scar puckered and distorted the flesh from brow to chin. Hedlow's words in the Council Chamber echoed. "...sorriest of all.... camp-followers .... scarred.... shunned by all."

Ketch thought there was much to be admired in Clerk Hedlow; not many public figures would house a former Royalist woman camp follower, if this were indeed the case. There was something else about that tall, graceful figure that sounded a note in his mind...

Your wine, sir!"

This from Robert, the manservant, proffering the last glass on a silver salver.

Ketch and Blake were ushered to their seats by a solicitous Hedlow, as Robert returned promptly with a huge pewter tray, laden with a succulent roast of pork, crusty bread and dishes of vegetables. Platters filled, the three men settled to their food and a conversation of general nature to aid the digestion. It was a simple meal, but the occasion was special for Ketch; clean linen, sparkling glasses and good plate reminded him of a time in his own life that seemed very far in the past.

His guests satisfactorily fed, Hedlow replenished all three glasses and only then directed the conversation to serious matters.

"So, Ketch. How do you see your situation now?"

"Well, Sir," replied Ketch.

"I and my Troopers are in a most difficult position. The local garrison will resent our being here, and I have no doubt that there will be those who will seek to show their resentment.This will be the case particularly in the next few days. To speak frankly, Sir, I see no purpose in spreading twenty Troopers thinly around this town. At the moment, that would be twenty opportunities for trouble! With your permission, I will keep my men out of sight in the Peacock Inn, where we are billeted.But, before you comment, sir, I also think that we must establish a presence that will show the town that the army has responded to the Council's request. I would, therefore, put ten Troopers within the Council House, directly at your disposal, to protect that building and the proceedings within. I would recommend a two-man guard, publicly, at the main entrance. To those two men I shall give clear instructions not to move from their post, whatever happens. If there is trouble, they will move inside, to be directed by you. I myself, and one or two men, will discreetly appraise the town."

Clerk Hedlow smiled.

"You would make an excellent diplomat, Ketch. Major, are all our Corporals of this metal?"

"No" replied Major Blake.

"I wish they were. Ketch has been recommended to me by his Cornet, and I must tell you, Hedlow, that I shall have other duties for him that must take precedence over all."

"I know" replied Hedlow, leaning forward to speak more directly to Blake.

"I know that you are here on your own purpose - a purpose of which I know nothing, save that it is a matter of state. Such matters offer great dangers, and great rewards, for which powerful men will hazard. Le Vaughn will know of your presence here, and he will wish to turn your affair to his own advantage."

"Who is this Le Vaughn?" enquired Ketch. "He sounds like a man who has both powerful friends and enemies."

Before replying, Hedlow rose and took from the sideboard a small wooden box and three clay pipes. "If I am to speak to you of Le Vaughn, then I must be tranquil - and I find a pipe of tobacco a pleasant, calm way to end the day. Will you gentlemen join me?" Both accepted the offer and, when all three pipes were drawing well and a haze of fragrant smoke rose in the air, Hedlow took up his tale.

"Francis, Lord Le Vaughn, is of Norman descent and owns estates in Lincolnshire, Essex and Northamptonshire. He is one of the richest men in England, with commercial interest throughout Europe. He is a member of many important guilds in the City of London, and on the outbreak of war, threw his strength behind the cause of Parliament. But, above all, Le Vaughn is ambitious, and he has trampled over many good men to further that ambition. He is a Freethinker, an Independent, and he challenges hard both those of Church and Presbyterian opinion. As a man, he has a magnetism that makes others his willing servants. He speaks well, rides magnificently and has fought and won duels. He is a man whose will has no boundaries; do his bidding and you are rewarded; oppose him, and one way or another he will cut you down.

"Le Vaughn's star is in the ascendant. Through his placemen, he virtually controls the main towns and Norfolk and Lincolnshire. I have heard that many members of Parliament have secretly sworn him their support. There is only one man with a stature and support greater than Le Vaughn, and that is our Lieutenant-General, Cromwell!"

Major Blake leaned forward to tap his pipe on the hearth.

"I understand" he said, throwing an enquiring glance at Hedlow.

"That Le Vaughn and Cromwell are enemies, that Le Vaughn seeks to disband the army and take to the Parliament all executive powers, whilst Cromwell dithers on all matters except disbanding the army.

"It is as you say," affirmed Hedlow, drawing firmly on a pipe that was now well aglow.

"But Charles Stuart is also part of this tapestry of power. I think both Le Vaughn and Cromwell would wish an accommodation with the King."

Hedlow paused, then, pointing with his pipe at Blake to emphasise his point, the old clerk continued.

"The issue is, will fair words or force bring the King to either side. I think our General would have an honest agreement with an honest King, something that would justify the rebellion and install a new form of government. My Lord Le Vaughn, on the other hand, is more direct, he would wish his foot on Charles Stuart's neck. However, my own concern, for the moment, is Northampton. It seems that Corporal Ketch has matters well in hand, and thanks to your note, or whatever it was you showed Colonel Fell, we have some protection whilst you are with us."

The three men spent a further hour debating the politics of the time until Hedlow rose unsteadily to his feet. "Gentleman you have much to do. May I offer Robert and a torch to see you safely home?"

Ketch and Major Blake declined Hedlow's offer of an escort and set off together on the short walk to the Council House, where their ways would part. Their talk was of the fine dinner, Fell and his Garrison, the Desborough family - but above all, the will and energy of Francis Le Vaughn, and his national ambitions.

The sentry guarding the virtuously sleeping troop assured Ketch that all was well, and the new Corporal thankfully reached his bed without disturbing any of his fellow soldiers. But weary though his body was, his mind continued to whirl with the events of the day. At last, he fell into an exhausted sleep and, as his mind relaxed, he dreamed of a slim, graceful figure lying beside him and of dark, silken hair spread over his chest; as the woman raised her head to look at him with warm, glowing eyes, he saw a face of exquisite beauty - with no sign of a scar....

Chapter 5

Ketch woke early the next morning, but the June sun was still ahead of him and preparing itself for another hot day. He rose from his straw bed in the corner of the stable loft, pulled on britches and stretched. He scratched his chin and decided that today he would thoroughly wash himself before undertaking the delicate task of shaving.

It was Cornet Marlowe's practice to count his Troopers every morning - a habit acquired from long experience - and Ketch knew that it was a most valuable exercise. Even through the thick of the war, soldiers had walked away from their military duties to the more urgent duties of husband, father and provider. Ketch determined to make a positive start to the day by taking a firm grip on the activities of the troop. He, too, would take up the habit of counting. Wide awake now, he slid his feet into the rough leather shoes that he always carried in his pack; a cavalryman could spend many hours of the day out of the saddle, and riding boots were not kind to walking feet. Collecting his belt and sword he moved across the loft floor to the ladder that led below. Once down in the yard he undertook his count of Troopers, the younger ones generally still asleep, the older ones starting to assemble the means of meeting their early morning needs.

"Hup, lads. Attention, Troopers!Rise, dress, and muster troop. You have the time it takes me to shave for there to be nineteen Troopers lined up here in the yard for my inspection."

Having stated his intentions, Ketch moved towards the kitchens of the Peacock to secure for himself a bowl of hot water that would ease the passage of his sharp blade. Nineteen Troopers were standing around the yard when Ketch had completed his morning preparations. He surveyed his new responsibilities. These were hard, tough men; each one an individual but, collectively, a frightening force to manage. Every man in this troop was a veteran and had at some time or other killed or supported the killing of others. Yesterday he had asserted his leadership by outfacing Trooper Mutch but he knew that the honeymoon period for new Corporals was very short, so firmness and clear orders were his objectives this morning.

"Holditch and eight men of his choosing will go to breakfast whilst Tull and the other nine feed, water and groom their horses: that arrangement will reverse on my order. But no-one goes to breakfast until they have clearly understood the following orders for the day."

Having clarified the matter of breakfast, Ketch knew that he had their attention for no more than a few minutes, but by the end of that time, each Trooper knew his task for the day and understood the general imperative to keep out of sight. The roster for guarding the Council House was given, as was the order to stay within the confines of the inn. With a final command to Tull and Holditch to report to him after their breakfast, Ketch strode off to report to Cornet Marlowe.

The Cornet was sitting up in bed eating a breakfast of bread and warm milk from a rough-hewn wooden bowl.

"Come in, man, come in!" he barked, and Ketch could see that his mood was sharp and flinty, and that his face carried the flush of pain. "Never, never break a limb, Ketch." he growled.

"The pain is terrible - the damned leg does nothing but throb. I cannot move, and I have not had an hour's sleep. How I shall endure five weeks, I do not know. And to complete this misery, I breakfast on pap!"

Ketch rubbed his nose thoughtfully. He was relieved that there was still some humour in the Cornet, but decided this was an occasion for military matters rather than sympathy. Briefly and clearly

Ketch outlined to Cornet Marlowe the incident with Colonel Fell, and his own concern to support the Council but to avoid incidents with the Garrison.

"You have been wise, Ketch" said Marlowe.

"You do well to go gently with Colonel Fell; he has an unpleasant reputation for brutality to his enemies and a harsh discipline for his troops. But, this is the point, he is canny, and has powerful friends. He's not a man to upset.Aye, I reckon you must report to him, Ketch, as a courtesy and hope and pray that he does not have the lot of us arrested and thrown into his dungeons."

Cornet Marlowe put aside his bowl and used his hands to heave himself into a more upright position. This brought an involuntary gasp of pain, and did not improve his temper.

"This is a very devil's brew, Ketch" he said.

"The Common Council and Colonel Fell may well grind my troop away in their opposition to each other and you have these other matters, courtesy of your Major Blake.Well, I warn you, Ketch - I want twenty Troopers alive and well when I get out of this room!"

"Yes, Cornet." replied Ketch, quietly.

He realised that Marlowe was throwing him a lifeline amidst all the factions surrounding him. The easy, straightforward priority of preserving his men would allow him to deny Major Blake and also to stand secure against Colonel Fell. He thought wryly.

"Stay a simple soldier", he thought.

"How often I have just done that. But now it is far too late; I'm committed to Major Blake.

"You may be assured, Cornet Marlowe, that all your men will be ready and waiting for you, on your recovery."

Marlowe reached beneath his pillow and drew out his familiar, well-worn bible. For one moment, Ketch thought he was going to bind him with some form of oath, but instead the Cornet held out the book to him.

"Perhaps you might read a passage for me"

Requested the older man.

"Start with the book of Samuel, Chapter 2, verse 22."

Ketch found the place, and read:

"With the loyal thou showest thyself loyal, and with the blameless man, blameless.With the savage man, though, showest thyself savage, and tortuous with the perverse."

"A sound text for any soldier" interrupted Marlowe.

He took the bible from Ketch, and looked at his Trooper.

"You will need God's help, Ketch."

"Amen to that" Ketch replied, softly.

Then, gathering himself, he stood to attention.

"I will report to you each morning and evening, Sir, on my activities and those of your troop. Today I shall look about this town and attend on Colonel Fell. I shall, with your approval, take leave of you now and report again this evening."

"To your duties, Corporal" responded Marlowe.

"Until this evening."

Ketch stepped out of the front door of the Peacock Inn into the now strong sunlight, and the hand that pulled down the shady brim of his hat paused to tap a thoughtful finger against the side of his nose. He now had a brief moment of independence to use as he pleased. He was jolted out of his pondering by the awareness that it was Market Day - and the square fronting the inn was thronged with people passing between and clustering around a considerable number of market stalls and carts.

Ketch knew from his youth that Northampton market had a considerable reputation that drew buyers and sellers from many miles around. The markets had continued to be held throughout the troubles, albeit at times with scant produce, for they were a source of news for the ordinary folk of the town on how national matters were progressing. Now that the King had surrendered and was tucked up in Holdenby House it seemed possible that life might return to normal as the markets drew larger and larger crowds. Ketch relaxed somewhat from the tensions and uncertainties he had been feeling, and his gaze wandered over the scene before him. Farmers, hawkers and entertainers now sought to coax money from the townspeople of Northampton. It was a colourful sight, not only in terms of the produce being sold and the people buying and selling, but also in their behaviour. Bargaining is not a quiet activity and the noise of primitive commerce filled the square. Ketch noticed that groups of off-duty soldiers sampling the market, and quite prepared to push and cuff anyone in their way, were being given plenty of room by even the most avid of the bargainers. Ketch knew that markets attracted trouble; thieves, cutpurses and fraudsters would be working their trades. Not a place for someone seeking to avoid confrontation, he thought to himself. He set of towards the Church of All Saints skirting the Market Square and avoiding contact with the crowds. He noted with satisfaction two Troopers smartly at sentry duty on the steps of the Council House, and then turned down towards the portico of All Saints.

A familiar voice came to his ears as he approached the front of the Church; Preacher Hyack was haranguing a steadily growing crowd. As he was about to turn away, Ketch's attention was caught by the still figure of a woman, half-concealed in the shadow of a doorway on the opposite side of the road. He would have dismissed her as just another good wife on her way home from market, pausing to rest her heavy basket and glean a little entertainment, but for the stillness of her form and the intensity with which she appeared to be listening to the Preacher. Ketch could not see her face, for the wide wings of her cap were pulled unfashionably forward and securely pinned in place. Perhaps the intensity of Ketch's regard disturbed her concentration, for her head turned towards him and a pair of large, dark eyes showed startled recognition. It was Ann, Clerk Hedlow's housekeeper; but before Ketch could smile an acknowledgement, she had bowed her head away from him and set off swiftly towards the Derngate. A strange encounter, thought Ketch, and what a tragedy that so much beauty should have been so destroyed; what other punishments had been inflicted by her persecutors did not bear thinking about....

Ketch had stood too long watching Ann, for Preacher Hyack had spotted the long, lean figure in the distinctive buff coat and was now pointing an accusing finger directly at him.

"Have care, citizens of Northampton!"

The voice was rising to a screech.

"We have soldiers from London sent to tell us how to live our lives, how to pray to our God, and there is one of the acolytes!"

The crowd turned to look at Ketch, their faces glowering. He quickly skirted the group, and moved down the street toward the Castle.

"Let him go" cried the Preacher.

"Leave him alone. Let him slink slyly past the word of God. He will one day regret his sin."

But even as his words turned the attention of the crowd back to him, the Preacher's eyes and a nod of his head dispatched a burly, bearded man in Ketch's direction.

Ketch had seen the nod, and quickly tagged his pursuer. He increased the pace of his walk and felt, rather than saw, that his bearded follower maintained a gap of about thirty paces between them. Ketch now turned into a quarter of the town that he did not know. Rickety, timber-built houses were grouped closely together in small squares and alleyways, blocking out much of the light. A pungent stench of rotting vegetable and human waste stung the nostrils; scrawny dogs snapped at him as he disturbed their scavenging. The few figures he glimpsed, disappeared rapidly at the sight of the uniformed Ironside, except for two bedraggled hags who called out an invitation to him from an upstairs room, and bared their breasts, laughing as he strode away from them. A bundle of rags in a doorway turned into a drunken, pockmarked beggar who caught at his legs causing him to stumble against a rotting barrel. As he grabbed at the barrel, trying to keep from falling into the oozing filth of the gutter, a rat leapt from it and vanished into dark places. Ketch was conscious that this stinking slum was doubly dangerous, for he was still being pursued.

He made a sharp turn down an unexpected gap between two houses, crossed the next street at a run, and turned into a way that seemed in the right direction to get him out of this quarter. Ten paces on and his heart sank; there was no way out, for a high half-timbered wall blocked the end. He turned quickly to face his pursuer, his hand on the pommel of his sword. The entry to the alley remained empty, and there was no sound of footsteps in pursuit. It suddenly felt very hot, and Ketch could feel the sweat building up around his neck and running down his back. Still nothing happened. His eyes checked the alley for a means of escape, but there was none. He was well and truly trapped in the narrow passage.

He was not surprised as the entrance darkened as the large form of the preacher's bearded lieutenant filled it. Dressed in dirty brown breeches and with what was once a white shirt struggling to cover huge arms, shoulders and chest, the great body went into a crouching position, and a curved knife caught the light as it was switched from hand to hand. It was a knife and a fighting style that Ketch recognised from the previous day; and although large of bulk, there was a lightness and sureness of touch in the manner in which his adversary moved his knife from hand to hand and there was almost a delicacy in the way he moved his feet.

"Have some Christian charity" reasoned Ketch.

"What quarrel have we? Come, let us go our separate ways in peace."

"Too clever a soldier" hissed his opponent.

"Too clever!"

With a quick lunge, his left-hand swung inwards and the point of the knife flicked towards Ketch's throat.

Ketch had been a soldier for some four years, but his exercise in the martial arts had begun at the age of seven. In his father's schoolroom the art of fencing had been part of the daily curriculum, even for the sons of grocers and drapers. But whilst their expertise was based on two or three years of schooling, for Ketch it had become a lifelong exercise. He had no fear of the large, quick-moving but probably slow-witted, figure now threatening him. But he also knew that even with the most ill-prepared of opponent's care must be taken. Ketch had been taught again and again that when facing a swordsman in single combat the great swordsmen watched neither hands nor eyes, for these were the great betrayers. It was the feet that communicated an opponent's true intent.He took two paces smartly backward, drew his sword and held it ready for the attack that was about to come. At the very instant his adversary's feet tensed and prepared to catapult body and knife forward, Ketch pre-empted the attack with a swift, accurate slice from the tip of his own blade that cut deeply into his opponent's wrist; the knife fell into the gutter and the great brute stared at his cut wrist welling blood. He cried aloud in pain as if it were a new experience to be so hurt and clutched his wrist to his stomach. Ketch moved in a pace and wove a pattern with the tip of his blade around his adversary's beard; as the man's arms reluctantly came up to protect his head; Ketch kicked him on the kneecap.

The colossus fell to ground, gurgling with pain. Ketch leapt over him and out of the alley. Catching sight of the sun through a gap between the houses, he set off rapidly to seek an exit that would take him away from this dishonourable brawl. He slowed his gait as he entered a less disreputable looking part of the town, and paused to wipe the sweat from his brow and the sides of his nose, puzzling over the two incidents involving Preacher Hyack. Clearly, he was a religious fanatic of the most extreme kind; anyone who opposed him was a target for revenge. Ketch shrugged his shoulders, and made a mental note to keep well out of the Preacher's way; he had quite enough problems, one of which was the need to report to Colonel Fell. This would most certainly be a difficult and unpleasant interview but, as he was now close to Northampton Castle, the main garrison centre for the town, Ketch steeled himself to face up to the task.

The main entrance to the Castle was on the southern side and, as Ketch approached it, he entered the familiar world of soldiers. The area before the main gate was a bustle of activity, but no-one paid him any attention as he strode past off-duty soldiers gambling in the dust, horses being groomed and an outdoor smithy alive with the noise of hammers beating metal.

"I would see your officer."

Ketch addressed a fresh-faced young man who was obviously in charge of the main gate, but equally obviously was not taking his responsibilities too seriously, as he sat on an empty cask and watched happily as soldiers, wives and tradesmen passed to and fro unchallenged.

"And what would your business be" replied the young man, raising himself from his seat.

"Most of our officers are drinking the Colonel's health, and that of Lord Le Vaughn. Today the good lord has unloosed his purse strings and every man in this garrison has received half his back pay. You are welcome to try and find whoever you wish, but by God there is some heavy drinking even at this hour!"

In his exuberance, he clapped an arm about Ketch's shoulders.

"Lord Le Vaughn is the finest gentleman in this county today, anyone who personally hands me six pounds has my support and that's an end to it."

"Amen to that" responded Ketch.

"Your Lord Le Vaughn, Fairfax and Cromwell will see us soldiers and the country aright."

The young guard spat on the floor.

"Those two will betray us; they'll trim their sails and accommodate Charles Stuart. No, it is patriots like Lord Le Vaughn who should rule the roost in London, and every man here in this county will follow him."

"Unfortunately, I know nothing of your Lord Le Vaughn" answered Ketch.

"But I am sure he is a fine leader."

Ketch was anxious to get away, for the young man's enthusiastic words had drawn the attention of a group of soldiers loitering on the other side of the main gate. Nodding their approval, they came to join in the conversation.

"Some more lads with money to spend!" cried Ketch loudly, slapping the young man on the shoulder.

"If only I had time to test their mettle through some honest games of chance. But now I must away on my errand to an officer."

He disengaged himself from the gathering group who started to debate some gambling arrangements of their own and walked through the shadow of the gatehouse into the bright sunlight of the main bailey. During the period of the troubles between King and Parliament, Northampton Castle had been a bulwark in the defences of Parliament. The county garrison had been almost totally based here and, in consequence, many adaptations and temporary buildings had been constructed. Ketch headed toward a finely built, two storey wooden building with glass mullion windows, set against the far wall of the bailey.

The sentry at the door was a large, dour-faced man who had clearly not been overwhelmed with euphoria at his recent financial advancement. Ketch explained that he had a duty to report to Colonel Fell; as he spoke, he could hear the sounds of convivial celebration going on inside the building.

"They have been drinking with enthusiasm for an hour" grumbled the guard.

"And Colonel Fell with them. I doubt that you will get much sense or patience from anyone here."

As he spoke, the door opened and Colonel Fell himself stepped out. His long black hair was tousled, his eyes blazed with a strange triumph and his face was alive with smiles. He took a sharp look at Ketch, and his look rapidly changed to annoyance.

"Cornet Marlowe has instructed me to report our presence here in Northampton to you, and to explain why..."

"Enough!" interrupted Fell.

"This is a fine day for Northampton's best soldiers, go away, and do not interfere in matters that are beyond your understanding."

He thrust his head forward into Ketch's face.

"I know why you are here, and I know you give hope to opponents of my Lord Le Vaughn"

Here his eyes flickered towards the great West Tower.

"All of 'em, will be crushed."

Wine had weakened the Colonel's self-control.

"Look to yourself, soldier. Forget the Common Council; forget Major Blake and his beloved Cromwell. Take your Cornet and hurry back to London."

With a scowl, he turned on his heel and strode across the bailey towards the West Tower, smoothing his hair and straightening his tunic. It appeared that he was to meet his superior, and that could only be Le Vaughn.

Thus dismissed, Ketch marched out of the Castle, thankful that the meeting had been so short. The distribution of largesse and the resultant drinking had undoubtedly focused the Colonel's mind on other matters, and Ketch and his troop were no more than a minor irritant to a man whose grip on Northampton seemed absolute. The eternal struggle for power, thought Ketch; Charles Stuart and John Pym; Cromwell and Le Vaughn - whoever it was, it was the ordinary people who made the sacrifices and collected the scars.

Ketch, thankful that he had survived the interview, resolutely put these thoughts from his mind, and directed his steps towards the Church of the Holy Sepulchre - and the house of Mary and Martha Desborough. There was still the matter of the King's missing letter to investigate!

The Desborough house sat at right angles to the burial ground of the Church of the Holy Sepulchre, known familiarly as "St Sepulchre's" to its parishioners. The small two-storey house was built of warm golden Northampton stone, with a Welsh slate roof. The solid front door opened directly onto the street, and as Ketch tapped lightly on the door, he noticed that the downstairs window was shadowed with a drape, preserving the privacy of the occupants. Some seconds passed, and he knocked again. There was still no reply. Ketch was turning to go, assuming the ladies were out, when the door opened, a reluctant few inches and the face of Martha Desborough peered suspiciously at the unwelcome visitor.

"Good morning, Mistress Desborough. May I enquire as to the health of your sister?"

Martha's demeanour and her reluctance to open the door any wider made it clear to Ketch that he would need to persevere if he hoped to be invited to enter.

"She is well, thank you." replied Martha.

"A good night's rest and quiet repose have been the best medicine."

"And she has suffered no real hurt?" pressed Ketch.

"No, no. She is quite well. Thank you for your enquiry."

Martha was clearly seeking to terminate the interview in order that the door could be closed without offence. Ketch realised that a more forceful tactic was required.

"I have come on another matter also," he said.

"I wish to discuss with you, certain matters concerning your father and your brother, Ralph Desborough. It would, I suggest, be the better for me to speak to you privately."

Martha's face became troubled at Ketch's words; glancing back into the house, she paused, then opened the front door wide.

"Come in if you must" she said.

"Family matters are, as you say, best discussed away from the hearing of others."

Ketch stepped across the threshold and was conducted across the narrow hallway and into the darkened front room. Martha drew back the drapes, and offered him a place on a solid oak chair. She took her seat on the couch, her back straight and rigid. Before Ketch could say anything, the door flew open and Mary Desborough entered the room.

"Look, Mary" said Martha, quickly.

"One of the soldiers who helped you yesterday has come to see us. But he wants to talk about father and Ralph."

This brought a frown to Mary's pretty face, and her blue eyes went cold. Recovering her composure, she crossed the room and sat on the couch next to her sister. Together, they formed a defence against any intrusion, and Ketch decided that the truth, carefully phrased would be the best approach; he hoped that they would recognise the truth, and respond to someone who wished them no harm. He chose his words judiciously.

"I know that you two ladies have experienced probably the worst years of your lives. You home, possessions, place in society, and your father have all been taken from you. You are two defenceless women, living in a time when disorder and brutality are everywhere. As part of a family, whose estates have been sequestered, you live on the goodwill of your enemies. I am surprised you stay in Northampton, where any drunken soldier or vindictive scoundrel can challenge your threshold."

"Do you wish to frighten us, Sir?" cried Martha.

"We try to be courageous in a place where few will even say 'good day' to us, but this talk will terrify us if you continue."

"I am sorry," said Ketch,

"But I wish you to know that I understand your position; and that what I say and what I ask is not an attempt to hurt and humiliate you. I would like you to think of me as a friend, someone you can turn to." The sincerity in Ketch's voice had clearly affected Mary, who blinked away tears from her eyes. Martha was a different case.

"You're are a Roundhead soldier" she snorted

"And you want to be our friend. You and your like have harried us unmercifully, and have brought us down to our present state. No, Sir! You are no friend of ours. Ask your question, and go! I tell you!"

Her face grew harder as she drove her points home.

"We have been questioned already by Major Blake, with whom you are, no doubt, in careful alliance. He has had all our answers."

Ketch leaned back into his chair in the face of such a torrent of words. Clearly securing any new information from this quarter was going to be extremely difficult.

"I must say this to you" he continued.

"Your father is dead - perhaps murdered. You yourselves found the body in Holcot Woods. There are many people interested in the details of that death; many people interested in who was close to him at that time."

"We last saw our father alive five years ago" said Martha.

Then, bitterly.

"The day he left us on our own to fend for ourselves.

"Ketch rose to his feet and paced thoughtfully about the room, his eyes casually noting every detail of the place.

"Amongst those desperately concerned with Sir Roger's death is your brother, Ralph. That concern may or may not be more than that of a son for a murdered father"

Out of the corner of his eye, Ketch noticed Mary Desborough give an involuntary little nod of assent to his words. He continued,

"Such concern could lead a loyal, possibly headstrong, you man to return to Northampton, to contact his family and perhaps to seek their help in the pursuance of his purposes.."

"Enough!" interrupted Martha, rising to her feet.

"This will upset Mary, who has suffered enough these last few days. Go to our room, Mary, and rest. I will see this gentleman soldier out."

"I think, Mistress, it would be wiser to help those who would help you." said Ketch.

As he spoke, he strained all his senses to try and catch some sign of a masculine presence that might reveal that Ralph Desborough was in this house, but his eyes, his sense of smell, his hearing, revealed nothing.

Martha ushered him out into the small hall as Mary obediently went up the stairs. Ketch gave a brief bow, and replaced his hat, automatically glancing into the ornate small mirror hanging above Martha's head as he adjusted the brim.

"I wish you well, ladies..."

He began his farewell, but stopped at the look of fright on Martha's face. The mirror was not in the right place for two small females to tidy their hair and bonnets before stepping out into the street. It was, however, at just the right height for a six-foot man. Ketch smiled as the door closed behind him with a definite thud. It might not be proof, but he felt sure that Ralph Desborough was using his sisters' house and that the two women were protecting him.

The June sun was well past noon when Ketch trudged into the stable yard of the Peacock. He was hot and tired: a cavalryman's uniform was not ideal for town reconnaissance in the height of summer. He helped himself to a drink from the water barrel, and noticed that some half-a-dozen of his Troopers were sitting around in the bright sunlight, looking sulky. Ketch knew that this was fairly normal for soldiers but, given the weather and their circumstances, Ketch thought they looked unnaturally glum. One or two were nursing cuts and bruises, and Trooper Ripley had a bandaged shin. Sitting on a flour barrel was Trooper Holditch; the plump Londoner was smoking a pipe and of all those present looked most at peace with the world.

"Well, Corporal" he greeted Ketch's approach.

"We have had a little bit of trouble in your absence. We changed over guard duty less than two hours ago, and it did not go smoothly!"

There were some full grain sacks piled alongside Holditch and with a weary sigh, Ketch sat himself down to hear the report. He remembered he was a Corporal, however, and pulled himself up straight.

"Tell me the worst. I leave you for a morning and things 'do not go smoothly'?"

"You should have been here, Ketch," interjected Ripley.

"We have had a hard time of it."

This drew murmurs of assent from all present. Ketch could see his men felt aggrieved - and they were, of course, going to make the most of it.

"All right" he said.

"Quiet yourselves. Trooper Holditch will now tell me what has made you brave soldiers so unhappy."

Holditch puffed on his pipe a few moments until his audience settled.

"You gave order, Corporal, that Tull should march eight men down to the Council House to relieve me and the nine others that were on guard. Now, Tull, he manages his bit well enough and down they come. Mr Hedlow, who was pleased enough with what me and my men had done - being very quiet and just pushing a couple out front to show we were there - he says, 'Off you go, Holditch. March your men back to Corporal Ketch, for the new guard can take over'!"

"Easy enough for Tull" came in Ripley again.

"In the Council House, safe and sound!"

"Yes,"

Added Trooper Larkin, determined to contribute to the growing tale of woe.

" Not running the gauntlet like us".

Holditch paused, stared the source of the interruption into silence, and continued.

"By the time we march out, there is a bit of a crowd outside; and they are none too friendly. I thought the troubles were over, but damn me if they don't start throwing things at us - fruit and rotten vegetable to start with, but there were some evil looking rascals who started to throw tiles and stones. Well, the upshot of all this was that we were jostled and pushed and given a very hard time. It's not much more than a hundred yards from the Council House to here, but we ended up legging the last few paces; and once here we had to turn and form and look business like with a few pistols cocked and swords drawn. We are not unscathed either for a few of us have cuts and bruises."

"What I can't understand" persisted Larkin. "Is why they are choosing us. I even saw uniformed soldiers in the crowd. I thought Northampton was supposed to be one of our garrisons."

"What about Tull?" asked Ketch.

"Oh, he is clever enough," said Holditch.

"He just shuts the doors of the Council House with every man inside, and he wouldn't come out! It's all right now, the crowd have gone back to the market, or to their dinner most like."

Holditch paused.

"The sentries are back outside the Council house, but it's clear we are not welcome here, Corporal."

"Well, you may be right," said Ketch.

"But it's time you lot started to earn your pay. Comfortable ale houses have made you soft."

Raising himself from his sacks, Ketch turned back to Holditch.

"We will not be caught again. I want one man all the time in the front room of the Peacock, watching the square."

Ketch determined that he was due some rest and thinking time so, leaving the Troopers with a range of tasks to perform, he climbed the ladder to the loft and stretched himself out on his hay bed and let his mind wander. His last thoughts before falling asleep were that Northampton was turning out to be anything but an easy billet.

Chapter 6

Francis Verney, better known throughout England as Lord Le Vaughn, sat at the large oak table that served as his desk in the upper room of the West Tower of Northampton Castle. He was clearly taking his ease, for his solid body was clad in a loosely girdled purple robe, and his bare feet were thrust into simple sandals. He enjoyed relaxing thus, for he knew that such dress reinforced his likeness to a Roman emperor. At fifty years of age, he was at the height of his powers; the large, almost totally bald head, the heavy eyelids over piercing eyes, and the large, hawk nose bespoke strength. This was a leader of men, not merely by virtue of physical strength; the slate-dark eyes flashed intelligence and willpower, and his voice could charm as well as command. There was but one corruption in him: he wished to rule everything and everyone, and those that opposed his will he destroyed.

Colonel Fell, standing at ease before the table, watched closely the man who was one of the six most powerful in England. Seven county Associations were controlled by Le Vaughn's supporters; the City of

London was dominated by his friends, as was the House of Lords, and his support was growing daily in the House of Commons. The captains of the four largest ships in the Parliamentary navy had sent him letters of support, as had the governors of Plymouth, Hull and Bristol. Only the New Model Army was proving to be resistant to his blandishments, but even here, he still had his hopes. The Commander-in-Chief, Fairfax, was sick of war and thought only of retiring to his estates in Yorkshire. The main opposition would come from Lieutenant-General Cromwell and his son-in-law, Ireton - but now they were at their most vulnerable. With the war won, Le Vaughn and his supporters would disband the army, press for the release of the King, and seek the election of a new Parliament based on a new franchise. His master, Le Vaughn, would be the new chief minister. He would manage a weak monarch and raise sufficient money to pay off the army. Cromwell would provide no opposition in the face of such demands for, at heart; he was a weak temporiser. Colonel Fell was confident that Le Vaughn could discredit Cromwell and bring the army over to his side. The Colonel stood watchful ready to perform his master's commands.

Lord Le Vaughn, however, was not in self-congratulatory mood.

"Fell" he snapped.

"We need that letter, I must see it, and hold it myself."

"My Lord" soothed Fell.

"Our spies are everywhere, we observe Major Blake and the Desborough sisters. We even have men close by their uncle's farm. There may well be no such letter, my Lord. It is only a Royalist rumour."

"That letter exists, Fell, and I intend to have it ", replied Le Vaughn. "With it I can bend Charles Stuart to my every wish. He would do anything to hide his dishonour. To invite a French army into England is unbelievable, but to break his coronation oath for the catholics was stupid"

Le Vaughn rose to his feet.

"Show in Major Blake ,I think we have kept him waiting long enough. Hold but a moment Fell whilst I change my clothes. I shall woo this Major first Fell, but if I know this man, I shall in the end have to frighten him".

When Fell announced Major Blake, Le Vaughn was again seated at his table, but now he was fully dressed in sober black, with nothing more than a white short collar to break the austerity of the image he presented.

"Come in, Major Blake", he said.

"Pray be seated" and he waved a hand to the chair on the opposite side of the desk.

"I thank you, my Lord" acknowledge Blake, taking the proffered place.

"It is indeed a privilege for me to meet you."

"Indeed, no!" exclaimed Le Vaughn.

"It is important that we old men meet the brave soldiers who have been winning this war for Parliament. May I offer you some refreshment?"

He indicated the sideboard where stood a tray with goblet and a decanter of wine. At Blake's polite refusal Le Vaughn continued smoothly.

"Very wise I personally drink only water. Strong drink has been the downfall of many good men."

Le Vaughn leaned back in his great carved chair, placing the tips of his fingers together in a reflective manner.

"Major Blake, I think you would agree that I have played my role with great loyalty for Parliament in this war against Charles Stuart. Northampton, both town and county, under my friend Lord Golby, has been the staunchest of bastions for the Parliamentary cause. What influence I have in the City of London and in both Lords and Commons has steadfastly been brought to bear in support of our common purpose. No one can claim to have risked more and given more than myself. Is this a just claim, Major, would you dispute this?"

"No, my Lord" replied Blake.

"Everyone knows that what you say is true, that you have dedicated your life to the Parliamentary cause."

"Tell me, Major," continued Le Vaughn.

"Does such a man deserve support from all those who, like him, have also fought long and hard for Parliament? Does he have some claim on their loyalty?"

"Yes, I am sure that is the case" replied Blake, feeling unsure of how this conversation was developing.

"Let me ask you a direct question" said Le Vaughn, his voice warm and friendly.

"Who should rule when this war is finally done? Should it be Charles Stuart? Can he be trusted? Can we believe any promises he will make? Should it rather be Parliament, Vane, Hasselrigg of the Commons, or some great lord, Essex or Fairfax, or...?"

The hooded eyes turned full on Blake.

"Should the army rule England? Tell me, Major, we have been fighting Charles Stuart for some four years over this question, what have you been fighting for?"

"For the People and Parliament" replied Blake,

"First and last. That is why the King's gauntlet was taken up."

"Why, then" asked Le Vaughn, still holding Blake with his eyes.

"Why then do you continue to work secretly for your Lieutenant-General Cromwell, who would have the army rule England? Come, Major, he might be a fine general, an open and honest man, but we have not fought a King to be ruled by the army."

His voice became warm once more.

"I need good men, Blake, to foster and support my cause in both Parliament and the army, so that the fruits of the war are not wasted, so that Parliament is strong, and so that our struggle is worthwhile, so that the people, with a humbled King, can live in peace."

The full force of the man's personality was overwhelming.

"Will you help me, Blake? Will you help England? Do not let the spilt blood be for nothing!"

The Major found this plea persuasive; he had joined the war in Parliament's cause, this was what he had been fighting for. And to be the confidant and supporter of such a great personage would be the climax of his career. The Major was almost overwhelmed by the offer of friendship, service and trust. All his instincts, however, screamed out that Le Vaughn could not be trusted; that whatever he said, this was not a man to whom England should be given.

Whilst these thoughts pulsed through the Major's mind, there was a long silence that filled the room with the tension between the two men and amplified the power of Le Vaughn's personality, which almost physically gripped the Major. With an enormous effort, Blake was able to give his own answer, rather than the one Le Vaughn had almost forced out of him.

"I am a soldier, my Lord. Great matters of state are not my concern. I continue only to take my orders. I cannot make the choice you wish of me"

As the words came out, they became progressively easier to say; at the end, perched at the back of his mind, was the rueful thought that even Majors, when pressed, used the 'simple soldier' argument.

Le Vaughn snapped out his irritation at Blake's answer.

"So be it, Major Blake. I know you now as an enemy, or at least not a friend, of Parliament - and one who has rejected my own offer of friendship and advancement. What would you say now if I were to order Colonel Fell to escort you to one of my dungeons? That would make you re-think your place, I have no doubt."

Major Blake knew that he was frightened of Le Vaughn, but he was determined not to show his fear and so he spoke calmly in reply, even though his heart was pounding

"You know, my Lord" he said.

"For I have no doubt that Colonel Fell has informed you, that I carry a Commission recognised by Parliament and signed by the highest in the army, and that Commission charges all to provide me with help and assistance."

Le Vaughn's eyes narrowed, and he leaned forward to impress himself even more forcibly on the Major.

"Do not place too much trust in your Commission, Blake, for one of those signatories will soon carry no influence in the world of affairs. Indeed" and he allowed himself a smile of satisfaction,

"I myself expect to become Secretary to the Committee of Both Kingdoms in the new Parliamentary session. Your Commission has little force with me, Major. I suggest you run back to your master and tell him that news. He will not thank you for it."

Slowly standing to his full height, Le Vaughn dismissed Major Blake coldly.

"Northampton can be a dangerous place, Major. For your safety, I would recommend an early return to London."

Colonel Fell entered the room in immediate response to the summons of a small silver bell.

"Escort the Major from the Castle, Fell" ordered Le Vaughn. "His safety then is his own matter."

Blake was guided down the stairs and into the bailey below.

"I can find my way out well enough, Colonel."

"I am charged to see you safely from our threshold." replied Fell and this he did.

At the main gate to the Castle there was no 'farewell', no wave of the hand , Colonel Fell turned his back on the Major and walked back to the West Tower. Major Blake felt very alone and very exposed. He had just insulted one of the most powerful men in England, someone whose influence, and therefore his capacity to destroy, was almost limitless. The Major was frightened, frightened by Le Vaughn and frightened at his own vulnerability. In the face of his fear he made up his mind very quickly, a swift return to London was not just advisable, but essential if he was to live and avoid the consequences of his interview. He had to abandon the Cornet and the Corporal, at least temporarily, to their fate.

In the West Tower, Le Vaughn and his henchman were toasting the event with Madeira wine.

"He will not concern us any more" smiled Le Vaughn.

"You will now have a clear field so that you may find and bring to me the King's letter."

At this point, he threw back his head and laughed.

"He thought I was making him a serious offer to join us. Had he accepted, I would have squeezed him dry of information and then left him to you. As it is, he lives a little longer - but not here, under our feet."

"Satisfactory either way" agreed Fell.

"As it should be!" added Le Vaughn, and two silver goblets glinted as they were raised in triumph.

Tull and eight men marched into the stableyard of the Peacock. On being dismissed, they stowed their arms and hurried to join the rest of the troop and take part in the soldiers' recreations of gambling and gossip.

"Move over!" ordered Tull, dumping himself next to Holditch on the shaded side of the bench occupied by his friend.

"All right, all right" grumbled Holditch.

"You can't be all that tired, for all you've done all day is to sit comfortably in the Council House. Did you have an easy passage back?" he enquired, changing the conversation to the main event of his day. "Do you know, we were pelted with rotten fruit and pushed and pulled by the so-called townsfolk on our return to the Peacock. And there were members of the Garrison helping them!"

"We had some ugly looks" said Tull.

"But no disturbance. So, it was you who has had today's excitement!" He searched out his old clay pipe and, for want of tobacco, sucked on it dry.

"What puzzles me is, what are we doing here? Who are we guarding the Council House against the townspeople? The Garrison? I don't mind telling you, Holditch, I find all this very strange. With the Cornet out of it, we're going to need every bit of Ketch's learning to see us right. I don't see twenty Troopers taking on the Northampton Garrison if it has a mind to do something.""

Us Troopers" said a resigned Holditch, "will do as orders tell us. But enough of this, I am ready for some food. When are we eating? I thought this inn was feeding us."

Ketch entered the yard, refreshed by his nap and ready to carry out his evening duties.

"Holditch" he ordered.

"You can take eight men into supper now, and Tull, when they have finished, you can take the rest in and look lively."

There was no twinkle in his eye, and his pale face had no crease of a smile. Tull and Holditch rose to carry out his orders and started shouting instructions to their fellow troopers. With half a mind on their activities, Ketch's attention was attracted by Botterill, the innkeeper, calling from the kitchen door, that Major Blake had arrived and was taking his evening meal in Cornet Marlowe's room, and could Corporal Ketch join them?

"I want everything peaceful." Ketch warned his two friends, as he turned to go. He had news for the Major, and he felt sure the Major had news for him.

Chapter 7

Ketch and Major Blake sat facing each other across the bed of the Cornet. Ketch sensed an uncertainty about the Major, a hesitation that concerned him. He was in some way different from the confident and assured man who had recruited him to the army's service. The Major had stopped looking him in the eye. Cornet Marlowe, Ketch could see, was restless. Pain had remorselessly lain alongside him for two days, and any movement at all was now clearly agony. Marlowe was sitting up in bed but lying perfectly still. This care, however, brought little relief. He had wrestled with his pain, fought it with all his strength, but his growing exhaustion was evident in his gaunt face and hollowed eyes. His mind remained clear, but the ever present hurt in his leg made it hard for him to concentrate on the words of his companions.

"Damn me!" he exclaimed.

"Blake, my leg is burning as if 'twere in the fiery pit itself. Ketch, I would ask you to get me some strong red wine, then you can tell me your news and what must be done."

Ketch filled three pewter mugs from the large flagon of rough red wine that stood amidst the debris of the evening meal on a tray that had been left on a small table at the far end of the room. As Major Blake and Ketch sipped at their mugs, Cornet Marlowe drank deep of his. The effect was positive; with a grunt of pain, he readjusted his sitting position in his bed.

"Right, Ketch. Tell me your news, and then perhaps the Major can inform us on the visit I know he has made to Lord Le Vaughn. But speak softly, for that Botterill fellow has been hanging around this room of late, and I would not be surprised if he repeats what he hears for money. Some time, not now, we must decide how we will deal with master Botterill."

Before Ketch could reply, Major Blake forestalled him.

"We will hear your news, Ketch, in a moment, but mine is bad, so perhaps we should consider it first."

At their nods of agreement, he continued.

"My interview with Le Vaughn did not go well. He first offered me a place amongst his counsellors; this being rejected, he as good as warned me to leave Northampton. I am clearly unwanted here, and I am sure Colonel Fell will give me no more than a day or so before enforcing his master's wishes."

"But your protection" interjected Marlowe. "Did you show him the letter?"

"Oh, yes," replied Blake.

"And he took great pleasure in telling me of its very limited life, and how he himself will replace one of the signatories in the next Parliamentary session. So, my friends, my life is at risk and, by consequence, your position here cannot be maintained. I had thought a Cornet and Troopers would provide eyes and ears for my main purpose in Northampton, but with my Commission devalued, we must all return to London."

He sighed, and asked.

"Can you manage this, Marlowe? Ketch, can he survive a trip in your supply wagon?"

Major" cried Ketch.

Cornet Marlowe's face was twisted with disappointment and apprehension.

"Are you sure, Major?" he said.

"Before Ketch arrived, you told me the substance of your search, are you sure that you are beaten in your quest?"

"I am certain," replied Major Blake.

“That Le Vaughn is on the brink of becoming the most important man in England, and that the Northampton Garrison will tear to shreds anyone who opposes him."

"Wait!" exclaimed Ketch.

"Major, the product of my day is simple. I am sure that Ralph Desborough is in the town, and that can only mean that he continues his search for the King's letter. You must be close, sir."

Ketch was desperate to follow the plan he had considered for securing Ralph Desborough.

"He may yet lead us to it. And with such a prize placed in the hands of Cromwell, Le Vaughn may yet fail in his intent to rule England."

Ketch leaned forward in his effort to persuade Blake.

"Major" he urged.

"A few days more may bring us what we search for. It is a risk, I know - but surely we can find a few days."

"Ketch" replied the Major.

"Your men have already been attacked publicly."

"What!" exclaimed Cornet Marlowe.

"This I did not know. What happened, Ketch?"

The Cornet grasped Ketch by the arm. Concern for his troop added to the pain creases on his face.

"The Major is right" acknowledged Ketch, gently unfolding the Cornets hand from his arm.

"The Council House guard was troubled by a crowd of townsfolk - and members of the garrison at mid-day as it returned to the Peacock. But nobody was hurt -just some rotten fruit was thrown, that was all."

Major Blake turned to Marlowe.

"Well, your advice, Cornet?" he said.

"Do we all run away? Do I go? Do some of us stay?"

"Major" Ketch could not hold back.

"You are the one who concerns Lord Le Vaughn and Colonel Fell, the rest of us are no more than a minor annoyance. Let you leave your lodgings tomorrow and publicly ride out for London. But go only as far as a day's ride say, to Newport Pagnell, by the river. Take lodgings there, and wait. We will announce that the troop will return to London just as soon as Cornet Marlowe can safely travel, in two or three days. I know this will upset Hedlow and the Common Council, but it seems the best we can do for all. It will, at least, give me perhaps three days to pursue our venture. I am sure Le Vaughn will not really worry about twenty Troopers and their winged Cornet!"

Marlowe laughed for the first time since his fall but his laughter was filled with cynicism.

"He is right, Major! With you out of the way, and me laid up, Le Vaughn is not going to pursue Ketch and his men."

"Agreed!" Exclaimed the major, enthusiasm once more lighting his face.

"Ketch, you and your three days will be our last roll of the dice in this affair, and by God, I hope you can find something, but if not, make certain that you get out without Le Vaughn knowing any more than he does now."

Ketch smiled grimly.

"It is agreed then ,the Major will go and we shall stay".

He rose to his feet.

"Time is not our friend in this, we must be about our matters at once. With your permission, Sirs I will leave you. I must supervise the evening duties of the troop before I may take our own special interests forward."

"Come and see me later" replied Major Blake. "I must give you a note to take to Clerk Hedlow. He will be upset with this news."

Major Blake stayed but a short while as the soporific effect of two tankards of wine took hold of Cornet Marlowe. He stepped out briskly towards his own lodgings to prepare for his departure the following morning, and as he walked, he composed the letter that Ketch would take to Clerk Hedlow.

Cornet Marlowe looked around his now darkening small room. He felt better, the pain in his leg was slightly dulled and his companion in arms still sought his advice. "Winged but not down" he chuckled to himself as he forced his body down beneath his sheets. "My task is to watch Botterill," he thought as his weary spirit gathered pace towards sleep.

James Hedlow sat in his small south-facing garden and, in the bright sunlight of the summer evening watched the gradual advance of cold shadows and dark, forbidding clouds rolling in from the south-west. He liked his garden with its well-cut grass, its wallflowers and small herb garden. But the worsening weather was this evening to drive him from it. He stretched and rose from his seat, gathering together papers and pens and pipe to take them into the house. Already the clouds were shading the sun, and he foresaw a dark, humid evening ahead, with the possibility of a storm after midnight. He had work to do, for he knew that his Council was determined to emerge from war as a powerful arbiter of events in Northampton.

"Not if Lord Le Vaughn has his way" he sighed to himself.

He was uncomfortably conscious that, as the Council's Clerk and servant, he was increasingly being identified as the man responsible for the disruption and thwarting of Le Vaughn's activities in Northampton. He knew that his position, and that of the Council, hung on the thread of the favour of the House of Commons for a town that had supported the Parliamentary cause from the outset. How long that favour would protect them from Colonel Fell's soldiers, he did not know.

On reflection, he thought, the request for soldiers from London was a mistake. In this matter, Councilman Parfitt had been right, and he and Trussell wrong. The Troopers were inadequate to defend the Council should they be seriously threatened by Colonel Fell; all they did was to antagonise Le Vaughn and underline the Council's opposition to him. Listening to the advice of Major Blake had added to the town's fear and discontent rather than relieving it. Hedlow managed a dry chuckle to himself.

"Of course," he thought.

"We really have dug a deep pit for ourselves, for if we send them away now, we will have publicly capitulated to Le Vaughn and his power."

Shaking his head in wry acknowledgement of the vagaries of life, Hedlow went in to the simple supper he knew Anne would have ready and waiting for him. Whilst his own affairs were, despite his characteristic irony, threatening, she, at least, was almost recovered. Hedlow was still concerned for Anne. He knew her as a troubled spirit who deserved better of the world. Physically, she was strong - but the state of her spirit - ah, that was something he could not divine.

"Anne" he called, pleasantly.

"I will have supper in the front parlour, for I have some work to do. Ask Robert to lock up early oh, and will you light candles for me, please?"

Anne came to the kitchen door and gave her employer the sad, small smile that hid a wealth of gratitude for the compassion of this kindly man.

"At once, sir," she replied. "And I have already asked Robert to light a fire in your room."

"She is a good and thoughtful woman" . He mused

"But life was still a burden for her. She dresses her hair carefully in an attempt to hide the terrible scar on her face, but what about the scar on her soul. I have not pried too deep into her circumstances, for fear of wounding her yet further. That the victors could so harm the defeated who were of the same stock and blood, that is the great tragedy of civil war.

Robert broke his thoughts by entering the hallway with his arms filled with logs.

"Beg pardon, sir. Could you open the parlour door for me? I've the fire to get going."

Hedlow watched his manservant as the dry kindling spluttered and was coaxed into flame.

"Robert, how is Anne?" he questioned.

"Oh - well enough, sir." Robert sat back on his heels. "She works hard, give her that; she can carry two buckets filled from the well. And she cooks fine, aye - and knows about herbs, and things. Seems honest enough, too. But in all these six months, I can't say as how she's been much in the way of company." Robert spoke with the easy freedom of a trusted member of the household. "She's a quiet one - after supper, it's straight off to her room. Mind you, I don't know that she sleeps all that well. I've heard her about late into the night - but no wonder, poor woman - she must have plenty of bad dreams to scare her from sleep. Well, I suppose it was a charitable act, to take her in when old Rachel died, but I had hoped she'd have brightened the place up with a bit of laughter and...."

"Well, keep a caring eye on her, Robert, for she is indeed still a suffering soul."

Hedlow cut the flow of words, for the fire was now burning healthily, and he had much work to do that night.

Hardly had he pushed away the supper dishes and taken up his pen, when Robert appeared at the door to announce that Trooper Ketch had a message to deliver. Resigned, Hedlow pushed away his writing materials, and bade Robert to show the Trooper into the parlour.

Ketch with his hand loosely on his sword strode firmly into the room.

"Good evening, Sir." he said, and, as Robert closed the door behind him.

"I bring you a message from Major Blake, one that it is hard for me to deliver and for you to receive, but he has commissioned me to answer any questions that it may pose for you."

Hedlow motioned Ketch to a seat, but paced absentmindedly himself as he read the letter. His face paled as the full import of the message became clear.

"Does the Major know what he is doing?" he cried.

"We have been abandoned to Lord Le Vaughn. What shall we do now!" he cried in despair.

For almost an hour, Hedlow cross-examined Ketch concerning the reason for the immediate return of the Major to London, and the later departure of Ketch and his men. Hedlow's questioning was remorseless, and many times Ketch nearly burst out that the only reason he and his Troopers were staying for three days was in the forlorn hope of finding the King's letter - but he did not. Rather he matched the skilful question with equally skilful answers. In his heart, Ketch felt sorry for Hedlow and the Council; in truth, they had been abandoned, and even the small hope that the Troopers had been sent by a supportive House of Commons to help them was, Ketch knew, a lie. There had never been any intent in London to defy Le Vaughn; the Troopers had been there to help the Major. At length, Hedlow slumped wearily into his chair.

"This is a terrible blow" he sighed.

"To be abandoned so publicly. Now we must all look to ourselves." Then, resignedly, "So be it, Ketch. The Major leaves tomorrow and you in three days. That is all the time we have to make our peace with my Lord Le Vaughn and bend our knee to his terms. Well, I thank you for coming to see me."

Ketch rose from his chair, and Hedlow took his hand.

"We have been allies for a short time, Trooper Ketch. I wish you and your men well. Tell them in London, if you can, about the power of Le Vaughn, although they probably know."

He managed a bitter laugh. "Farewell, Ketch."

"We shall guard your Council House for three more days, Sir." reminded Ketch.

"So farewell' is premature."

Hedlow slapped him on the shoulder.

"You are right, lad." he said.

And, with his arm around Ketch's shoulder, he showed him to the door and into the now blackening June evening. The street seemed deserted - men, women, dogs, cats and all were indoors, awaiting the threatening storm.

"Hurry home," warned Hedlow. "Your quickest way is past the old well, and up along by the Derngate."

He turned back into his house and locked and barred his door against the coming storm.

Ketch hurried from Hedlow's house towards Beckett's Well along a well-trodden path, which was now empty of other human beings. The night air was humid and full of the storm to come. As he strode on, his mind dwelt on Hedlow's staunch courage, and on the problems that Ketch and Major Blake had posed for the town; his mind travelled on to Colonel Fell - and the dangerous Le Vaughn, whom he had yet to see but whose power he had keenly felt.

He was totally unprepared when two large muscular arms wrapped themselves around his chest, pinning his arms to his sides. Desperately struggling to free himself, he could do nothing against those powerful arms. His helmet was roughly dragged from his head, and a heavy blow brought searing pain, then blackness. Ketch fell to the ground; he was still dimly conscious of a large weight pinning his legs, and his shoulders were pressed down against the earth.

"Now!" crowed a voice.

"Well done, Titus. We have our man. The one who flaunts the servants of the Lord. Let me get a better look at him. I must mark him, like the harlots he protects."

Summoning up all his strength, Ketch partially moved the weight of flesh holding him down, for he began to realise the peril he was in. But to no effect - he was trapped by the huge strength of his assailant from the alleyway.

"That's it - hold him well, Titus, and stop his mouth."

Ketch recognised the voice of Preacher Hyack just as Titus's hand clamped itself over his mouth and jaw.

"I've a sharp knife her, Trooper" said Hyack, at which Titus gave a strange giggle.

"A knife that marks those who help the devil and his works; Titus and I use it well and often, Gentlemen and ladies, and soldiers, it doesn't matter to us, does it, Titus?"

"No, Preacher, it don't" replied Titus

He giggled in anticipation.

"And we have a little pleasure when we do the Lord's work!"

Ketch continued to struggle, but it was in vain. He was having difficulty in seeing, and his breathing became shallow. Slowly, the distorted face of the Preacher was thrust close to his; he felt a sharp pain in his right cheek, and blood trickled down on to his neck.

"The first stroke of this knife is for our heavenly Father" chanted Hyack. "The second is.... "

Suddenly, Preacher Hyack was flung to one side, and Titus gave a grunt as he was roughly rolled off Ketch's legs. Ketch instinctively rolled away onto his side, and saw, standing between him and his attacker, a tall young man in the dress of a Cavalier gentleman. In a daze, Ketch noted a grimy red sash, with a strange pendant hanging from a chain round the young man's neck.

"Assassins" hissed the strange figure. "Who is it you seek to murder? Will you take on a gentleman of quality?"

His sword point flickered between the Preacher and his acolyte, both of whom were struggling to their knees. It was Titus who stayed on his knees as he saw the man who had knocked him to the ground. Titus looked stunned; his eyes bulged, and his mouth fell open. He covered his face with his hands and whimpered.

"It's him, Preacher!" he moaned. Back from the grave you put him in! I know him!"

"Quiet, you fool" snapped Hyack.

"Come, let's go" he said

He grasped the moaning Titus by the arms.

"'Tis only a man, Titus. This is no ghost - it's only a lad!"

Dragged to his feet, Titus took a hard look at the rescuer.

"My God, Preacher, you're right! Tis nowt but a lad, but I thought." His voice trailed away, and in a surge of rage he lurched towards the Cavalier.But Preacher Hyack was ready for this, and hung onto him.

"Another day, Titus, my friend" he hissed.

They both turned away from the confrontation, stumbling off into the gloom.

Ralph Desborough stood quietly for a moment. He began to tremble, his mind flooded with excitement; at last he had found someone who recognised his father's clothes someone who would know about his father's death. He now had names and faces. He was about to set off in pursuit when a groan from the figure on the ground forced his attention. As Ralph knelt to check the victim's injuries, Ketch was raised on one elbow, his right hand covering his face where the Preacher's knife had cut. Ketch took his hand away and looked at the blood covering it, then he raised his eyes and looked into Ralph Desborough's face. Ketch, too, had heard Titus's words; and noting the strange royalist costume, he guessed his helper was Ralph Desborough and that Ralph had some strange connection and significance for the preacher and Titus.

"You've been cut," said Ralph.

"But I think not too deep..."

"I know you, Ralph Desborough", cried Ketch.

He clutched at the arm still holding the sword. Ralph wrenched away in alarm and fled silently into the concealing night.

"Stay!" cried Ketch desperately.

"I have not thanked you..." But his words were in vain.

"Dear Heaven!", cried the apprehensive voice of Robert, Hedlow's manservant, as he approached the still prone figure of Ketch.

"What has happened? More violence in this town! Why, Mr Ketch, are you badly hurt?" he exclaimed.

He gently helped Ketch to his feet, and a lantern was pushed up to his face revealing the cut. Clerk Hedlow's voice was also brought to bear for he had followed behind his manservant.

"Bring him back to my house. We will look after him there. The cut to his face looks shallow enough, but there are signs of a hard blow to the head. Robert! do you go ahead and warn Anne to prepare?"Hedlow put Ketch's left arm over his own plump shoulders and, half supporting him, led the shaky Trooper back to his house. Thanking the straggling crowd that had followed them, in the hope of more excitement or information, Hedlow took Ketch into the parlour to the waiting Robert and Anne.

"Robert, lock up again" ordered Hedlow.

"Anne, will you clean the cuts suffered by this young man, and do it steadily."

He said it kindly, for he saw her eyes widen and her body stiffen at the sight and nature of Ketch's facial injury. The effect on Anne was more than could be quietened with a few kind words. Her hands flew to her mouth and with a small, strangled cry she turned and left the room.

"Help me, Robert," said Hedlow, and he and his manservant gently guided Ketch to the couch.

"Lie there, young man" soothed Hedlow.

"Robert will bathe your wound."

Turning to Robert, he said

"When that has been done, find him some blankets and let him sleep the night here. We will watch over him by turn. I must now find Anne and quieten her. She has had a shock - and I should have foreseen this."

Hedlow left the room and Robert began to help Ketch take of his jacket and boots.

"Hmmm, there will be no scar, soldier for it is a light straight cut, so the ladies will still look at you. You can even make up a tale of bravery and daring to go with it."

As Robert chattered on, Ketch gradually allowed himself to relax into the comfort of Hedlow's couch. Hedlow was not long in returning to the parlour.

"Anne is recovered" he informed them.

"I'm afraid the sight of a wound to your face, even such a slight one has brought back memories of her own hideous experiences. But she is herself once more, and is bringing water and poultices. She will help nurse you through this night."

Before Ketch could protest about the need to return to his troop, Hedlow intervened.

"I am Clerk to the Council here, young man, and you will follow my orders. You have a cut face and a bruised head. You will rest the night here. Your men will not worry about you until the morning, and you will have returned to them by then. You will have at least one night's sound rest and care."

Ketch realised the futility of argument, and welcomed the blanket that Robert was now placing over him. He closed his eyes and tried to put together the pieces of the puzzle, Preacher Hyack, Ralph Desborough ... ..

The door opened quietly, there was a murmuring, and then he sensed a soft, warm presence by his side. He struggled to open his eyes, and caught a glimpse of long, dark hair and eyes full of compassion, before a cool hand was laid over them, and a low, concerned voice whispered almost inaudibly.

"No, don't try to open your eyes. I am going to bathe your wounds, and then I shall use a healing ointment on your cuts. Tis a wondrous remedy, and will lessen the hurt...as I do know."

The sting of the water on his face and head wound made Ketch wince, but so gentle was the touch that wielded the cloth that soon his body relaxed. Sensitive fingers touched his face and head with a cool, pungent cream and he felt the pain easing and his mind calming; the darting pictures of Hayek, Ralph Desborough and the event of the night disappeared and his senses swam as he gave himself up to the perfume of Anne's body and soothing, almost sensuous, touch of her fingers.

A finger on his lips quietened his child-like gasp of disappointment as the hand left his face.

"I shall be but a moment." she said.

"I am going to prepare a drink that will ensure your rest, do not move, you are safe here."

Ketch despite his hurts, delighted in the sound of her voice and he sighed, with some comfort and pleasure.

Chapter 8

Ralph Desborough's eyes were ablaze with hope as he paced the small back bedroom of his sisters' house. At last he had found a possible link to his father's death and the key that would unlock the path to the King's letter. Hurriedly, he began to change; he no longer had any need of his father's jewellery, or such obvious cavalier clothes. The weeks of roaming the streets of Northampton during the dark hours were now ended. His task was clear. The preacher and Titus had known his father; Titus had blurted out the word "grave". They had killed his father; they would know the fate of the letter. His mood turned cold. He would kill them, he thought grimly to himself, but first they would tell him everything. In quiet and sober dress, he would go back into the night to continue his work. He had a known quarry and a clear task. He pulled on dark woollen breeches, a linen shirt and a countryman's jacket, and then reached for his sword. His hand hesitated for a moment, but his doubts were quickly resolved and he buckled the weapon comfortably over his left hip. There was a soft tap on his door, and Martha came in at his bidding.

"Ralph" she chided.

"You have not eaten..."

Sensing the fire and energy within him, she was troubled.

"What is it that excites you so? You are trembling! What has happened?"

"Nothing, Martha" he reassured her.

"I have to go out again tonight."

"Oh, why are you taking such risks?" she burst out.

Ralph caught in his arms and held her to him.

"Martha, dear little sister" he soothed.

"Fear not. Our trial is nearly over. Fortune smiles on us. My presence here, and the danger it brings you, has been my greatest burden; but events now move in our favour. Soon, God willing, my task will be finished, and I can away to France and await a more peaceful time for England. Please, Martha" he pleaded

"Stay strong a little while longer." He gave her a last hug. "Now, I must go!" And he picked up his cloak and was out of the room.

Martha stood, dejected with her shoulders slumped, looking at the empty doorway. None of her appeals could touch him; he was determined to pursue his quest, alone. "*Very well*" she thought to herself.

"But this time, Ralph Desborough, you will not go alone. Your excitement betrays a climax in this matter. You will need help."

Quickly she hurried upstairs to check that Mary was still sleeping peacefully and, returning downstairs, she collected her own cloak and slipped out into the humid darkness of the June night.

Porteus Botterill sat on a stool in the dark, damp cellar deep below his alehouse. The light of a single candle guttered and gave a wavering pool of light. He came down here more often these days, to think; and tonight, he was thinking very hard. He had heard conversations in Cornet Marlowe's room, which could be turned to profit in the right quarter. Certainly, he had names of people and a little information which would be of interest to the Colonel, and for which he could expect some coinage. He had been sitting for some time but now he had made up his mind. Heaving his bulk from the low stool, he snuffed out the candle and, with easy familiarity, climbed the cellar stairs up to the door that led into his pantry.

"I shall be out for an hour" he called to his wife, who was still swilling out pewter beer tankards in the scullery.

"Watch the household, and have a light in the parlour window for my return."

He took up his heavy walking stick, feeling the weight solid in his hands, and let himself out of the side door of the alehouse, the one that opened out onto the market square.

The house of James Hedlow was alive with the events of the night. Whilst the master watched over John Ketch, both Robert and Anne were organising and preparing matters to support the night watch. Robert was cutting bread and cheese and filling a small platter that already held slices of cold mutton.

"Just a little ale to go with it" he thought.

"And my watch tonight will not be too much of a hardship."

He still had to collect water from the well for their reserves had been used in caring for the young soldier. He placed a clean napkin over his feast, and picked up the wooden pails from their place by the kitchen door.

"Anne" he called softly at the storeroom door.

"I am going to collect our first call for water. I'll not be long."

Anne came to the door, a spray of dried herbs in her hand.

"Take care" she said anxiously.

"Those evil monsters that call themselves honest, religious, men may still be abroad. Strike hard and fast, Robert, if you see them."

Robert took a lantern from the hook by the main door, struck a flame from the tinderbox and lit the wick. His eyes fell on the rack of walking sticks and, heeding Anne's warning, he helped himself to a good strong wand. Thus armed, he discovered that one bucket was all he could manage to carry in addition. Well, it would have to do. Once out of the front door, Robert marched off briskly towards the well.

Titus clutched the pain in his side. However hard he pushed, however much he begged and prayed, it still hurt. He reeled across the grass. "Damn him to hell!" he moaned.

"It wasn't my fault!" He did the killing of the old man."

The pain was agonising; he did not care about the preacher, or the apparition he had seen that evening. He had to get home; he had to lie down; he needed help. He knew that he was badly hurt.

"I hope I got the murdering swine. I hope he rots in hell."

Such vicious thoughts helped a little, but Titus could feel the flow of warm blood now pouring over the hand that was clamped desperately to the wound. His strength, too, was beginning to leave him, and a coldness descended upon his limbs. He staggered, but did not fall, and the darkness of the alleyway swallowed him up. He had to reach the right door; inside would be warmth and rest and help. There was now an urgency about Titus's movement. Energy could not be wasted, and he moved straight to his goal of the ill-made door that led to his meagre two rooms. He crashed through the door, stepped into a pool of light made by one thin taper and, with all strength gone, collapsed to the floor, only dimly hearing the girl's muted scream.

James Hedlow pulled the blanket more tightly around his shoulders. It was a cursory action, for the small fire in the parlour gave out a steady heat and the night was not especially cold. He picked a small thorn from his blanket, and thought that he must have caught the little rosebush by his garden door on his way back inside. He had stretched his legs for but five minutes and Ketch appeared to have come to no harm in his absence and was sleeping soundly.

"A fine young man" thought Hedlow.

"It's no fault of his that matters stand as they do."

He could not stop picking over in his mind the recent events and the sorry spiritual state of his town. He felt himself to be a sort of custodian for it, and he was close to failure. If only someone other than Le Vaughn would prevail in Northampton then steps could be taken to restore quiet and good order, and ruffians and troublemakers could be got rid of. "Robert will relieve me soon" he yawned. "And then I can take my wild thoughts to bed. I've had enough dangerous activity tonight!"

Ketch's mind struggled almost to the surface of consciousness footsteps ...an outer door somewhere.... opening, closing.... a muted thud .... the door to the parlour opened gently, he could feel the cooler air cross his brown.... and he sank back into his heavy sleep.

The impending storm did not break that night, so it remained warm and sultry, and coal black. With no wind to provide some small stream of air, most townspeople found it difficult to sleep; and throughout the rounds of the clock, the restless sounds of windows opening and people coughing could be heard across the still night air. Despite such open windows, however, there were none to say that they saw what happened that night.

The young boy, no more than ten years old, ran as fast as he could over the dry green grass. Occasionally stumbling, and once falling flat on his face, he sped towards his destination. His small, tightly fitting shoes made no sound until they hit the paved stones that fronted Clerk Hedlow's house. It was a breathless messenger that faced Anne, the housekeeper, when she answered the door to his repeated blows.

"Why, Master Gilpin" she smiled.

"So much noise, to what purpose? What bothers you at such an early hour?"

Gulping in air, his shrill voice finally gave out his words.

"Father says, come quickly. Preacher Hyack has been killed, perhaps murdered, alongside Beckett's Well, and mother and me found him on our way to draw water. Mother is in a faint, and so I ran to get father, and he told me to run some more to tell Mr Hedlow." The words poured out of the boy in one breathless sentence.

"Come," said Anne, calmly taking his hand.

"You shall come with me and deliver your message yourself, and then you shall have something from the kitchen."

She led him into the house and guided him towards James Hedlow, who was not only Town Clerk, but Magistrate's Clerk, and Coroner for the town of Northampton.

Ketch was sitting on the couch rubbing sleep from his eyes under the gaze of Robert, when Hedlow brought Master Gilpin into the parlour.

"I think you had better hear this, Ketch," said Hedlow.

"But before anything is said, Robert! Since taking my place last night, has Trooper Ketch moved from that couch for any reason at all - and have you been awake all the time?

Robert's honest face looked first at Ketch, and then back to his master.

"I've been awake all night, sir" he said.

"And well tired I am now. And to your first question, the answer is 'No'. This soldier has remained here on this couch in this room the whole time, and I might tell you that a noisy sleeper he is, too!"

Before Robert could expound further, on Ketch's sleeping habits, Hedlow intervened.

"Thank you, Robert, but this is a serious matter. News has been brought that Preacher Hyack has been murdered, and as Trooper Ketch here was involved in a fight with him last night, he would be the prime suspect, and asked to account for himself. Well, we can now account for him to anyone's satisfaction; between us, we had our eyes on you, Ketch, all night" he continued, turning to Ketch.

"And it's lucky for you that we insisted you stay."

Ketch now had his full wits about him. Preacher Hyack murdered was news that he had to digest quickly and lay alongside the other events of the night. Ketch turned towards Hedlow urgently.

"I suggest, sir, that we go quickly to see the body and the circumstances of this death. Such events draw people to them very quickly; the curious, and also the petty thief will possibly be there already."

"No time for breakfast, Robert" said Hedlow.

"Come, Ketch. You are right, we must hurry."

Ketch and the clerk hurried from the room; they paused briefly to refresh themselves from the two buckets of water that stood by the front door. Such was the thinnest of breakfasts they took, as they hurried to the scene of death.

It was but a short distance from the clerk's house to the well and as they approached, Ketch could see the lone figure of a slightly stooping, thin man standing by what looked like a bundle at the base of the low stone wall. With each step forward it became clearer that this was no bundle, but the body of Preacher Hyack.

"Good morning, Rufus. This is an unhappy charge for you" Hedlow saluted the watcher.

"Yes, sir and Mrs Gilpin has taken to her bed with the horror of it. She and the boy found him this morning, not ten minutes since. So, I sent the lad for you."

"You've done your duty, Rufus. I would ask you for one more act on my behalf. Fetch my nephew, Stephen Hedlow. As Constable of this parish, he must be informed."

"Aye, sir, that I know. But he's nowt but a young lad, and I thought you would want to know about this first."

And with a quick nod, Rufus set off to find the Constable. Ketch and Hedlow looked down at the body of Preacher Hyack.

"This matter touches our affairs deeply," said Ketch.

"This is no simple murder, but has an import on what has brought Major Blake and the Cornet's troop to Northampton. I tell you quietly, Hedlow; this preacher had secrets that young Ralph Desborough seemed desperate to know. I must be quick to understand this or we shall lose our race. There will be crowds here soon" he continued.

"We must look with care at the marks that can be found, for sometimes a piece of thread or cloth or hair may help tell us who has been here."

Hedlow gave Ketch a sideways glance.

"You are familiar with these things, Ketch?"

My father acted as secretary to the Coroner's Court in my home town of Bedford, and many times he told us of deaths that were found to be not what they seemed, sometimes on the evidence of the smallest hair. It was of such matters that I learnt most from him."

"As Coroner for this Borough, I, too, have had some strange deaths to consider; but my eyes have grown dim over the years, Ketch. Now it is you who must use the cunning of your eyes to see how this was done, and what marks may betray the murderer."

Ketch looked first at the ground around the well. This had been worn flat by the passage of those who used the well daily, and a ring of plain, hard-baked earth surrounded the well for some six feet before the grass was reached. This circle of dry earth was broken by a patch of slightly moister ground, where the filled buckets had slopped over some of their contents as they were taken from the well. In this, Ketch could discern the print of a small, narrow boot, but no other marks of significance were yielded up by the parched earth.

He turned his attention to the corpse, dwelling for some moments on the strangely peaceful face of Preacher Hyack. In life, it had so often been twisted in hate; in death, with torment gone, it was now quite handsome. Ketch recognised the black trouser, jerkin and coat, and bent to examine them more closely. He trailed his fingers lightly over the fabric of the coat, and stopped at some light stain on the Preacher's jerkin, on the front of his chest.

"*Most likely food stains*" he thought to himself.

But he leaned forward and was surprised to smell the easily recognised fragrance of lavender, together with some other pungency that he did not know. Beyond these faint aromas, there was nothing to note in the Preacher's clothing; no unusual hair, or thread, or scraps of cloth. He was even uncertain about the fragrance; did it mean the involvement of a woman?

"*Not necessarily*" he said to himself. For many men, even those not cavaliers, carried perfumed handkerchiefs in their cuffs or pockets. Ketch sighed inwardly, and forced himself to consider the wounds evident on the Preacher's body.

The body was lying on its right side, almost in a foetal position, with knees drawn up and both elbows held close into the stomach. The Preacher had been badly served for, at first glance, the impression gained by Ketch was much blood; thick, congealing blood seemed everywhere around the body, and dried blood covered the Preacher's head. Ketch knew that, in a matter of blood, careful observation could yield much information.

"He has been grievously done to" sighed Hedlow.

"He was a trouble-maker, a man of deep and bitter hatreds, and many in this town will be pleased at his death, but in Christian charity, no man should die in this way."

"Amen to that" agreed Ketch.

He pulled aside the edge of the Preacher's coat.

"This is the blow that killed him, I would say."

And he pointed to the abdomen, which was still partly obscured by the knees and elbows. The hilt of a knife that had been plunged deep into the body could be seen, a knife that was clearly the source of the blood, that stained the surrounding earth.

"I think that is his own knife," said Hedlow. "I have seen him with it before. Was he injured in the melee with you?

Ketch carefully withdrew the knife from the body, with no little difficulty, and showed it to Hedlow.

"I've seen some blood, Mr Hedlow, but even troopers who have fought in many a battle, do not easily manage such a blow, and the position of his body would suggest that this was the fatal stroke.... Is there anything else to see?"

Ketch went down on to one knee, avoiding the stained earth, and carefully examined the dried blood on the Preacher's forehead.

"He has another wound here. See, in the hairline in the centre of his forehead, and the path of the blood from this wound can be seen."

Hedlow stooped to scrutinise the dried blood of the head wound, and Ketch's fingers traced the path of the main flow of blood down the left side of the nose to the left of the mouth and chin; but from this main flow, he observed further channels running down the left cheek to the left ear. Ketch pushed himself to his feet. "This would appear to be an earlier wound" he pondered. " A wound received some time afore the death blow, of that I'm sure. That blood ran straight and true down his face, and his head would have been upright. But later, he must have been turned, or have fallen, onto his left side."

"Are you sure that he was not injured in the melee with you, Ketch?" inquired Hedlow. "He might have received that blow then."

"No, he definitely left that battle unscathed. He and his partner were untouched."

"So" summed up Hedlow, "He has been involved in at least two struggles in the night. Is there more, Ketch?"

Ketch resumed his kneeling position and carefully looked over the rest of the body.

"The back of the scalp has also received a blow" he announced.

In order to observe the wound more closely, he placed his arm under the Preacher's head and lifted the back of it into the light.

"Dear Heaven!"

Shaking his head in distress, Hedlow turned away from the gory sight.... "Ketch!"

He interrupted himself, striding towards the edge of the grass circle. He stooped, and turned back towards Ketch with something in his hand. "We have <u>two</u> knives!"

"And another one I recognise!" replied Ketch grimly.

He gently replaced the Preacher's head back on the dry ground, and rose quickly to his feet to look more closely at the knife found by Hedlow. "That knife belongs to the Preacher's friend and ally - the one he calls Titus. I met that knife in the alleyway of one of the more unpleasant parts of Northampton."

"Aha, that would suggest he is involved" Hedlow was excited.

"I shall instruct the Constable to find this villain for us."

"There is a further puzzle for us here" continued Ketch.

"The wound at the back of the scalp has also bled profusely, and also down to the left ear, but at the back of the head."

Ketch tried to make some sense of the bloody state of the corpse. "Three blows have been struck," he said. "That much we know. First, a blow to the forehead, which bled much and with the Preacher upright; a second blow to the back of the head that knocked him onto his left side; much later, his murderer found him and killed him, and left him on his right side. I know no more who is his assailant, or assailants, when or why this was done."

"You've done well, Ketch" approved Hedlow.

"We must relate all this my nephew, Stephen. He's a good lad, with some wit and quickness of mind."

He nodded his head towards a broad-shouldered man approaching from the town at a good pace. Ketch stood to welcome him, but Stephen Hedlow stopped before reaching his watcher and bent to his knee to examine something in the grass. He carefully wiped his hand, and came up to the head of his family.

"There is blood on the grass over there, Uncle" he said.

"And I see you have a body here."

"More blood!", exclaimed Hedlow.

"Good God, what has happened here this night?"

The Constable examined the Preacher's body and the surrounding area, all the while listening to Hedlow and Ketch as they explained their knowledge of events, and their theory of the sequence of blows. A curious crowd was forming as Stephen Hedlow widened the area of search. His uncle considered it wise to leave the scene of the murder.

"I will leave matters with you, Stephen" said Hedlow, in a low voice. "Remove the corpse to the mortuary, and prepare for a Coroner's Court."He turned to Ketch.

"I will need you for that, Trooper. But for the moment, I doubt that there is much more to be done. Later in the day, we must take up these matters again."

"Yes, sir. And I must return to my troop, for they will get themselves into trouble if I am not there. Until later, Master Hedlow." Ketch turned away, leaving the Constable to direct affairs, and headed for the town centre and the Peacock Inn. He was a soldier with a bed-ridden officer and nineteen Troopers to look after in a hostile town; on top of these problems; he had the clandestine affairs of Major Blake. Ketch sighed to himself - this murder was not wanted; Preacher Hyack had been the key to the Desborough affair and the king's letter, which now seemed to be even further from his grasp.

Chapter 9

Hand on sword, Ketch strode briskly along the path that led from Beckett's Well up to the Market Square. He enjoyed the physical exercise, but his mind was a-whirl with the cascading events of the last two days.

"Right", he said to himself.

"This five-minute walk was is an opportunity to think clearly about Major Blake's mission to find the King's letter, Ralph Desborough's presence in the town, and the murder of Preacher Hyack. There is a link, and it must be explored."

The morning air was warm and humid, for the promised storm had still not broken. Ketch's head was throbbing, and his hand was drawn to it regularly, to try and ease the pain. His clothes felt uncomfortable, for he had slept in them. These physical irritants waylaid his thinking, but he did not give up and, by the time he entered the stable yard of the Peacock he knew that he must break his fast quickly and act swiftly.

"Ah, the Corporal has returned!"

Observed Tull, easing himself from the barrel that had become his personal place in the yard.

"Back like the Good Shepherd to look after his lambs."

The stable yard came to life as Troopers emerged from barns and haylofts to see the Corporal returned. A grinning face appeared at the upper hayloft door, Holditch was in good form.

"Less noise, you rabble. Honest Troopers are trying to rest up here! If you cannot keep quiet, tell the serving wenches that a brave soldier now requires his breakfast."

Hoots and shouts greeted this sally from Holditch, and Ketch was reassured that his men had enjoyed a comfortable night and an easy early morning. He felt it was time to reassert his position as corporal.

"Right, Troopers, breakfast or not, you've work to do," he ordered."Duties are the same as yesterday. That means you, Holditch, take your eight lads and mount your guard over the Council House in the same way. I know it's a difficult guard, but we are only here a few more days, until the Cornet can travel, so stand firm. The rest of you - prepare yourselves for some action; but swords only, leave your pistols behind. You, Larkin! You are the lucky one. You can mount guard over the yard. Tull! Get these men ready. Holditch! You should be on your way."

The barrage of orders set the Troopers into motion. Holditch began lining up his guard for the short march to the Council House, and Tull began checking the Troopers who were to remain. Ketch felt that a few words with Cornet Marlowe were in order, if only to explain his absence through the night.

Ketch knocked lightly on the door of the Cornet's room. Before he could enter, the door opened in his face and the apothecary, together with one of the serving girls, came out.

"Your Cornet has a fever" grunted the apothecary.

"I've given instructions to this girl, but in no circumstances is he to be moved or disturbed. I must get my instruments to bleed him at once."

This news from the apothecary was not good. Fever from a broken leg, Ketch knew, often meant much worse was to follow.

"Is there anything I can do?" he asked.

"No" replied the apothecary, gathering up his robe to descend the steps. "You could see that his rest is not disturbed and that your men are quiet. His life, like our own, is a matter for God."

"Amen to that" said Ketch, and for a moment his hand rested on the closed door, as if it would have rested on the shoulder of the sick man to comfort him.

Back in the stableyard, Ketch called Tull over to him. Briefly, he directed the Trooper to Abington Street, there to request Major Blake for his help as

Cornet Marlowe had a fever."And on your return, which must be speedy, muster your men in the yard, then call me. Go now, quietly and discreetly; let as few as possible know what you are doing."

"Let him rest."

Ketch turned towards the kitchens. He managed a quick breakfast, and a sluice of his head at the pump, and felt ready to face what was likely to turn out to be a long day.

"Right lads, gather round and listen to me and mark carefully what I say," instructed Ketch.

Tull, back from delivering his message, and the remaining Troopers bound by these words stood alert and tense. To ensure their concentration, Ketch made them sit in a circle with him crouching in the middle.

"That preacher who caused the trouble by the Church and argued with the Cornet has been murdered, stabbed with his own knife down by the Archbishop's Well. It's a nasty business."

He gazes sternly at them.

"There was a lot of blood about, and I've had two set-tos with him myself, but thankfully I have solid witnesses in Clerk Hedlow and his household as to where I was last night."

The Troopers looked at each other, and began murmuring, but Ketch raised his hand and they fell silent.

"I know, I know" he exclaimed, "someone must pay, and there are those in the town who would be quite happy for the cause to be placed on Cornet Marlowe's Troopers. But I also know that this same preacher had a brush with a certain royalist gentleman called Ralph Desborough, who was very sharp to meet him again."

"From what I've heard," said Tull.

“That preacher had more enemies than is natural for a man of God - and there are many as would be quite happy to stick a knife in him." Murmurs of assent for Tull's views came from the seated Troopers.

"For a number of reasons" Ketch interrupted their muttering.

"Major Blake and myself want this Ralph Desborough, and you boys are going to help me flush him out."

"Your mysterious Major again" said Tull. "He'll be getting you into trouble, Ketch."

"'Corporal' Ketch to you, Tull,” said Ketch, reminding the lean Trooper exactly who was managing affairs. "And never mind the arguments - we have a job to do."

Ketch outlined to the men his suspicions that Ralph Desborough was hiding in his sisters' house by St Sepulchre's Church. He drew a simple plan in the dust of the yard, and gave each man a position to take up that would leave the little complex of house, garden and church totally surrounded. Talking softly but urgently, he went around each Trooper to make certain that every individual knew his station and his task. Finally satisfied that all knew their parts, he rose to his feet.

"Now. I want each man to leave here individually, and to make his way to his own place. No noise! No rushing! Just a quiet walk which draws no attention from anyone. This has to be done quietly, with as few as possible catching onto what we are doing."

The Troopers bustled about, whispering excitedly to each other. This was action; this was going to be fun. Some smiled at the idea of the trap that Ketch had laid.

"Well, Corporal" reported Tull, "I think we are ready."

Quietly and without fuss, Ketch and his Troopers slipped through the market square and made their ways to the crusader church and the little house that flanked its graveyard wall. Keeping Tull by his side, Ketch waited in the shadows cast by the church as the men took up their positions.

"Now, Tull" said Ketch.

"It is up to you. I shall now visit the Desborough ladies. Give me but two minutes, and then you and your three lads can start to search the church. No noise going in, but once inside you can rattle around a bit. I want you to flush him out without drawing any interest from the Garrison."

Over the low town buildings, Ketch could see the battlements of the Castle just a short distance away and he had no wish to renew his acquaintance with Colonel Fell. With a nod to Tull, Ketch moved down the street and rapped lightly on the door of the Desborough residence and as Mary's face appearedin answer to his knock, he smiled.

"May I come in Mistress?" he asked.

"I would speak with you and your sister."

"My sister is unwell"..."She can see no one ".... faltered Mary, her face apprehensive at the sight of Ketch at her door.

Firmly and brooking no obstruction, Ketch pushed open the door and propelled Mary ahead of him into the small front parlour. Mary tried to scream, but the sound would not come out of a throat taught with fear; nevertheless, although terrified, she managed to deal Ketch a sound, stinging slap to his injured face, which brought an unaccustomed colour to his pale cheek.

"Steady, Mistress" he cried, gripping her firmly by both wrists.

"I shall not harm you."

He held her fixed for a few seconds, so that she was clearly in his control. Acknowledging his strength, the spirit of defiance within Mary fled; when

Ketch released her, she staggered towards the couch, her shoulders slumped and tears in her eyes.

It was not Mary Desborough who claimed Ketch's attention. In the instant of mastering Mary's fear, Ketch had caught sight of Martha Desborough sitting in the corner of the room.Her appearance startled him; she sat in her brown dress with an old green shawl around her shoulders, gently rubbing her hands together. The once proud, spirited woman seemed no longer to be there. She paid no attention to Ketch, or her sister Mary. Her focus seemed entirely inward, bent upon her own thoughts.

Mary Desborough turned from the couch to face Ketch, and defiance now filled her frame. As one who had been constantly protected by her elder sister, she seemed to find a new strength in having to defend them both.

"Now you see" she snapped at Ketch; her pretty face flushed with rage.

"This is how she returned last night. Someone or somebody has done her a grievous hurt."

She moved to her sister and placed her arms about her, but Martha appeared not to notice. She continued to look down at her lap and at her locked hands. Ketch knelt before her and placed his hands gently over hers. He searched for some words of comfort. So distracted was he by her plight that the sudden sounds of confusion coming from the garden took him by surprise. He sprang to his feet and ran through the kitchen to the garden door. There, rolling in the dust, with three stout Troopers hanging on to him, was the figure of Ralph Desborough. The captive kicked and struggled, fighting, despite the numbers against him, for his liberty. But the Troopers had their own hard strength that finally held him..

"Bind his arms and bring him into the house" ordered Ketch.

As he spoke, Tull and the remaining Troopers climbed over the low wall that separated the churchyard from the garden.

"You were right, Ketch" crowed Tull,

"Er, sorry, Corporal. We stamped around the church like fifty new recruits, and he was away across the churchyard and into your arms." There was pleasure in Tull's face at a job well done, and some admiration for his Corporal.

"Well done, Corporal!" said one of the Troopers, and another slapped him on the back.

"The citizens of Northampton should be well-pleased that you have caught their murderer," said Tull

"They might think a bit more- kindly on us for this". Ketch stood a moment, enjoying his success; then he frowned.

"Get him inside the house, Tull" he commanded. "Hurry up! We still ce inside the house, Ketch instructed the Troopers to return to the inn as they had left it, singly and without drawing attention to themselves. One Trooper was detailed to report to Clerk Hedlow, discreetly and quietly, that Ralph Desborough, the possible murderer of Preacher Hayeck had been apprehended, and could the Clerk come at once to the Desborough home.

"Tull, you stay with me," said Ketch.

"And watch out for the younger sister; she's a spitting cat at the moment, and now we have netted her brother, she is going to be troublesome."

Together, the two men brought the bound and silent Ralph Desborough into the parlour. The impact on the two sisters was immediate; Mary sank limply onto the couch.

"Oh, Ralph!" she wailed.

"Why, oh, why have you come back?" and she started quietly sobbing.

Martha seemed to regain her faculties. There was little life or spirit in her movements, but she was now aware of herself and her surroundings, including the people in it, and she regarded them with a cold calmness.

"What will you do with us?" she inquired of Ketch.

"Madam, your brother is a known enemy of the people and parliament" replied Ketch.

"At least, that is what will be said. I know that, in reality, he is just another supporter of young Charles

Stuart and, it may surprise you, that he in all probability saved my life last night; but his presence here has done for him. He is the prime suspect for the murder of Preacher Hayeck."

Both sisters and the brother started at this news.

"Dead!" exclaimed Ralph.

"Are you sure?" asked Martha.

"No doubt at all" said Ketch.

"He was found, a bloody corpse, by Beckett's Well at dawn this morning."

"And we all know that the Desborough and the Capsticks had no liking for him" interjected Tull.

"My comrade" said Ketch, putting his hand on Tull's shoulder, "You must not alarm these ladies. Please step outside and keep watch for Mr Hedlow whilst I keep an eye on our prisoners."

"Will you be safe, Corporal?" asked Tull. "Watch the women - they can be dangerous!" he winked at Ketch, and left the room. Ketch turned back to Ralph Desborough.

"I have not forgotten how you saved me from the Preacher and his mad companion last night. Both you and I are known to have quarrelled with him; but I was with James Hedlow, under the care of himself and his manservant all through the night - and you are the main suspect. But. I think I may be able to help you in this matter - if you can provide information on another."Ralph Desborough regarded

Ketch with some uncertainty. "If you can help me clear my name of a charge of murder, I thank you, and would regard any debt you feel you may owe me as settled. But," he paused and looked carefully at Ketch's pale face. "On any other matter, there is nothing to be said."

"Well said, Ralph," cried Mary. She had regained some composure and her face was once again fierce. "I don't know how you helped this Trooper Ketch - or whether you now regret it - but don't let him trade favours with a Desborough." She turned for support to Martha, who was clearly shaken at the news of the Preacher's murder and the charge against Ralph.

"So be it" shrugged Ketch. "Let me help you face the charge of the Preacher's murder. The rest can wait between us. But Clerk Hedlow will be here soon, and there are some questions I must ask. Will you answer truthfully, Sir, and tell me all you can about you and the Preacher?"

"Only inasmuch as it does not affect the family honour" assented Ralph. "I am sorry" he added desperately, "I know you wish to help us."

Ketch helped Ralph to sit on a small chair in the centre of the room. Martha stumbled rather than walked to join her sister on the couch. There they sat side by side watching the confrontation between their bound brother and his inquisitor.

"Very well" said Ketch. "We will do what we can. Now - late last night you rescued me from Hayeck and Titus; and you were dressed in the garments of a cavalier gentleman. Something - some word, or comment - that passed between Titus and the Preacher excited you, and made me believe that you wished to talk to them again and at length. Did you, Ralph? Did you see the Preacher again last night? Answer me - I think I can help."

Ralph seemed to ponder Ketch's words while his sisters gazed at him mutely. Finally, with an indrawn breath, he seemed to make up his mind.

"It will do no harm" he said, "to tell the truth. It can now have no effect on my wider purpose." He turned to Ketch. "Yes, I saw them again. After our encounter I returned home, took some refreshment and changed my clothing, then I went out in search of those two cut-throats - I had questions for them." As he spoke, Ralph began to relax, and the tension in his body and the emotion is his voice ebbed away.

"I found them all right - again by the well. It was not quite dark, and there was just light enough to see them. They had clearly fallen out, and even as I approached them, unseen, their quarrel became a vicious fight. I could half hear some of the words that passed between them; the Preacher was enraged at Titus, that he had betrayed him; and Titus was in turn ranting at Hayeck's lust for blood. Their struggle became a deadly one, for the Preacher drew his knife and plunged it into the body of Titus, who shrieked and fell to his knees; I could see the blood flow from his hands to the ground. The Preacher went to the well and refreshed his face with water, then turned to look at the wounded Titus. He, in turn, staggered to his feet, and cursed the Preacher with foul words; but he did not approach him, for I could see that he was sorely wounded and was looking for some underhand way of striking back. He gave a final curse and staggered off into the dark. The Preacher turned again to the well - I heard a grunt of pain, and a knife fell not far from the Preacher. It seemed that Titus had tried a last murderous throw, but it was wide of the mark - and I could hear him lurching through the bushes."

"Did you approach the Preacher?" questioned Ketch.

"Yes" replied Ralph. "I thought that now was the time to tackle him."

"You thought he knew something of your father's death?"

Ralph threw a sharp glance at Ketch. "You know why I am here!" he said.

"Who are you, Ketch - a Roundhead spy? For sure, you are no simple soldier."

Ketch raised his hand to quieten Ralph's anger.

"In that matter", he said,

"We have different purposes. But in the matter of Preacher Hayeck's death, believe me", he implored, "I can help you."

Ralph's voice, as he continued his tale, was careful and guarded. Now he felt in the grip of an enemy who knew all about him and his quest to save his family honour. He felt impotent, and, increasingly, that his quest was futile.

"Can I have a little water "; he asked hoarsely "for my throat is dry".Ketch spent a few moments to go to the kitchen and return with water that he fed to Ralph who drank greedily. With his thirst satisfied, Ralph had decided to continue his tale.

"I approached the Preacher and confronted him by the well. I had the advantage of him and I placed my sword at his throat. He laughed at me, and damned me and my family as papists and enemies of the people. And then, in mid-sentence, he leapt at me in a treacherous attack. It was not his voice, but his face and eyes that warned me of his villainous thrust with his knife. As he leapt at me, I twisted my body and avoided the knife. Instinct governed my blow, that felled him. I wish I had not struck him; he could have told me much that I wished to know, but I could not help myself."

Ralph's tone was one of both antagonism and despair.

"So, you see, Ketch, I struck the Preacher down with one blow. He fell like a stricken ox to the ground."

Martha Desborough leapt to her feet, pale and panting, but before a sound could come from her lips the whole small group was startled by a heavy pounding at the door. Ketch crossed swiftly to open and revealed Clerk Hedlow and his nephew, the Constable.

"Quick, Hedlow" urged Ketch.

"We do not want too many eyes turned this way."

He closed the door rapidly behind the two men as they entered.

"As you say, Ketch" said the Clerk. "The less we have to do with Colonel Fell and the Garrison, the better."

Hedlow's voice faltered as he saw the bound figure of Ralph Desborough sitting on the couch next to his two sisters.

"So, Ketch, you have found the proscribed Ralph Desborough!"

He turned towards that forlorn figure.

"Foolish youth! Why have you returned to this town, where you are known as a King's man? Do you not realise that by being found in your sisters' home they now run the risk of further fine and punishment?"

Ralph did not respond to the Clerk's chiding. The line of his jaw hardened as he faced the representatives of civic power and punishment. To explain to a man whose life he had saved, and who was a soldier like himself, was one thing, but to converse with Clerk Hedlow and his nephew was another. They represented the new order, and could only be a source of danger to him.

"Master Hedlow, and Constable Hedlow, you come at an apposite time" said Ketch, turning towards them.

"Ralph Desborough has just confessed to the murder of Preacher Hayeck."

A gasp escaped Ralph at this betrayal; both sisters hissed at Ketch, and Mary, her blonde hair straggling across her face, moved to strike Ketch another blow.

"How can you!", she cried.

"You say my brother saved your life from this preacher and his mercenary, and now you repay him with a charge of murder!"

Martha Desborough, wearing an angry frown, confronted Ketch. He moved to her and took her by the shoulders.

"Quiet, quiet, Mistress" he soothed.

"It's all right. I know the truth. Fear not."

He pushed her gently but firmly back to her seat on the couch.

"Master Hedlow" he continued, keeping one hand on Martha's shoulder.

"I was careful to say that Ralph Desborough had confessed to the murder of Preacher Hayeck. Before we go further, I must ask him but one question."

He turned to Ralph. "Where did the blow land that felled the Preacher with such force?"

"On the forehead" replied Ralph, touching his own to indicate the spot.

"He fell to the ground and lay still. Before I could do anything, I heard a rustle behind me and an exclamation of some sort - people were coming. I knew I must not be discovered, so I fled to what I thought was safety here at the house and the church."

"As I surmised" said Ketch, and he stroked his nose thoughtfully. "Ralph, you did not murder Preacher Hyack, despite what you have told us. Yes, you struck him a blow - a blow that drew blood - but I think the Preacher was less hurt than he pretended. Is that not so, Martha?"

He turned towards the now silent sister. Slowly, Martha nodded her head.

"Yes" she said softly, "he was far from dead."

All in the room suddenly realised that Martha had some, until now hidden, involvement in this matter. Ketch took Martha's hands in his.

"I found some white stains on the Preacher's jerkin; at first I thought they were but remnants of food, but on closer examination, they had a cream like appearance, and smelt of lavender. There may be others in this town, but Martha, here, has such a scent always about her probably to ease her hands."

With these words, Ketch released Martha's hands, and on his own was the smell of lavender.

"Ralph did not kill that terrible man," said Martha. "I did."

"Martha!" interposed clerk Hedlow,

"Careful now what you say! I have heard what Ketch has said, and there are matters to be explained, but words before witnesses must be spoken carefully, and may do you great harm."

"I am composed, Master Hedlow", she said and rose and stood next to Ralph, in the centre of the room, to face full square the clerk.

"I have been so fearful for myself and Mary and Ralph, and this fear has taken my strength, and nearly my mind, but now I am glad that this Trooper has guessed my secret. And for good or ill, you must know." So saying, she looked at her brother, who sat still and defiant in intention, but even so, his eyes flashed her a warning about his own secret.

"You know that my sister and I have been sheltering our brother, Ralph, for some weeks. Why he has returned to danger, we do not know, and he will not tell us."

This was clearly bitterly felt by Martha, for not only had she been abandoned by father and brother, but she had also been refused the confidence of her brother.

"Last night" she continued.

"Ralph returned home excited and more alive than I have ever seen him before. He stopped only to change out of father's clothes, which he always wore when going out at night. More sensibly dressed he left the house in a tremendous rush. It was too much for me. In a rage of frustration, I put on my own cloak and followed him."

"Oh, Martha!" cried her younger sister.

"What torment you have had. You are the strong one of the family, but even you have been hurt."

As her sister continued her tale, Mary also rose to stand next to her, one arm protectively and lovingly on her older sister's shoulder Martha had temporarily stopped but, with a deep breath, continued her tale.

"Ralph quickly criss-crossed the town; he was clearly looking for someone, but he was heading towards Beckett's well, at the other side of town. It was getting quite dark, for a storm was threatening, but I was able to be but some thirty paces from Ralph, for he took no heed of any pursuer - he was too hot upon his business."

At this point James Hedlow rose from the hard dining chair he had occupied and quietly walked into the kitchen, to return with a cup of water, which he handed to Martha.

"Drink this" he said,

"And be gentle in telling your tale young lady. If you are determined, speak slow and true."

Martha nodded her head in thanks for the water but otherwise ignored everyone else in the room. As her story moved to its climax, she seemed to draw inwards upon herself and physically she turned away from her kin, directing her gaze at Ketch.

"I think you know what happened," she said. "I saw Ralph confront the preacher, and the preacher laughed and cursed at him. I could not hear what was said, but both Ralph and the preacher were angry. Then the preacher leapt at Ralph, who struck him a blow on the head with the hilt of his sword. The preacher collapsed. I could not help but cry out, and in so doing, I saw that I had caused Ralph to turn and flee."

"One question, Martha" said Ketch.

"When the preacher fell, how did he fall."

"Face down" came the reply."

He had twisted as he fell. I could not see his face - he was peering at hell itself, I have no doubt, for he was evil and vicious! I approached him fearful at what Ralph had done, but he was not dead - he was not even badly hurt, for as I knelt to turn him over to see his wound, he grabbed my arm, and he laughed at me. He raised himself to his feet, and his hand gripped my arms until I cried in pain. He said terrible things - words no woman should hear, least of all from a preacher!"

Martha was becoming distressed at the memory of her ordeal, and Ketch turned to Mary. "I think your sister should sit down" he said, "And if there is some small quantity of brandy in the house it might be beneficial."

Mary nodded, and took from a small wooden chest a pewter mug and a bottle. Pouring a generous measure, she moved Martha to the couch and pushed the mug to her lips. Obediently Martha drank the brandy, and then continued her story.

"Preacher Hyack was strong and he had hold of my arms with a grip I could not break. With his face pushed up close to mine and his foul breath all over me, I was near to fainting. I pushed at him with all my might, and he must have caught his foot, for he stumbled and fell backwards, right on to the rim of the well. His head gave a crack as it hit the stone, and I could see blood running from the back of his head. His eyes rolled - and closed - and he slowly slumped over on to his side."

"One moment" said Ketch, his voice tense.

"And please be certain of this Martha, onto which side did he fall?"

"He fell." Her brow furrowed, then.

"Yes, of course - he fell to his left side for he fell away from me, and I could no longer see his face.

Then I turned and fled. My heart was pounding with fear, I rushed home to find Ralph ahead of me, but I could not speak, and went straight to my bed, and from that moment, I have not left the house."

Hedlow and Ketch exchanged glances and with a quiet word to the Trooper they both left the assembled Desborough family in the charge of the constable and walked out of the small house into the peace of the garden for a more private conversation.

"I mind your thoughts when we first found the body, Ketch," said Hedlow.

"A first blow to the front of the head, a second to the back, leaving the preacher on his left side. You are an extraordinary man, Ketch, for that is the very tale that these Desboroughs have given us. And I've not forgotten that a third blow was struck which left the preacher dead, on his right side. Have you thoughts about that?"

"Perhaps..." mused Ketch.

"But, whatever, I feel confident that no Desborough is responsible for the preacher's death."

The sun now beat heavily upon the two figures in the garden, and the heat and the brightness made concentration difficult. The wild flowers and shrubs that the sisters had lovingly tended brought pleasure to the eyes, and the scent of summer was strong about the place.

"Let us sit a moment in the shade" said Ketch.

"There are some further matters I must discuss with you."

And he guided the clerk to a small bench that pleasantly drew shade from an elderly oak. Sitting comradely side by side with the clerk, Ketch knew that he needed this man's help if he were to go further in that quest that he had commenced with Major Blake. Choosing his words with care, he sought to win the favour he needed.

"Hedlow, you know something of Major Blake. You know him as a loyal and trusted servant of Parliament and the army, a friend of Northampton, and one of those who would pit his wits and strength against Lord Le Vaughn's mighty power. I know he has left Northampton, and your joint venture of Cornet Marlowe and his Troopers, against Le Vaughn have failed.

"Yes, it is so, my soldier friend" sighed Hedlow.

"And very speedily my council and I will bend the knee to Lord Le Vaughn and seek his pardon. There is nothing I can do to stop this, Ketch.Le Vaughn is the master of Northampton."

"That may be so," replied Ketch,

"But there is another part of this Northampton chess board where Le Vaughn is as uncertain and unknowing as the Major, a matter of even greater importance than who rules Northampton."

Hedlow, like the good public servant that he was, began to tell Ketch that there was little he knew of that was more important than who ruled in Northampton, but Ketch cut across the words of the clerk.

"Master Hedlow" he said firmly.

"What happens to Charles Stuart, Lord Le Vaughn and Oliver Cromwell himself may well be determined by the Major's quest, and he and I need your help in this matter. It does not put you at risk- I merely require some co-operation. Both you and I know that Ralph and Martha Desborough are innocent of the preacher's death, but, in this other matter, I need to precipitate events. I need to hurry them into mistakes, to press their minds. So, will you return to the room, arrest both sisters and brother, be hard with them, frighten them just a little, but then confine them to the house on their surety to appear before you tomorrow. I am trying, Hedlow" he explained.

"To make them talk to each other when you have gone. Will you help me?"

The dark figure sitting next to him pondered a moment.

"It is a small matter, Ketch" he replied."

"I cannot see how these three Desboroughs threaten Le Vaughn or the town. You know, or can surmise, the governance of Northampton that I would have and so, I will do as you say. But, all in ignorance, and that is probably the best. Come," he said, rising to his feet,

"Let me play my part."

"Thank you, Sir" cried Ketch with relief.

"But let me precede you to your stage."

Ketch, followed by Hedlow, returned to the parlour and Ketch took position by the garden window as clerk Hedlow addressed the three anxious faces turned towards him.

"It is time," said Hedlow gravely,"

"We must bring this matter to a head. Ralph Desborough went out into the night searching for preacher Hyack, found him, quarrelled, and struck him a grievous and bloody blow. Martha Desborough, following her brother, also struggled and murderously harmed him. This same preacher is now dead; his body lies in the crypt of All Saints' Church demanding justice and the verdict of the coroner. You are both at the very heart of this matter, and will be brought before me to account for yourselves."

Turning to Ralph Desborough, he continued,

"You and your sisters can be imprisoned by my constable in the Council House."

He paused

"On your honour as a gentleman, if you promise not to leave this house, and all three to present yourselves to my judgement as coroner at noon tomorrow, I will let you enjoy that amount of liberty. What say you to this?"

"So be it," said Ralph Desborough.

"Loosen my bonds. My sisters and I give our word we will not stray from this house, and we will come to your judgement tomorrow."

"So, shall it be" said Hedlow.

"Come, Ketch! Constable!We have other matters to attend to."

The three men left the house briskly, but as they turned to walk back towards the town centre, Ketch slipped away from his companions.Straddling the garden wall, he took one quick look around and dropped quietly into the garden. Three long strides, and then he sank to his haunches below the window of the room where the three Desboroughs still sat.

The brother and the two sisters sat in a line on the couch at an angle to the window where Ketch crouched beneath the sill. All was quiet, and no one spoke for some minutes. Ketch could feel the heat of the sun on his back.

Softly Martha spoke to her brother.

"Ralph, you and father have given everything to the cause of Charles Stuart. You have lost your wealth, position, home - and abandoned your sisters. We have had no part in these matters, but despite all that we have suffered, our love for you and father has never wavered. You are our only brother, and you know that we would give up what little we have if you asked us. Now, Ralph, you are deeply involved in matters that affect our lives and liberty, family honour does not give you the right to hide them from us. We have been your soldiers, Ralph, in your struggle. We have the right to know why we may once again lose everything."

"Yes, Ralph," murmured Mary Desborough, her blond hair heavy with sweat and her face salted with tears.

"We should know matters."

Ralph Desborough rose to his feet and absently moved to close the window.

"Leave room for some air, John," cried Martha.

"We are still stifled by this weather."

Ralph therefore did not fully close the window, and the few inches left open were sufficient for Corporal Ketch to hear the full story that was told to the two Desborough sisters.

"Father and I were both with the King for much of this war, and it was with great pride that I saw father rise in the council of the King," said Ralph.

"Before Naseby, I had been away from the King and thus rejoined father on the very eve of the battle. He was confident of victory, and we agreed that, after pursuing the vanquished enemy we would seek to meet each other at the landmark of the ruined Church of St James, by the village of Moulton."

"Of course, all this was vain-glory; the King and his army were crushed, and those that could fled for their lives. I crossed to the Low Countries with the Prince and other allies, and many refugees from the battle joined us. From the most important of these I learned of a terrible mistake by Charles Stuart that put father and our family honour in the greatest of peril."

In a voice thick with tension, Ralph told the story of the King's damning letter, and how Sir Roger Desborough had ridden away from the field of Naseby never to be seen again. How both Roundhead and Stuart spies, each for their own reasons, sought high and low for Sir Roger and the letter. The two Desborough girls stared at Ralph as if transfixed. No words came from their lips, and their faces registered fear as he recounted his own personal oath to return to England to find his father and the evidence of a King's folly. He told them of his decision to visit the old ruined Church at Moulton, and his grim discovery of his father's body.

"So!" exclaimed Martha.

"That was where you really found father!"

"Yes" said Ralph.

"I could not risk anyone knowing the truth. I had to enlist your help in the deception that father was found close to home in Holcot Woods, for I knew many would wish to know his true final resting place."

"I think I begin to see," said Mary Desborough.

"Why you dressed yourself in father's clothes and jewellery. You hoped to jolt or frighten someone into revealing that they were a party to father's death, and that way you might learn the whereabouts of the letter - for plainly it was not on father when you found him."

Ketch rose quietly to his feet and stole from the garden. He had heard enough. Roger Desborough, with the King's letter, had gone to the Church of St James by Moulton to meet his son, only to be met and foully murdered by Preacher Hayeck and Titus Oats and their ruffian band. Ketch set off through the now hot and dusty streets, he thought with sympathy on the shattered Desborough family and of the price they had paid for loyalty to an undeserving monarch. He clenched his fist, and dragged his mind away from such thoughts, he focused on the two key tasks he had to perform. First, he had to communicate all concerning the King's letter to Major Blake, who waited but a day's ride away at Newport Pagnell, second, as far as they knew Titus Oats was the only man alive who knew exactly what had taken place at that Church by Moulton, and how Sir Roger had died. Ketch had to find Titus and quickly, for Preacher Hayeck had plunged a knife deep into him.

Chapter 10

Some fourteen miles away, in the front parlour of the Saracen's Head Inn at Towcester, Francis Le Vaughn sat in a finely carved chair by the cold hearth. Such was the heat of the day that even the dark stone-flagged room was warm. He turned to his companion, a slim young man of some twenty-five years, dressed in silken hose and a rich doublet, sporting fine buttoned shoes; a young man of wealth and position.

"Tell me about the King" said Le Vaughn.

"Oh ... he frets a little, which is natural. But he finds his confinement acceptable; he even visits Althorpe from time to time. He has visitors - Cromwell himself has been to see him; what they talked of, I do not know, but the General left in a bad humour. Holdenby is not the finest house in the land, but as a gaol, the King finds it passing pleasant."

The young man stood lazily beside the inn window casually viewing the countryside scene. It was not difficult to get our King lodged in a county that has given such support to Parliament" said Le Vaughn.

"And to have him close by allows me to protect him from those who would do him personal harm."

"May God save you!"

Lord Easton was duly grateful. Although to the casual observer an indolent young man, Lord Easton was one of a small band of royalist supporters who risked their lives being close to the king in his captivity. They had pledged themselves to protect his person and were prepared to both die and kill for him

"But, when will he be King again? ", he inquired of Le Vaughn.

"When do you plan to see off Cromwell, and Vale; when will their heads adorn the Tower gate?"

"Patience, my friend" soothed Le Vaughn.

"Slowly Parliament begins to see my way, that we should trust our King. We have no other, so it is with him that we must treat. Ah, if only we could disband the army! Then matters would be easy; but alas, for the moment, that instrument is not ours. All we can do is to continue to foment passions between Parliament and the army."

"But the King's person must be protected" interjected the young man.

"But "Of course" snapped Le Vaughn, then collected himself.

"Whilst he remains at Holdenby he is safe, and they have neither the strength nor the pretext to take him."

He rose to his feet.

"Tell your friends, all is well; we are all working to restore Charles Stuart to his own- he may hope to rule more than Holdenby within the year."

Le Vaughn swept a deep bow and left the room, hiding the mockery in his eyes.

Outside, twenty dragoons stood by their chargers, awaiting their orders.

"We return to Northampton" ordered Le Vaughn.

"His feet slipped easily into the stirrups of his horse and he took up the reins. With him in the lead, the party of horsemen clattered over the cobbled main street of Towcester, once trodden by Roman legions, and out onto the dirt road that led through some of the richest fields in England. Towcester itself had been besieged during the war, and Parliament and the King's men had foraged the country bare; but two years without predators had given time for people and the land to recover.

Le Vaughn exuded satisfaction as he led his men through the countryside. It was a fine day; he was rich in coin, plate and land; regiments looked towards him, as did towns and cities. The King was lodged in his county, and his friends in Parliament were beginning the task of taming the army. Le Vaughn, though arrogant, was intelligent and resourceful. He knew that, despite all, he was at risk. His enemies, led by Cromwell, were powerful; the army was unpredictable; Parliament was fickle, and Charles Stuart was not popular. Power in England could be his, or, if the balance tipped the other way, if, for example, that damned letter was found and made public, both he and Charles Stuart would be lost, crushed in a fury of religious outrage.

"That, letter remains crucial. Fell must find it and hand it to me and with it, the King would do as I, Le Vaughn, bid.Of course, it might not exist, or lost by that fool, Desborough. Fell must bear down more fiercely onto the Desborough family, it is time to squeeze the women on this matter.

Le Vaughn considered the position of his enemies and gave a grunt of satisfaction.

"I have time yet, Cromwell's Major Blake is gone, and the Cornet, with his broken leg and handful of Troopers, were unimportant."

Le Vaughn laughed out loud.

"Today, that stiff-necked Clerk and his Council had will beg an audience to offer their respects and to secure my good offices. That is an audience I shall enjoy, and Hedlow? Hedlow, he mused, will retire."

That self-same clerk Hedlow was once again sitting by the bed of Cornet Marlowe in the best bedroom of the Peacock Inn. He, Marlowe and Ketch had resumed their council of war. Ketch, with Marlowe's approval, had appraised Hedlow of all that he had heard and all that he knew concerning the King's letter. The Cornet seemed in better spirits for his recent rest and he vigorously gnawed a leg of chicken whilst the remains of the stripped carcass lay on a plate precariously poised on the bump in the blankets created by his generous stomach.

"It seems to me, Ketch" said Hedlow, "that the sooner you find this ruffian Titus Oats the better."

"Yes" replied Ketch. "One way or another, Titus will settle the matter of Sir Roger's death and what happened to the letter."

"If there is a letter" interjected the Cornet, resting between mouthfuls of chicken. "All this chasing about stems from the royalist rumour. No one is sure about it."

"That is so" replied Hedlow.

"But I think we should be quite clear in our minds as to the importance of this game we play."

The old clerk took from his pocket his favourite clay pipe, ready filled with tobacco and with a coal lifted by tongs from the small bright fire in the hearth, he lit up.

"It is about two years since Naseby, and some months since the Scots handed Charles Stuart over to the English Parliament, and the truth be that for some time nobody has known what to do with him."

Hedlow drew strongly until his pipe glowed, then continued in the carefully pronounced speech with which he had often addressed the Council.

"But matters are now drawing to a climax. Parliament and the Presbyterians would try to bind the King with contracts and laws, the army would take the King into their own hands. That division is now becoming clear. Behind the Parliament, using all his power to reach a settlement with the King is Le Vaughn. He sees a future as the King's Chief Minister, especially a weak King, fettered by Parliament. The King would reign, but Le Vaughn would rule. And then, God help us all!"

Hedlow spat into the fire.

"We in Northampton have experienced the vicious and cruel nature of his hand. England would groan under such a man.

"But the army would not stand for it!" Exclaimed Ketch.

"The army's power is slowly being undermined by Le Vaughn" replied Hedlow.

"And the one army commander who can outface Le Vaughn is General Cromwell, and he vacillates, still seeing good in the King, and reluctant to see through what most of us know is inevitable."

"So, this letter which damns the King before every Englishman would destroy Le Vaughn's plans and push Cromwell into supporting his army comrades?"

"Just so." affirmed Hedlow.

"Royalists, Le Vaughn and the army are all searching wildly for this King's letter so they may play their political game. But For us, better the Royalists or the army be successful, for should Le Vaughn find the letter, he will use it to bind the King to him completely, or he will destroy it and all those who know of its existence - Royalists, women, Trooper, Cornets....."

"And clerks" concluded Cornet Marlowe, with a grimace.

"At the moment, we are ahead in this race.," said Ketch.

"We know Titus Oats is the key to this letter, and only the Desboroughs safely in their house are also so appraised."

"This secret we must keep to ourselves" warned Hedlow.

"God's Teeth!" exclaimed Cornet Marlowe.

"We sit talking at our peril. Ketch, find this damn fellow, and get that letter to Major Blake fast. These matters are too deep for me, Hedlow. The sooner Ketch does what he can, then the sooner we can be away. Such affairs of state take from my courage.I'd sooner face a loaded battery than stay involved in this Italian type affair!"

Ketch left the Cornet and Hedlow talking and retalking the matter to hand, and he stepped out into the inn yard, now bathed in the lengthening shadows of late afternoon. Tull had returned with the guard from the Council House, and the Troopers were greeting each other with oaths and jests and complaints, as do all soldiers prior to expected food and a comfortable evening.

"Tull, Holditch, to me" exclaimed Ketch.

"Oh Corporal" complained Tull.

"I'm just off duty, and I need a pipe and a spot of comfort before you start chasing me around."

"Not much of a Trooper is he, Corporal?" interjected Holditch.

"A couple of hours duty in the Town Council House, and all he can do is sit around in an inn yard asking for his pipe."

"Enough!" ordered Ketch.

"We have no time for your pleasures. I need your help, and I need it now."Tull and Holditch immediately became all attention. The Corporal was asking for help. This was serious. Ketch outlined to his two friends that he needed to find Titus Oats quietly and without fuss, but quickly.

"Is it to do with all that rumpus in the churchyard and that spy, Major Blake? Asked Holditch.

"You are in deep now, Ketch" he continued.

"Yes, I am" replied Ketch.

"And you are both going to help me. I want you to organise the troop to search this town quietly. I want men in taverns, whorehouses, bakers. I want their ears open, mouths closed and looking for someone helping a man who's had a knife in him. You'll take eight men each. Larkin can stay with me."

Ketch stroked his nose before giving his final instructions.

"I want this search done without drawing attention to ourselves. I want craft and cunning. I want the men to use their heads and not go shouting about what they are doing. Make that clear to them you two".

With orders to report back every half-hour, Ketch's Troopers fanned out across the town of Northampton. Quiet, well-behaved soldiers are welcome in most public places, and these Troopers, with Tull's and Holditch's admonitions ringing in their ears, were both quiet and attentive to what was about them. In tavern and barbershop, they made their enquiries.

Ketch and Trooper Larkin stayed in the inn yard. Larkin was the oldest man in Ketch's troop. Born in the last year of the last Tudor, he had strong independent religious beliefs that produced radical political views. But Larkin rarely spoke out, keeping his thoughts to himself. Generally confining himself to reflections on the iniquities of all kings, popes and rulers and how none of them was any good for the common man. The value of Larkin to Ketch was that he was a Northampton man.

"Now, Larkin," said Ketch. "This is your home town, and when we get news of Titus Oats' lodgings you will take me straight there without fuss or flutter."

"Yes, Ketch" replied Larkin.

"But it is some years since I was last here. I've no relatives, no kin, left in this town - I'm not sure I know it like I used to."

"You just put your mind to it" replied Ketch.

"And I want you looking like a townsman, not a soldier. So off with that top and belt, and wear this cloak. We will not want to draw attention to ourselves."

"Corporal, I'm a soldier. I don't know about these dark, spying ways you're into" complained Larkin.

"Just do as I tell you, Larkin. You are supposed to have a bit of sense, or so Tull tells me. Though God knows why I listen to him."

Larkin seemed mollified by Tull's recommendation and, muttering put on the clothes Ketch had provided. Ketch wrapped himself in a full-length cloak, which he could wear bareheaded.

For two hours they had to wait, thus prepared, and during that time troopers had regularly wandered into the inn yard with no news. Then, just as the first fingers of despair began to clutch at Ketch, Trooper Holditch walked casually and at ease into the inn yard. Out of public sight, he ran to Ketch

"Got 'im!" he crowed.

"The preacher and Titus have rooms with a blacksmith's family by the Horse Market. I got to talking with a saddler's wife, who thought Missus Blacksmith was getting all high and mighty, having a preacher in the house."

"Well done!" cried Ketch. "There is use after all for your cheery, well-fed face! Bring all the men back" ordered Ketch.

"I want every man safe in this inn yard. I want them ready, with horses fit and watered, and with their boots on. I don't want that Colonel Fell sneaking up on them, and we may have to move in a hurry. I want you and Tull thinking and watching, not sleeping. Now, go!" With these orders ringing in his ears, Holditch went about the business Ketch had given him.

Ketch and Larkin made their way from the Peacock Inn, across the Market Square towards the horse market. As they walked briskly side by side, they saw one or two of their Troopers drifting back quietly to the inn. Ketch stroked his nose thoughtfully; he was anxious about the troop, anxious about Cornet Marlowe. Now that Major Blake had gone, the murder of the preacher had added to the atmosphere of fear and uncertainty that pervaded the town. He was relieved, like all generals, that at least his little force was concentrating.

There was only one Blacksmith's Yard by the horse market and Ketch and Larkin swiftly found their way to it. As with most buildings in Northampton, it was dominated by the shadow of the Castle. Le Vaughn covered everything, thought Ketch, but he comforted himself with the thought that Le Vaughn knew nothing of Ralph Desborough, the preacher, or Titus, and of their significance for the King's letter.

He came to sudden halt.

"Damn!" he exclaimed.

He realised that Mary and Martha Desborough were alone in their house, with Ralph honour bound to remain there. It would not be long before it came to Le Vaughn's ears that there had been Troopers searching the church and graveyard next to the Desborough home. Someone might even have seen the capture of Ralph. If Le Vaughn were to seize the three Desboroughs, he would soon find out everything they knew. Ketch could guess the sort of methods for extracting information that would be employed by Colonel Fell and Lord Le Vaughn.

Ketch cursed himself for his slowness of thought. What should he do now? His irritation focused upon the hilt of his sword, which he tightly clenched. Larkin must be sent to warn them he decided. His first hope, that the Peacock Inn or the Council House would be a haven, but these he dismissed. Nowhere in Northampton would be safe from Le Vaughn.

"Larkin" he snapped. "Go to the Desborough house quickly. Warn them that they are at risk, and should fly Northampton. Tell them that they are still under parole to me but that for their own safety they should leave the town.They have relatives at a nearby village. Let them hide there. Go, now, and Larkin, try not to frighten them but be serious in intent!"

Ketch cursed himself. "Major Blake would not be impressed" he thought. It was a Ketch, worried and full of self-recrimination that entered the blacksmith's yard.

Lord Le Vaughn, once more in his favourite purple robe, stood by the window of his room overlooking the courtyard of Northampton Castle. He held a silver goblet of fine wine, and casually fingered the jewel that hung around his neck on a heavy gold chain. Even he felt excitement as his long-held plans began to unfold, plans that could lead him to the highest seat of power in the land. He closed his eyes in the late evening sun, and enjoyed its warmth on his head that was full of a dazzling future. In three days, time, on the third of June, he would move the King to Northampton Castle, where the people would clamour for his return to the throne. Then, in triumphal procession, he, Le Vaughn, the newly appointed Chief Minister, would lead the King to London and Parliament for a grand reconciliation. Simultaneously the navy, his County Associations and the City of London would welcome and support this new start for a war-weary England. The army, Fairfax and Cromwell would not dare to oppose him. He had the wealth to pay off enough regiments to undermine their strength, and sufficient support in Parliament to secure the disbandment of the army. He smiled, contemplating the triumph of his will over his enemies. In particular, the upstart Cromwell, who still agonised and mewed about the sanctity of the King's person, failing to use the army, the one instrument of power that could deny Le Vaughn.

"*Cromwell's own weakness of purpose will deliver him to me*" thought Le Vaughn, and his lips curved into a thin smile.

"The process starts tonight. When the Town Council of Northampton, the most stalwart for Parliament, will agree to petition me in the market square tomorrow, the first day of the new month, for the return of the King."

Colonel Fell entered the room, his bulbous eyes bright with triumph.

"The Town Council will wait upon you within the hour, my Lord" he said.

"They wish to know your pleasure and how they can regain your favour. That grey-pated, clever clerk of theirs will lead them in begging your forgiveness. I hope you will be merciful, my Lord!"

"Oh, I shall!" replied Le Vaughn.

"In their paltry way they have sought to frustrate my will, but tonight I will be generous, for to seek their support tomorrow. But, once they have clamoured for the King, and placed the town squarely in our camp, Hedlow and Trussel and the rest will feel my anger."

"My Lord, there is other news" said Fell.

"A Royalist, probably Ralph Desborough, has been taken in the town, and rumour has it that he has given his parole to stay in his sisters' home. Are they still a danger to your Lordship, should I take them?"

Le Vaughn considered the possible threat of the Desboroughs, the King's letter, and its impact on a vacillating army leadership. It is all so uncertain, and of little import, he thought. Parliament, the City, securing the King's person, was what mattered now. Great matters were to be managed; this was now a minor detail.

"Scoop them up if you can, Fell" he said.

"But it is of little matter now. If you can squeeze any King's letter out of them, do so, and hold it for me. I will now prepare to meet the Council."

"It shall be done, my Lord" said Fell.

"May I inquire as to when Charles Stuart joins us?"

"On the third of June" replied Le Vaughn.

"Lord Easton and a small group of supporters will bring the King to the Saracen's Head at Towcester.

There I will meet him and escort him to the safety of Northampton Castle."

"Is that fop of a lord and his young friends to be trusted, my lord", asked Colonel Fell.

"Do not be too deceived by them Fell" replied Le Vaughn.

"In the matter of the king's person they are fanatics and dangerous to those that oppose them, but they are with us and I have no doubt will perform the task that they have been set."

Colonel Fell drew his sword, and saluted Le Vaughn.

"Then when you have the King's person, you will have England" he cried.

"And you" said Le Vaughn, "Shall be a General of Horse!" Both men laughed long and loud at their good fortune.

Ketch found himself looking at the honest and slightly perplexed face of Stephen Hedlow, Constable, and nephew to the Clerk of the Council.

"There is a man dying upstairs" said the Constable.

"And he is the companion of the preacher whose body we found this morning. It looks like we have two murders to report to my uncle, the town clerk. A nasty business" he mused aloud.

"Some folk are too friendly with knives..........Ketch! What exactly are you doing here?"

Ketch thought quickly. He needed to talk to Titus at once; Stephen Hedlow could help or prevent this. What sort of man was this nephew of Hedlow's? Ketch decided to trust to family traits. He rapidly told Stephen that he and his uncle believed that the preacher had knifed Titus previous to his own murder, and that Titus had possession of knowledge that affected the good of the town. Whilst trusting to the honest nature of Stephen, Ketch, stressed his closeness to his uncle and how they were working together. The respect that Stephen had for his kin showed clearly, and was Ketch's passport through the yard into the blacksmith's kitchen, past a large, dark man and a red-eyed woman, up some stairs to a small dank bedroom at the back of the house.

Titus Oates, alone in the room, lay on a low bed underneath a lone small window that cast a little light on his sweating body. Dressed only in rough trousers and a torn shirt, he lay on top of filthy, dark blankets, holding a bloody cloth to his side. His eyes were shut tight with pain, and his hand holding the cloth was clamped hard to a body that was rigid with the struggle for life.

Ketch knelt beside him and whispered his name. The sound of another human voice seemed to release some of the tension within Titus. The struggle for life had been long, but was now lost. Someone was now here, and he could relax and wait for death, knowing that he would not die alone.

Ketch leaned over the faintly groaning Titus, who opened his eyes to see who was with him.

"You!" he gasped. A flash of recognition in his eyes was followed by a dull acceptance.

"You could have killed me" he whispered.

"But you didn't.I've never liked you soldiers."

Titus croaked with the effort of speech.

"I've had trouble enough with you all, but you could have done for me, but you didn't.....and that bastard preacher did!"

The words came stumbling out from Titus, and Ketch could see that death was closing in fast. Gently he held the dying man's hand.

He seemed to have little time for his task for Titus was clearly drawing close to his end. There was no time for soft words that would ease death. Ketch had questions that required answers. He had to get the information before death stole it from him.

"We know the preacher stabbed you and we know it was because you revealed to Ralph Desborough that you knew something about the death of his father".

Titus groaned "God help me", he gasped.

"I've done bad things in my life, but that man's death was terrible. No one deserves to die like that. The Preacher was a devil that night. I swear he enjoyed it."

Titus began looking around him widely.

"Is there a priest here? "He said.

"I need a priest someone to absolve me from that sin."

Again, he moaned but even this was now costing him his remaining strength.

"Tell me" urged Ketch, "And I can tell the priest for you."

"No good" moaned Titus.

"I've too many bad things to fear for, and that damn preacher did it, him and me, about six of us, we strung up that fine cavalier. Oh, he danced and struggled. The preacher knows, oh, he knows all right!" Titus was beginning to rave, and his voice grew weaker, his breath coming quickly in fetid pants.

"The preacher is dead" said Ketch, desperately trying to shock the dying Titus into some temporary rationality.

"Ah!" choked Titus.

"Dead afore me.Well, well" he chuckled.

"Who got 'im? Tough, was the preacher, he'd be a hard man to kill. Gone to hell before poor old Titus ..." A short chuckle became a wheeze, and then a choking cough.

Ketch bent his mouth down to Titus's ear.

"You are the only one who can tell us how that cavalier, Sir Roger Desborough, died, and what was taken from him!"

With a feeble giggle, Titus said.

"He died in church, St James by Moulton. He came walking into our camp in the old tower. Preacher killed him, and stripped him, but all we got were some fine clothes and jewellery. We searched every bit of him and his clothes, hat and boots even, for coin, but he'd nothing. But he died in church ...."

Titus was now breathing in short rasping pants. A crescendo of death seemed but moments away.

"What about a letter?" hissed Ketch.

"Was there a letter on him?"

"No, no letter" gasped Titus.

"Preacher can read, Titus can't.... But there wasn't no letter. Rings, and a pendant we had, and we sold, but he died horribly and slow. "Preacher dead, eh?"

Again, Titus coughed and choked, and his words became a loud nonsense delirium. 'Preacher' and 'church' and 'preacher dead' were the final words Ketch heard. Titus suddenly fell silent, and then, with a final effort raised himself up by grasping Ketch by the coat. He looked, mad-eyed, at Ketch, and then fell back on to the bed, dead.
Ketch became aware of Stephen Hedlow standing behind him. He left the Constable to deal with the corpse and the blacksmith's family. He had their trust, and Ketch was confident that Stephen would recount Titus's final words to his uncle. Once out into the early

evening air, Ketch made his way from the horse market back to the Peacock Inn.

He was now horribly confused; his mind raced over what Titus had said. There was no letter. So much energy had been spent for something that did not exist. Major Blake, Ralph Desborough, and God knew who else, had been searching for those who had killed Sir Roger Desborough, certain that this would bring them to the incriminating letter written by Charles Stuart. He, Ketch, had won this race, had found Titus and achieved absolutely nothing.

"Titus was certain there was no letter, so Sir Roger did not have the letter when he was killed. Perhaps he had destroyed it, lost it, and hidden it somewhere...."

Not only confused, but also depressed, Ketch strode back to the more certain task of managing a troop of horse. His mind leapt to Trooper Larkin and his mission to the Desboroughs. He hoped that the precaution was unnecessary - but also, that it had been in time.

Martha Desborough lit two candles for, despite the light outside; it was becoming gloomy in the Desborough house. Mary and Ralph were sitting at table eating their evening meal of cheese and hard bread. Martha herself could not eat; the terrors and tensions of preacher Hayeck's death, and her and

Ralph's involvement, had been too frightening an experience.

"Come, Martha. Do sit down." Said Mary.

"Ralph and I have finished our meal."

Martha sat at table with them, and they returned once more to the subject of their father's death, the King's letter and the mystery surrounding it.

"What if father hid the letter," said Mary.

"He was a clever and cautious man. He expected to meet you, Ralph, but a battle had just been lost, and there was danger everywhere. He could well have hidden it where he knew you would find it if anything happened to him. Think, Ralph!" she exclaimed. "Father would want you to see this through."

"But where?" groaned Ralph.

"Again, and again I have thought this. Nowhere in the tower could he hide it, there was only the overgrown churchyard. If he hid it there, nobody could find it."

"What about a mark?" asked Martha.

"A sign, a pointer, something that was not as it should be...?

"There was no mark," said Ralph.

"It was months later when I found him. If there was a mark, it was long lost."

Silence followed this inconclusive end to their thoughts. With a sigh, Martha rose to her feet.

"Come, let us give thanks for our food."

Bowing their heads, and with hands together in prayer, they listened to Martha saying Grace.

"...In the name of the Father, and of the Son, and of the Holy Ghost. Amen." said Martha.

"Amen." said Mary. Ralph said nothing: his body stiffened; his mind began to race. Pictures of his dead father flashed in his mind: the tower open to the sky: the churchyard: the tombstones... Not the name of the father, but the name of the son! His name - Ralph - cleared of grime and moss on one of the tombstones. A mark!

Ralph's mind was a blur of excitement.

"I think I understand", he exclaimed.

"I have the sign," he cried.

"The grave with my name on it. Father hid the letter by the gravestone with my name on it. It was cleared and fresh of mould."Ralph leapt to his feet.

"I must go!"

He grabbed his cloak and hat.

"I must find a horse," he said.

"But your parole!" cried Martha.

"You gave your word of honour, Ralph!"

Ralph halted.

"I will give up my own honour to save that of father, and the name of the King" he cried, and rushed to the front door of the house, pulled it wide open, and ran out, straight into the arms of a waiting trooper.

Chapter 11

Trooper Larkin was hot, thirsty and tired. Despatched by Ketch to warn the Desborough family to flee the town, he had hurried through the small streets of Northampton, a cloak covering his heavy clothing. Now his boots hurt his feet and his heavy wool jerkin was making him sweat. He had, however, successfully traversed the town and, making easy work of the last few downhill steps past the Church of the Holy Sepulchre, he stepped up to the door of the Desborough residence to deliver his message.

Before his gloved hand could hit the door to announce his presence, it swung open and a tall figure hurtled into him, sending them both to the ground in a single mass of waving arms and kicking feet. Amidst oaths, and some pushing and pulling, the accidental assailant got to his feet and, without any sort of apology, ran off in the direction of the Church and the town centre.

"God's Teeth!" exploded Larkin, still winded and sitting on his rump with his legs splayed out before him.

Two women seemed to appear instantly, and with cries of sympathy and gentle help, Larkin was slowly raised to his feet by Mary and Martha.

"Where's he off to, in such a rush?" cried Larkin.

"Knocking Troopers to the floor is uncivil and uncalled for - especially when the party being damaged is here to give warning and help to them that's giving out the buffets."

"Oh, we are most sorry," said Martha. "Our broth........er! friend is in a hurry, and I am sure meant no harm. He is impetuous and always in a rush."

"Please let us help you," said Mary, who had secretly been much amused at the sight of a dusty and cross Trooper Larkin sitting in the road.

"Come! Come into the house, and take a cup of water."

Larkin, who was beginning to recover himself in the company of two ladies anxious for his health, began to feel that indeed his injuries required further female cosseting, and that perhaps a cup of water was appropriate. With Mary and Martha either side of him, he allowed himself to be eased over the threshold and into the parlour at the front of the house. Permitting the concerned attention of Mary and Martha to sit him down, Larkin began to feel much better. Only then did his urgent message from Ketch to the Desboroughs flood back to him.

"Ah" he cleared his throat.

"I am a messenger to you gentlewomen, sent by Corporal Ketch, he says, aah - Oh, yes - you should leave Northampton quickly for there are those that would wish you harm perhaps even imprisonment."

Larkin nodded his head in approval at having got out the words so accurately.

"And, ladies, I must say our Corporal Ketch is not one to frighten easily so I think you ladies should take what he says, and I deliver, seriously, and go quickly."

Having delivered what Larkin thought was a rather fine, well-spoken message, he paused, first to draw breath, and then a sip of water from the cup which Mary Desborough had thrust in his hand.

"What nonsense is this?" questioned Martha.

"Who would want to harass two feeble royalist women, any more than what we suffer already. I'm not sure about your Corporal Ketch, and whether or not he is well-disposed to the Desboroughs." So, saying, she turned to her sister, Mary, who was looking thoughtful and concerned.

"What you say is unfair, Martha" said the younger sister.

"Corporal Ketch was only doing his duty in taking Ralph, and do not forget that he and that Major Blake rescued me from the preacher and his mob, and that his quick wits saved you from a charge of murder. Think on it, Martha" she continued.

"News of Ralph being taken but still here with us will by now be about the town. There are those that would be happier with all the Desboroughs safely locked away."

"Alas so!" mocked a voice from the doorway, and three faces turned to see Colonel Fell blocking the entrance to the parlour.

"The front door was open," he said.

"And I have an order to escort Ralph, Mary and Martha Desborough to greater safety in Northampton Castle."

The two women looked at each other in dismay. Corporal Ketch had been right, and had sought to warn them. A short, doubting delay had been their undoing.

"We protest," cried Martha.

"By what authority and in whose name is this done?"

"My authority is my own" replied Fell.

"The order is that of Lord Le Vaughn. You have been harbouring your brother, Ralph Desborough, a proscribed Royalist - do you deny it?"

The reality of their guilt took away all their power to object to Colonel Fell's commands. Accepting their powerlessness, the two sisters prepared to be led by Fell out onto the roadway where six pikemen were waiting to take them away.

"I see your brother has flown," said Fell.

"Broken a gentleman's parole, not much honour in the Desborough family" he sneered.

Trooper Larkin did not like the look of Colonel Fell. He could tell an autocrat easily enough, but this man had a feel of evil about him; for a single Trooper to oppose him now would end badly.

"A young man knocked me down in his flight, Sir." He said.

"The ladies have been helping me with my injuries."

Fell looked dismissively at Larkin.

"You'll be one of Marlowe's fools" he snapped.

"Get out, and get back to London, go on!" and he raised his arm to encourage Larkin on his way.

The Trooper needed no bidding.

"Thank you for the water, ladies" and picking up his cloak, he hurried out of the house, around the six pikemen, and sped on his way towards the Peacock Inn to find Ketch.

A last backward glance over his shoulder as he hurried past the church showed him the two sisters being marched away. He thought they looked so delicate and forlorn, holding hands and surrounded by the armed men of Le Vaughn.

By the time Ketch had returned from the horsemarket to Cornet Marlowe's room, Clerk Hedlow had gone, and the Cornet was able to tell Ketch that the old servant of the Council had been resolved to lead his senior councillors before Lord Le Vaughn to seek the restoration of his favour to them.

"An awful big bite to swallow for Hedlow, is this," said Cornet Marlowe.

"He's a proud man, and does not expect to survive in his post after this snivelling capitulation of the town council to Le Vaughn."

The Cornet had been reading his bible but, preparing for conversation, he put it on the bed.

"You look sombre, Ketch" he continued.

"How goes your search?" he asked.

He pulled himself up to a more comfortable position in his bed, and motioned Ketch to the chair beside him. Ketch moved to the chair and recounted to the Cornet his success in finding Titus, but his total dismay that Titus insisted with his dying breath that there was no King's letter. That nothing had been taken from Sir Roger Desborough at his murder in the old Church of St James at Moulton.

"He was adamant" sighed Ketch, "And I believe him."

"Well then, Ketch" said Marlowe.

"You have done your best, there is no letter or, if there was, it's gone, and that's an end to it. The doings of Major Blake and Cromwell, Le Vaughn and England I have no doubt will carry on apace without us." Leaning forward, Marlowe spoke in a friendly, almost fatherly, tone to his new Corporal.

"I know you had a liking for the excitement of this work that the Major gave you, but you are a good soldier, Ketch, now a Corporal, and that is steady work and, in God's service, honest work. We must now put all this behind us. In two days, if we procede slowly, I shall be fit to travel in the wagon, so I want everyone for those two days off the streets. No guarding the Council House, everyone confined to the Peacock: and I don't want any drunkenness, Ketch. By Heaven, you'll have your work cut out there."

Marlowe was well pleased that his troop could now leave Northampton and go back to the regiment.

Ketch was grateful for the words of the Cornet. He had been excited by the Major's mission and he had hoped to play a part in the high fortunes of his country; but it was not to be. Tomorrow, the first day of June, he would take the troop out on exercise. The horses needed it, and it would keep the men away from ale. With an early start, they could ride Newport Pagnell way, and he could report to the Major his failure. The Major, Ketch mused, would no doubt slap him on the back and tell him he had done his best and that the Major himself must get to London to report to his army commander. And Ketch? Well, Ketch must return to Northampton and return his Cornet safely to Colonel Butler's regiment. Ketch would be back to being a soldier, probably back to being a Trooper.

Ketch acknowledged the kindly smile on Marlowe's face.

"Well" he though.,

"Straight soldiering is not so bad, and at least I've got a good officer."

He got up from the chair and, checking that the Cornet was comfortable and pausing only to impress on Botterill, the innkeeper, the need to be alert to the patient's every need, Ketch stepped out into the inn yard where his men were sitting around a small fire, finishing their evening meal. The sun had gone down behind the two-story building of their inn and casting dark shadows. Ketch joined his men and took the opportunity to tell them of the ride he required of them the following day. He was surprised how cheerfully the prospect was taken up by them. Inaction, even in the precinct of an inn, had clearly weighed heavily on them, as had the insults and blows they had been forced to accept from the townspeople. Thus, Ketch's troop was in fine spirits at the prospect of leaving Northampton for some fresh country air. But Ketch himself was in a brown mood. Even the banter of Tull and Hoditch, to which he dutifully rejoined, failed to lift his spirits. He sought to occupy himself by checking and cleaning his pistols, and testing the sharpness of his blade. This activity was taken up by the troop as a whole, and match and ball, and flint and steel, became the source of animated comparison and conversation. In this way, Ketch began the process of unwinding himself from the other world of politics and spies that he had briefly entered.

It suddenly struck him that he was a Trooper short. Nineteen men stood or lounged about the inn yard, including Ketch himself; there should have been twenty.

"Where the devil is Larkin?" thought Ketch.

As if in response to his thought, Trooper Larkin entered the inn yard. Hot and flustered, he went straight to a small water barrel and, with the tin cup there for all men, drew himself a full measure and gulped it down. Having met his most urgent need, he turned to Ketch and, wiping his sleeve across his mouth, said

"I've had an adventure that you won't credit, Corporal. You sent your oldest Trooper for your most difficult task. I've been bundled over by a violent young man, soothed by young women, and scared to death by a full Colonel of Horse."

General jeering was the response to Larkin's outburst, together with graphic remarks from Tull and Holditch on Larkin's capabilities with young women. Impatient to hear the full details of Larkin's news, Ketch dragged him to where some sacks of grain were stacked by the inn wall and, sitting Larkin down, got him eventually to tell his story in simple straightforward words. Thus, with the light beginning to fade, Ketch heard that Colonel Fell, Lord Le Vaughn's man, had taken Mary and Martha Desborough into custody in Northampton Castle. Annoying and sad news, but Ralph Desborough breaking his parole and rushing off before Larkin or Fell had arrived sent Ketch's mind racing. What was so important, thought Ketch, that Ralph Desborough would break his word of honour and abandon his sisters. Ketch's heart began to pound; the excitement he had begun to dismiss now raced back into him. The game was not yet over; he was still involved in great matters. Ralph Desborough now knew where lay the King's letter, Ketch was sure of it! Only that would cause such a man to break his personal parole. He must find Ralph, find the letter and, through the Major, get it to those who could forestall the plots of Lord Le Vaughn. He also had an idea, a prospect that he knew the destination of Ralph Desborough.

"Tull, Holditch" he snapped.

"Saddle my horse, and your own, we are going hunting. "Mutch!" He called, and turned to the Trooper whom he had once thought would challenge his Corporal's authority.

"You will keep the troop here, and safe, and you may inform the Cornet that Corporal Ketch may yet resolve a matter for Major Blake!"

"Yes, Ketch" said Mutch. He clearly enjoyed such new responsibility, Standing tall, by his looks and manner he spread his physical authority in support of his Corporal as Ketch, Tull and Holditch rode their horses out of the inn yard.

Lord Easton pushed away the pewter platter on which the remains of a boiled chicken congealed, and turned his gaze towards the other two occupants of Lord Le Vaughn's private room in Northampton Castle. They too were sitting at the oak table and sharing the meal with him."This is like dining with two beasts from Africa," thought Easton, for opposite him, Colonel Fell was gnawing at a chicken carcass and, and to his right, Le Vaughn was expertly dissecting an apple with a vicious looking dagger.

"You plans are fully laid?" Asked Easton, helping himself to a fresh linen napkin and carefully washing his fingers in the silver bowl placed at his right hand.

"Of course," snapped Le Vaughn.

"Deliver Charles Stuart to the appointed place in three day's time. After acclamation in Northampton, I will happily reconcile him to Parliament, and he will be a true King again. The City, the Commons, the House of Lords, the Navy and my own regiment support me."

"And the army?" enquired Easton.

"The army is leaderless, and will be disbanded. Fairfax and Cromwell are without any resolution or strength of purpose. I shall destroy them"

Le Vaughn smiled and speared a piece of apple on the point of the dagger.

"And reap your due reward" replied Easton.

He continued in a light, ironic tone.

"The King's new chief minister is a post reserved for those who can so serve his majesty."

Lord Le Vaughn picked up the silver goblet before him and rose to his feet.

"A toast, gentlemen. To Charles Stuart, may our plans to restore him to his true glory bear fruit."

"Amen to that" grunted Fell.

"The King" said Easton.

"Good fortune to you all."

He drank deep from his goblet and, taking up his knife, began to push at the remaining food on his platter in an absent minded and desultory fashion. Taking up his courage, he continued.

"My Lord Le Vaughn, you are perhaps the most powerful and dangerous man in England, and as I sit here now, I know your will covers parts of this country of which I know nothing. In the next few days, you risk everything to take the person of the King and restore him to his throne, with all his prerogatives, as of old. The King has agreed to place his life and power at your disposal. Success will bring you riches and power but, should your adventure fail, the position of the King would be weakened. Perhaps fatally weakened, and such failure would have a price, my Lord, even for such as yourself."

Le Vaughn fixed Easton with steel-like blue eyes. Slowly he spoke.

"I have risked everything, more than ever before in my life, and I know that if I fail in this endeavour, nothing will be saved of me. Everything, including my life, is forfeit. It matters not to me whether the blow comes from a disappointed King or a triumphant Cromwell. All I can say, my Lord Easton, is that, when I succeed, I shall remember that you felt it necessary to spell out the terms of failure."

Easton started at this reply and for a moment considered a further retort, but thought better of it. Colonel Fell saw and understood his indecision and laughed. Le Vaughn remained silent for a while, staring with blank eyes at Lord Easton.

"My Lords" interjected Fell,

"This is morbid talk when our designs stand at the threshold of success. My Lord Le Vaughn, tell Lord Easton of this evening's meeting with the town council. It is worth telling, and will assure him that all goes well."

The tension between them was broken by the Colonel's remarks and Le Vaughn began his tale of how the town council, some hours earlier, had waited upon him, requesting a moment to secure his good opinion.

"They were all there" he said.

"Trussel, Lugg, Parfitt, and their mouthpiece, Hedlow. Oh, how Hedlow hated it!" chuckled Le Vaughn.

"Their opposition to me has ended. Hedlow has resigned as Clerk to the Council and I am asked to make a new appointment for tomorrow."

"I thought Trussel was going to burst with anger when you suggested that Nathaniel Parfitt would make an excellent mayor," added Fell.

"And, of course, they did not like the beating my men gave Councillor Lugg, who now sits with the Desborough women as your guests in the castle."

Le Vaughn smiled at the memory, and Fell refilled all three goblets with the rich red wine.

"Tomorrow" continued Le Vaughn, "Nathaniel Parfitt will lead Northampton Council in a public declaration to myself in the market square that the King be restored to Parliament in line with the ancient laws of England, and I shall be begged to secure this for them. I shall, of course, demur, and say that such high matters of state must involve the army. They will rail against the tyranny of the army, but I will declare that I can do nothing unless it be the overwhelming wish of the people and Parliament.

"Such scenes of overwhelming support" interrupted Fell.

"Will of course take place, as they have already in Bristol, Hull and Oxford. Tomorrow it happens in Northampton, and on the second day of June it will happen in the City of London."

"On the third day" continued Le Vaughn, his voice taut with triumph,

"Charles Stuart will join his faithful people in Northampton and lodge in the strongest most fortified town in England. From here, he will march upon London and reclaim his throne, and no one shall stop him."

Chapter 12

Ketch rode his horse furiously, and his two companions were hard-pressed to stay with him. Ketch knew the way and, once outside the town walls and the more recent fortifications, he set a racing gallop along the track that led to the Northeast. His goal was the church of St James. He had no certainty that was where Ralph was heading, but it was the last place that Sir Roger Desborough was known to have visited. If this hope was wrong, Ketch knew he had lost his last gamble. The light was failing, and Ketch had no idea whether Ralph was ahead or behind them. He knew Ralph would have to find a horse; how quickly that could be done, he did not know. He hoped he would arrive first; a trap sprung speedily on the unknowing was preferable to trying to surprise someone engaged in secret work, with their senses all alert.

The deserted Church of St James at Moulton was some way North of the village and thus was bounded by fields, hedges and ditches rather than habitations. Ketch headed his party to approach cautiously and, some hundred paces short of the broken-down old church walls, he halted. Leaving Tull to hold the horses and to keep them well away and quiet, he and Holditch stealthily picked their way through an ever-darkening evening to the edge of the churchyard. The two Troopers moved to the tower, the only unseen part of the terrain, and a quick glance within told them that no one was at present sharing this part of Northamptonshire with them.

"*Good*" thought Ketch, though he prayed that he had chosen rightly.

"We can now prepare for Master Ralph Desborough for there are no signs that he has been here before us."

Having no idea what Ralph would do, or whether or not this was his destination, Ketch positioned Holditch just inside the doorway to the tower; a place from which he could see the position taken by Ketch which was close to a gap in the ruined churchyard wall. From here, Ketch could see the track from Northampton and could signal Ralph's arrival to Holditch, and the two of them could watch his movements. Ketch had no intention of telling Holditch about the letter, but his instructions were quite explicit.

"We will give him two hours, if by then we remain alone my gamble will have failed but if our luck holds and this is his destination, do nothing until I call for you. At the first smell of a Trooper he will be away. When I shout, you come running hard, unsheath your sword - have it ready, but out of moonlight."

So instructed, Holditch took up his position, and Ketch retreated to his.

"Nothing to do but wait," thought Ketch.

He hoped Tull would stay put and keep the horses quiet. If not, their time would be wasted. He would have to trust to luck, he dared not leave his position now.

Being deserted, St James' Church was well away from any regularly travelled track and so, when within some small part of time, Ketch heard the soft footfalls of a carefully walked horse, he was certain that his guesswork had proven right and that indeed Ralph Desborough hoped to find the King's letter here in the churchyard. Relief swept over him, with a wave of his hand he put Holditch on guard and, pressing himself down close by the remaining wall, he desperately sought to see his quarry in the now darkened churchyard.

Ralph Desborough still cursed his foolishness. He had stolen a horse quite easily from the long rails in the Market Square, although he had heard shouts in the distance as the owner discovered his loss. Once out of the northern gate, he had ridden for some five minutes in the gathering gloom before he realised the need for a lantern. Searching for a name on a gravestone at night would be impossible without light. Stealing horses was one thing - finding a full lantern was another! Steel, flint and tinder he always kept about him, but lanterns were not easily borrowed, especially at night. Thankfully the warm night had left windows open and, scouting round the houses that edged the town, a sleeping child's bedroom had eventually yielded him a treasured candle lantern. But time had been wasted, and now that he was so close to his goal, he was impatient to settle the matter.

Ralph rode on quietly through the night, grasping the lantern tight with one hand and holding the reins lightly in the other. He was an expert horseman and knew this countryside well; he slowed his horse to a walk as he approached the ruined church. It was now dark, but a new moon threw a very faint light so that some outlines were to be seen. On the light breeze Ralph could hear the usual nocturnal sounds of the countryside, but all seemed well. He knew roughly his goal, and it would take but a minute to locate the exact tombstone and retrieve the hoped-for King's letter, which he resolved he would not read other than to verify his find and immediately destroy, burning it with fire from his lantern. Ralph was swinging between the emotions of hope and excitement and yet he prepared himself, also, for a crushing disappointment and failure. One way or another soon his hopeless quest would be realised.

He dismounted, and tethered his horse loosely to a tree. Sheltering by the wall, he quickly struck a light to the candle and placed it in its haven of the lamp. Shuttering three sides, he cast the remaining beam of light in front of his feet; there was now sufficient light to guide him to the stone marked "Ralph."

Ketch watched with grim anticipation as the shadowy figure of Ralph Desborough, guided by the light of his lantern, moved through the gap in the broken walls of the churchyard. He had removed his boots and filled the foot of a stocking with loose earth. He knew it as a footpad's weapon that would knock a man unconscious but with little danger of more serious hurt. He waited as Ralph began moving from one gravestone to the next, throwing the lantern's light over the face of each stone. Ketch slowly moved from his own position to get closer to Ralph. There were sufficient gravestones, thorn bushes and piles of rubble for Ketch to move with little chance of being observed, and Ralph was too totally absorbed in his own task to be sensitive to anything outside his immediate vision. Ketch knew that his great enemy was sound - the snap of a twig or the scrape of a rock would echo in the summer night and warn his quarry. He moved with great care, gently testing each spot where he placed his now bare feet.

Ralph stopped before a gravestone in a small group of six, some fifteen paces from the dark entrance to the roofless tower - an entrance that Ketch hoped still contained Trooper Holditch. Placing the lantern so that its light now shone on the base of the stone, Ralph went down on to his knees and began feverishly to search the gap between stone and turf. Almost immediately, he seemed to withdraw something and hold it under the light of the lamp. Ketch knew that this was the moment. Lightly running forward, and enduring the cuts and pain of bare feet on unseen and rough ground, Ketch struck Ralph a blow on the back of the head with the stocking. The limp body of Ralph Desborough slumped to the ground with a dull thud.

Such a tactic was that of the cutthroat and the highwayman, but Ketch had spent some of the time waiting for Ralph deliberating on the safest way to take him. Ralph was young and strong; even with the advantage of surprise; Ketch was not certain that he could hold him down long enough for Holditch to come to his aid. Even then, three men rolling around in the dark could provide many opportunities for mistake. A strong word of authority and a sword to the throat might have worked, but a startled man might instinctively lash out, and Ketch had no desire to use his sword, especially in the dark. The weighted stocking had seemed the best guarantee of success, and indeed the prone figure of Ralph Desborough bore testimony to Ketch's foresight. Even the lamp was undisturbed. Ketch called out to Holditch and, as he heard the Trooper scrambling to him, he knelt and from the still fingers of Ralph's left hand took a sealed package wrapped in waxed paper.

Ketch deliberated for a few moments, then broke open the package; by the light of the lamp close to the fallen Ralph and watched silently by Trooper Holditch, he opened the letter it contained, and quickly scanned its contents. It was, he saw, everything that Major Blake had said. His task was clear; he must take it to the Major, then his job would be done. He would have succeeded where so many had failed. He felt well satisfied. The affairs of state and all their subtleties he would leave to others. He, Ketch, had performed his task.

"What are we going to do with him?" whispered Holditch, still embraced by the atmosphere of spies and secrets. .

"We can leave him." Ketch whispered back.

"He is a fine young man, what would we do with him? We can not turn him over to Le Vaughn. No, let him lie! We have other work to do."

Ketch placed the letter deep inside his shirt and recovered and replaced his stockings and boots. He and Holditch used the lantern to guide them to Tull and the horses. In a few low whispers Ketch briefly gave Tull a version of what had taken place. He knew Holditch would give a full and detailed account on the ride back into town and many other occasions. As they neared the town walls Ketch bade them to be silent and they passed easily back through the northern gate and rode on to the Peacock Inn. On arrival they stabled their horses and threw themselves into the luxury of sleep amidst the hay and sacking of the stable loft. Ketch had not forgotten, however, to both check with Mutch that all was well and to double the guard that night, for he knew the importance of the paper that pressed close to his chest.

June 1st 1647 was a fine, bright summer's day, and Ketch rose early. He had now abandoned his plan to take the troop on exercise; rather, alone, he would deliver his prize to Major Blake. He had to appraise Cornet Marlowe of his movements, and ask him to manage the troop from his sickbed. So, entering the rear entrance to the inn, he tapped lightly on the door of the bedroom occupied by the Cornet.

"By God, Ketch" exclaimed the Cornet, on seeing him.

"I'm glad you are back."

He hauled himself into a sitting position.

"I'm bored, and you have news and matters to tell me, I've no doubt."

In low tones, Ketch swiftly explained to the Cornet how Larkin's news had sent him to the church mentioned by Titus, and how he had secured a certain paper from Ralph Desborough.

"Ketch" said Marlowe.

"I'm dumbfounded at your success but, I fear for your safety. You are now perhaps the most wanted man in England. Every faction will be hunting you. Take my advice and get that paper to your Major Blake as fast as you can. You've done your work, and to survive, you must pass on that responsibility. Don't stay here; I'll manage the troop. Go now - that's an order!"

With the Cornet's urgencies behind him, Ketch returned to the yard and saddled and prepared the strongest horse in the troop - the Cornet's own.

"Tull!" He called the West countryman to him.

"I have other business this day, and the Cornet has resumed control of the troop. He will want you to report to him on each hour for orders." Ketch fixed a hard gaze on his friend.

"You will keep matters secure here, Tull, I know you can manage it."

"I'll not ask your purpose" replied Tull.

"The sooner this business is over, the better. With the Cornet winged, and you gone, I shall do my best but it will all go to the devil if you are long gone."

With this gloomy comment pressing in upon him, Ketch mounted his horse, and pressed his hand against his heart to check that the letter was still in place. Seeing Tull entering the inn, he felt confident to take on his new challenge, and with a nod to Larkin and Mutch, he moved out of the yard, his horse's hooves clattering on the sets of the market square as he headed for the South Bridge and the London Road. Bridge Street was quiet as he rode past its houses and shops. It was too early even for those who opened betimes to catch the first trade, so few took any notice of the solitary Trooper as he rode out of the town, up the hill past the Cross and on towards Newport Pagnell and Major Blake.

The ride was uneventful. Ketch himself was nervous and carefully scrutinised every traveller as a possible Royalist spy or Presbyterian agitator. Although the roads were still dangerous, it required numbers and courage to take on even a solitary mounted Trooper, who might well have companions nearby. Although early, the day was warm, and Ketch had to stop twice for water, and to rest his horse. Despite this, his progress was good and, in less than two hours, he sighted the bridge over the river that led to the small town of Newport Pagnell.

Military guards still controlled the bridge. Ketch informed the sergeant in charge that he had a message for a Major Blake, who was in the town. The sergeant was able to direct Ketch to Major Blake's lodgings but, as he walked his tired horse along the wide high street, his progress was considerably interrupted by the weight of armed troops in the town. "Clearly" thought Ketch, "something is afoot. There is a reason for all this military preparedness." Being unable to provide an answer, Ketch remembered his own mission and concentrated on finding the Major's place of refuge.

Major Blake had taken a room above a cabinetmaker's workshop, and the yard at the back contained stacks of sweet-smelling, newly cut wood drying in the sun. Ketch tethered his horse next to a water trough, and saw a small, weathered man of about forty years, stripped to the waist and stirring a pot of what Ketch, from the smell, took to be glue. The man was sitting on a stool, and puffing on a clay pipe whilst performing his task. Before Ketch could speak, the man cleared his throat and spat into the bubbling mixture before him. Ketch's humour was such that he smiled at such a basis for manufacture. He enquired of the man if this was the lodging place of a Major Blake, and was the Major at home?

The cabinetmaker looked up from his pot and grinned at Ketch.

"Not a Guild secret" he said.

"Just a foul habit!"

Raising himself from his stool, he told Ketch that yes, Major Blake had taken the upstairs room and was indeed in, having just finished his breakfast. Ketch climbed the set of wooden stairs set against the side of the house, which led to the Major's room. After a brisk tap on the door, he pushed it open, stepped inside and closed it behind him. Major Blake was sitting in shadow for the early morning sun had not yet filled the room. He looked tired and, for a man of energy and self-regard, seemed lethargic and unkempt. He was wearing his uniform rather than his lawyer's clothes. His eyes brightened on first seeing Ketch, but the dullness speedily returned to them.

"Ketch, he said.

"Come in and report. You find me tired and weary; I have spent a night on matters of state, trying to meet my master's needs - but affairs do not go well. Those who seek to accommodate Charles Stuart are in the ascendant. I fear the army will be disbanded, for Parliament has now agreed to it. All that has been fought for, all the sacrifice, will be lost."

Waving Ketch to the sister chair of his own, he continued.

"Come, sit and rest, and tell me your news. Has Le Vaughn full control of Northampton?"

Ketch knew he should tell the Major at once his momentous news, but he could not help guarding for a few more seconds the sole enjoyment of his secret. Once the Major knew, he would take over and direct events, and Ketch would move to the side of the stage.

"Indeed, Major, Le Vaughn's power grows. Hedlow is no longer Clerk to the Council, and the full council have begged Le Vaughn to be reconciled to them; perhaps of even greater concern is that they demand he secures the person of Charles Stuart to be reconciled with his people."

Major Blake's face hardened, and Ketch could see that, despite his bone-numbing weariness, the Major was still adamant in his defiance to Le Vaughn's plans to restore the King. Ketch decided that this brave man, this spinner of secrets, this constant servant of the common good, should have some hope.

"But, Major" he said, "I have the King's letter, and you were right. In his own hand, he begs the French King and his chief minister for a Catholic army and swears to take the faith himself."

So, saying, Ketch triumphantly produced from his breast the letter and, smiling handed it to the Major.

Blake, a man of iron control, could not help but let Ketch see his amazement. He snatched the paper and quickly read the contents.

“My God Ketch”, he said. “How! When! Tell me quickly how you came by this. Where was it? Who had it?

Ketch gave the Major a swift telling of his tale and the Major laughed with delight at the success of Ketch’s venture.

"By all the saints, Ketch" he said, "This is it! This proves the sort of man Charles Stuart is. Surely, Fairfax and Cromwell will now act!"

The Major leapt up out of his chair and began to pace the room. The lethargic, defeated man that Ketch had seen on entering the room was now transformed into the man of action and self-confidence of their first meeting.

"Time" growled the Major, as he paced the room.

"Time means it must be Cromwell," he debated with himself.

It took several more paces up and down for the Major to come to a plan of action.

"Ketch, I hope your horse is in good fettle, for you are coming with me. We are going to meet a General, the most famous soldier in England. And you are going to tell him your tale."

Alive with excitement, the Major took his sword and belt from the corner of the room, and led Ketch out and down the stairs into the yard.

"Breach" he yelled at the startled cabinet maker.

"Fetch me my horse, and quickly, man. This Trooper and I have urgent matters to attend to."

As the Major quickly secured and prepared his horse, Ketch tightened the girth on his and, within ten minutes, Major Blake was leading Ketch out of Newport Pagnell on to the London Road.

The two men rode for a good half-hour before the Major turned to the East, and began to follow a cross-country route along little-used tracks. Blake had remained silent as they rode, but after some ten minutes he turned and spoke to Ketch.

"You may have noticed, Ketch, a higher than normal level of military activity about this area. Garrison comrades have been told that very senior officers are in the vicinity, so of course they are all seeking to show how prepared they are. A very senior officer is close by, Ketch. Here at a time of great political crisis, and at a time of great personal trial, we are going to add to his agony by showing him the letter."

As he spoke, he led Ketch through a gap in the high hedge they had been following, into spacious, open parkland. Clearly still maintained, the change from hedgerow and thicket to wide-open grass and single mature trees was a very definite one. This had undoubtedly been the personal hunting ground for a grand lord. Some two miles further on the parkland narrowed into a gentle sloping valley. Pausing at the top of a small rise to allow the horses to rest, Major Blake pointed out to Ketch a fine Tudor residence, almost completely hidden by trees, nestling in a fold of land.

"Although that house looks quiet, even deserted," said Major Blake. "It is in fact strongly guarded. The important person who stayed there last night is well-loved by the army. So, let us approach openly, and without subterfuge. There will be muskets pointed at us as we arrive."

The two men rode from the parkland onto a tree-lined drive that led up to the main entrance to the house. As they walked their horses calmly forward, soldiers emerged from various unseen places and took up positions on each side and behind the strangers, so that on arrival at the great wooden doors they were escorted by some dozen companions, all well-armed. The main doors opened and a man in civilian dress hailed the soldiers.

"All is well. This officer is close to the General, and welcome here, though his companion is unknown to me."

"Secretary Thurloe" cried Blake.

"I would wish to see the General. I have news that will cause him great thought, and I would have him talk to this Trooper, a good soldier, that I will vouch for."

"So be it," said the man called Thurloe.

"Look after their horses" he instructed the guards.

"And, of course, search, and take all weapons."

Blake and Ketch offered up their swords and were carefully and expertly searched in case they retained other weapons. Having been cleared, Thurloe led them both into the main hall of the house and thence into a small empty side room.

“Secretary Thurloe”, said Major Blake this is Corporal Ketch part of a detachment under Cornet Marlowe who have been on duty in Northampton. He is a man I have brought in to our confidence and who has done us a great service. He has brought us what we have so desperately been searching for.”

At this point, Major Blake whispered for a few moments' words into Thurloe's ears that Ketch could not hear. The Secretary gave an exclamation of joy.

“You have done well Blake," he said.

“ As has your new friend.”

He turned to face Ketch.

“Excuse our secret ways corporal”, he continued.

“You will have some knowledge of our employment and the caution it brings.

"Wait here, " he said. "I shall soon return."

As the two men waited in the dark-panelled room, Blake questioned Ketch on the details of his acquisition of the letter. These he dutifully answered; when finished, he asked Major Blake a question of his own.

"Who" he asked "is Secretary Thurloe?"

Blake smiled to himself.

"Secretary Thurloe is probably the cleverest man in England. He is devoted to Cromwell, and it is he who has secured my attachment to his office. That, Ketch, is the man who gives me my orders. He is a man who knows many secrets, and, though he is but a clerk, generals in the army listen to his words. Few people know his name, you are now one of some score of men who have an idea of his importance. He is now your master, Ketch. Both you and I work for spymaster Thurloe."

At this point the object of the Major's comments returned and Ketch was able to get a quick look at such a secret and powerful man. Secretary Thurloe was of middle years with close-cropped reddish hair. He wore all brown; jerkin, breeches, stockings and shoes. Only a white shirt and small silver buckles on his shoes, broke the dominance of that colour . There was a restless prowling energy about him; he looked a man of great intellect with a clear face that was free of disease. His eyes, Ketch noted, were an unusual grey that attracted and held the eyes of whomsoever he addressed. His energy seemed barely contained by his speed of gesture and movement.

"Ah, Major Blake" he said, "

"you must come with me. You, Trooper" turning to Ketch.

"Must wait".

Ketch felt disappointment at this; he was being left out. Having won the race, others, more important than he, were to take the prize.

"Well" he thought ruefully, "So be it. I have had an exciting time - it is a pity that it's over, but it may well be back to soldiering for me."

He sat for some fifteen minutes on a plain wooden window seat considering his future, when his thoughts were interrupted by the return once more of Thurloe with the request that Ketch should now accompany him. Dutifully, Ketch obeyed and followed his new master. They crossed the hall and entered a large, airy room, also well appointed with oak panelling. A full mullioned window flooded light onto the fine furnishings. Thurloe took his place behind the huge desk set in front of the window, and looked every inch the clerk.Blake sat to the left of Thurloe's desk, and to the right was another heavy door to the room.

"The Major has told me of your work for us, and your success in securing a certain paper. He seems to thinks highly of you."

Thurloe's voice was slightly shrill, but he spoke deliberately and, as he spoke, his dark grey eyes seemed to take in not just every physical feature and movement of Ketch but every thought as well.

Above all, Ketch felt that he wanted to talk to this man, to tell him what he wanted to know. Thurloe did not consciously inspire fear, but his manner and look conveyed a message of focused opposition to those who resisted him. Ketch, however, refused to bend his will totally to this man, and he in turn looked hard with his own deep blue eyes at Secretary

Thurloe. Ketch spotted a hint of surprise in the Secretary's eyes, and then came a smile.

"Well, Trooper" he said.

"You are now a part of our very secret little band. You are now attached to the department of the Secretary for Extra Papers, and we are now going to affect great matters of state. In the room through that door is Oliver Cromwell, the greatest man in all England, and the most honest and god-fearing man I have every met, to whom I have devoted my life and service. Even now, he still tries to hold the country together - King, Parliament and the army. Despite all the evidence that the King and the Majority faction in Parliament are willing to betray him and all that has been fought for, to reach their own treacherous accommodations. Although I have provided him with enough evidence of all this, he even now will not place himself at the head of the army and face the placemen and profiteers who swarm on the body politic of England."

Major Blake turned to look at Ketch, and added to Thurloe's explanation.

"Cromwell now clearly recognises the ambitions of those in Parliament, like Le Vaughn, who will, under a restored Charles Stuart, pillage the country for their own purposes and pleasures. But he still has some respect for the King, as a man and as a Christian."

Thurloe leaned forward and looked Ketch full in the face.

"The letter you will now show to Oliver Cromwell damns Charles Stuart as false to his Coronation Oath to preserve the Protestant religion, he would embrace the Catholic religion to save his position and his throne. We three, therefore, are seeking to galvanise this Cromwell into action, we are gentlemen playing for the highest of stakes."

Thurloe rose to his feet.

"You have the letter, Major Blake?" Receiving an affirmative reply, Thurloe continued

"Come, then. Let us meet our general."

He pushed back his chair, led his two associates to the nearer door, tapped briefly upon it and entered. They came into a private room set aside for the visit of General Cromwell. Like the room they had just left, it was oak-panelled, with high ceiling and large windows that looked out onto the parkland. There was a patterned carpet on the highly polished floor, and high wooden chairs on either side of a large and ornate fireplace. Cromwell himself sat at a large plain desk, with his back to the windows. The desk was covered with papers and maps. Clearly, the General was hard at work.

"Come in, Thurloe" he said, laying down his pen.

"Introduce me to your companions."

Ketch looked carefully at the General. He had seen him before, just once, a few days before Naseby, but that had been at a distance. This was the first time he had seen Cromwell close to. He saw a man of medium build, with shoulder length light brown hair. His face was of a pale complexion and dominated by one feature, his nose. Set above this bulbous lump of flesh were two piercing blue eyes.

"But it is a strong face" thought Ketch.

"A countryman's face; coarse perhaps, but powerful."

Simply dressed in knee breeches with a white shirt and short black jacket, the General looked like a prosperous farmer. Only a broad, bright red sash denoted his senior military rank. The General seemed tired but purposively cheerful.

"My Lord General" said Thurloe.

"Major Blake I believe you already know. His associate is Trooper Ketch, of Colonel Butler's regiment. He was part of a small troop sent to support the town council of Northampton in preserving local peace and order. He has been helping Major Blake in the matter of the supposed letter written by Charles Stuart at Naseby, a matter to which I know you give little credence."

"Despite your energetic entreaties" smiled Cromwell.

"But, my Lord" said Thurloe quietly, holding up the letter,.

"We now have it! We have the very same letter written by Charles Stuart in his own hand, abandoning his Protestant faith and seeking a French army to suppress his people."

Cromwell frowned at this news, and looked hard at Thurloe.

"In God's name" he cried.

"Can this be true? Is there no faith in this man?"

He rose to his feet.

"Show me the letter" he commanded, and Major Blake dutifully handed it over.

Cromwell moved from his desk, carefully examining the folded letter and the now broken seal. He opened out the heavily creased paper, and scanned the contents swiftly.

"It is the King's handwriting" he confirmed, wearily.

"How came you by this, Thurloe?" he demanded.

"Major Blake, no doubt, and his new recruit, God damn them!" he said, and turned on Major Blake and Ketch.

"You gentlemen are responsible for destroying the honour and good name of the King of England."

The sharpness of Cromwell's voice was like a slap across the face for Ketch. He thought he had done well, he had used his talents to find that for which half of the secret world of England was searching. Now he was being taken to task.

"My Lord General" he said.

"Major Blake and I have brought you a particular letter written by Charles Stuart after Naseby. He is responsible for its contents and its consequences, not we who have recovered it."

Cromwell's tone remained terse, but not so sharp.

"I see, Major Blake, that your colleague is not afraid to speak for himself, and to correct, if only very respectfully, the views of a General of Horse."

"Yes, my Lord" replied Blake.

"Perhaps Trooper Ketch can quickly tell you how he came by the letter."

"So be it" replied Cromwell, seating himself once more at his desk.

"You have five minutes, Ketch."

Ketch used his time to good effect, and the details of the Desboroughs, the murdered preacher, the terrorising of Northampton by Lord Le Vaugn and the scene in the churchyard were swiftly and accurately recounted. When he was finished, Cromwell questioned Ketch for a further ten minutes before wearily clearing a place on his desk and setting the open letter prominently before him.

"Thank you, gentlemen" he said.

He addressed both Blake and Ketch.

"You have served Secretary Thurloe well, and I have no doubt he and I will continue to have need of your special talents. You are all dismissed."

The three men turned towards the door, when Cromwell spoke again.

"One moment, Ketch. A word with you."

Ketch turned and remained in the room whilst Thurloe and Blake left. The general sat Ketch in one the fireside chairs, and took the other himself. He sat upright, with each arm lightly placed on the wing of the chair.

"Ketch" he sai.

"Despite your involvement with Major Blake, I suspect you may be seen as an ordinary Trooper in our army. I need to know how men like you feel about our times. How far will the men go? Will they face up to King and Parliament, and yet not themselves become tyrants? I tell you now that my purpose is uncertain. I have spent the better part of my life helping Parliament bring the King back to the laws of England and a tolerant Protestant religion. I had not thought to see a day when King and Parliament conspire against the people and the only hope of England lies in its army and its generals. I have prayed on this, Ketch, and the letter you bring throws me into turmoil. Charles Stuart would sacrifice the Protestant religion, that is a matter of damning import!" Ketch looked with sympathy at his General, who sat still and quiet after his outburst. He could see that Cromwell was still in a spiritual struggle and practical indecision.

"General" said Ketch. " I am an ordinary soldier in your army, perhaps fortunate to have been schooled better than many, and to have travelled in France and the Low Countries, but this army is one that hates war and wants peace. But above all, it wishes to take its pay and look to as free and as gentle a life as can be had for its people. If Charles Stuart and men like Lord Le Vaugn share out England, then God help us, and God damn those that let it happen!"

Ketch realised that, in the emotion of his response to Cromwell's promptings, he had perhaps overstepped the mark.

"Begging your pardon, General but I think many of my troop would put it in that fashion, if not stronger."

Cromwell nodded and paused and then after a moment of stillness he saw the General's body relax as if some inner contradiction had been reconciled. Then his mood changed and suddenly he became all urgency and for a further hour he cross-questioned Ketch on the state of the army and the views of the ordinary solder. Again, and again, he pressed Ketch on detail and justification of his views. Finally, he rose from the chair and walked to the door, and called in Thurloe and Blake.

"Gentlemen" he addressed them.

"I have now, with much regret. made a decision. Charles Stuart by this letter condemns himself. He is not fit to govern. His conspiracies with ambitious Parliamentarians will destroy our people and enslave them. Independent conscience will disappear under the rule of those whose religion is bent to their political needs."

He paused briefly, took a deep breath, and determination rang in his voice.

"I will join the army at Newmarket and we shall march on London and deal with this Parliament that cannot be trusted. To this my energies will be directed, Thurloe we must to work, but" he turned to the desk and picked up the King's letter.

"Firstly we must deal with this.I know not how a man like Charles Stuart could write such, on a matter of religion, even at a lost battle. For the people of England to know that he promised to become a Catholic and lead a Catholic French army against his own people would not only destroy him but also throw all England into total fear and confusion. This news would not bind factions together, it would add to chaos and fear. It is sufficient that I alone know this. Thurloe, Blake, Ketch for you, this letter never existed."

So, saying, Cromwell took the King's letter and threw it onto the small fire in the hearth. The four men were silent as they watched it slowly take fire, and then burn in bright flames. Cromwell took a poker from the hearth and spread the ashes that remained.

"Even you, Blake, with your methods, can not rediscover that!" he said grimly.

The burning of the letter gave Cromwell some further cathartic release and, briskly full of energy, he came a General, and started to issue his commands.

"You, Thurloe" he said, turning to his Secretary, "Will take steps to secure the King. Some of my Lord Fairfax's officers are below. Cornet Joyce is ambitious and not to be outfaced by the well bred. He may well be suitable."

Cromwell returned to his desk and immediately commenced writing instructions.At the same time, Thurloe and Major Blake were bombarded with orders and requests. A bell was rung and other officers were called in and orders given for a speedy departure. Fresh secretaries were called to his desk and letters were dictated at great speed to army units and garrison commanders. Ketch was overwhelmed by the whirlwind of activity that had suddenly sprung up around him. He suddenly realised that Thurloe was at his side.

"Come, lad," urged the Secretary.

"We have unleashed our General, and your part in this matter is ended."

He took Ketch into his own room and thanked him for his great efforts.

"We will talk again," said Thurloe.

"But for now, you must return to Northampton, your troop and regiment. You are party to our plans, Ketch, so not a word of this to anyone. Sometime soon, the Major will contact you."

Major Blake was nowhere to be seen as Thurloe escorted Ketch to the outer door, secured the return of his horse, and waved a brief farewell. The last words Ketch heard as he turned his horse away from the house were:

"We shall not forget you, Ketch. There is always more work for us to do!"

Chapter 13

Ketch rode back through the parkland towards the Northampton road. His mind was a whirl as he rethought the events of the last few hours. He listed in his mind the major events he had experienced. He had just been in close conversation with the most powerful man in England. He had been recruited to an unusual civil department of state, that of "Extra Papers". He was now in the service of clerk Thurloe, the man Major Blake had described as a spymaster. Certain it was that this man Thurloe, directed the activities of the mysterious Major and now had a control over his own life. Ketch was disappointed that after the heady excitement of his meeting with Oliver Cromwell matters had closed so speedily. The clerk Thurloe had but warmly congratulated him on his success, shown him to the door and bid him a safe return to Northampton. He had had no further lengthy conversation with Thurloe, no confirmation of any special position or new task just an allusion as to possible further work and Major Blake had just disappeared.

The first day of June was now of full summer strength, and Ketch, fatigued from the events of the night and the exertions of the day, was lulled into somnolence by the rhythm of his horse and the heat of the day. His thoughts turned to what had become an ever-growing presence in his mind. How pleasant it would be, to lie once more on the couch in Hedlow's house and be ministered to by Anne, the housekeeper. How caring had been her touch as she washed his wounds with cool well water. How soothing yet stirring had been her presence at his side? Ketch drew a strange and new pleasure from thinking about her. He enjoyed whilst gently riding the indulgence of remembrance. How graceful was her form, and how fragrant her hair. How lithe and quick were her footsteps as she returned to the house with more water - and how thirsty he was now in this enervating heat!

Some hours later he once more directed his horse down the hill past Eleanor's Cross, clattered across the South Bridge, and rode up to the Market Square and the Peacock Inn. On entering the yard, leading his horse, Ketch found his troop idle. The men were lying around the Inn yard, looking bored and restless. Larkin and Holditch were playing dice, and Tull was sitting on a small stool repeatedly throwing a small knife into the top of a barrel he had propped up in front of him."You promised us a ride out today,

Corporal" said Larkin, in an aggrieved tone. "We've been sitting around listening to Tull and Holditch all morning, and the best part of the afternoon. Nobody's moved out of this yard.
"Right, Larkin" said Ketch, and he addressed his Troopers briskly.

"I know you lads have been sitting around and doing nothing for most of the day, but that's going to change now. It's about time we really looked to our horses, cleaned out our quarters, checked and prepared pistols and swords."

A great groan went up from the assembled Troopers, but Ketch was not to be denied.

"Larkin, Hodge, start moving that" he ordered, pointing to a pile of vegetable peelings and general rubbish.

"Tull, take four men to secure lots of water for washing out the stables."

Swiftly and competently Ketch chased and chivvied the Troopers into authorised controlled activity. He was not above detailing a few men into activity for their benefit rather than for any particular value gained for the army from their efforts. Thus, he detailed Holditch and three other Troopers to carry sacks of grain from the upper granary down the ladder to the barn below and stack them in three separate piles. Later, he would order other Troopers to take them back up again. Ketch, like all in authority, knew that idleness undermined morale. Activity - preferably exhausting physical exercise - stems complaints, slows down those with surplus energy and eventually creates a glow of well being when the jobs are done. Having assured himself that all his troop would be busy for the next hour, Ketch went into the Inn to talk to Cornet Marlowe.

As Ketch entered the room, he saw that the Cornet was lying on top of the bed in his night-shirt with his strapped leg stretched out straight whilst the other dangled over the side of the bed.

"This heat is insufferable" grumbled Marlowe.

He struggled to lift himself to a sitting position. The effort was clearly painful, for a furrow crossed the Cornet's brow, and he grimaced as he rocked sideways to secure a pushing place. Ketch discreetly helped his officer to a more comfortable position and, pulling a small chair up to the side of the bed, he outlined to Marlowe the substance of his visit to the country house and his meetings with Thurloe and Cromwell. Ketch was not certain how far he should reveal these matters, but the Cornet was still his commanding officer, his position with Thurloe's department had not been in any way formalised or confirmed, and Major Blake had not bothered to explain his position to him.

"Also, the Cornet has been in this matter from the beginning" thought Ketch.

"He deserves some return for the pain of a broken leg."

"So" mused the Cornet aloud.

"That letter you recovered really sent Oliver Cromwell into action. Now, I wonder,what will he do? The army's at Newmarket and the King's at Holdenby. I suspect he had better hurry up, whatever it is.... Oh!" he exclaimed. "You don't know this, Ketch. Whilst you have been away, we have had important events here in Northampton. This morning the full Town Council, missing a few of its more prominent members , led by Nathaniel Parfitt and without our friend Hedlow who, I understand, has resigned, made a miserable grovelling salutation to Lord Le Vaugn. Hailed him as "Father of the County", called upon him to secure the King's person amongst his loving Northampton subjects so that he will be safe from the army! Le Vaugn, of course, had his garrison troops on hand to cheer, and Colonel Fell had secured the support of some of the townspeople. Botterill, the innkeeper, couldn't wait to recount all this to me, and I have no doubt that Le Vaughn is seeking a popular clamour for him to step forward to release the King and establish a new government. Certainly, Parfitt and his cronies were urging this upon him and, of course, Le Vaugn was gracious and condescending and spoke of the need for Parliament, King and army to settle their difference. But this is going on in other towns, Ketch. Oxford, Lincoln, to name but two. I believe unless Cromwell does something soon, he is lost."

"Well, Cornet" said Ketch.

"There is not much that we can now do about it. Matters must now take their course."

"Amen to that!" agreed the Cornet.

"Now, I will be able to make short journeys in the cart in a day or two, Ketch, so keep the men together, keep them busy. Try and give them a ride out but, above all, keep them away from townsfolk or any of the garrison."

The Cornet was clearly feeling better and itching to get out of Northampton and the unpleasant situation he had ridden into. He was obviously tired of Le Vaughn, secrets, high politics - and his Corporal dashing off.

"Are you still part of my troop, Ketch, or are you under orders from any of your new high-ranking associates?"

"I thought I was to be part of the "Department of Extra Papers" and help Cromwell's secretary, Thurloe, and Major Blake" explained Ketch."But they sent me back to the troop - so, here I am."

"Good. I can use you to good effect here" continued Marlowe.

"Get back to the men, and let's return to normal soldiering."

Ralph Desborough was sick at heart, and exhausted in mind and body. Since being struck on the head and losing the King's letter - to whom he did not know - he had also lost his horse, and had to walk the four miles back to Northampton. What was especially bitter for Ralph was that he had held in his hand that for which he had made every sacrifice. He had for an instant had possession of the King's letter before blackness descended on him. This sickness of failure was enhanced by the raging question - how could anyone have known of his discovery to so waylay him? The assailant had not robbed him of money, jewels or clothing, but took only the letter. So, it was someone who knew of it, and of its value, and they had been hiding in the churchyard for only one purpose.

As he made his painful way home in the darkness, he had thought long and hard as to who his assailants could have been, but he had no answer. Only Mary and Martha had known the true location of his father's murder, and only they knew his destination. His sisters, whatever their thoughts on how he and father had abandoned them, would never betray him in this matter.

In the early dawn light Ralph had arrived at the Desborough house by the Church only to find it empty. Exhausted, he had slipped into the house via the kitchen window and, after a cold meal of hard bread and bacon, he had tried to sleep. But the disappearance of his sisters was an added mystery that he had to address. Perhaps whoever held his sisters was the person who now had the King's letter! He knew that his sisters could not face cross-questioning, or torture - perhaps they had been forced to reveal his quest... Before sleep claimed him, Ralph resolved to find his sisters, to rescue them, and secure the King's letter - little knowing how futile such thoughts were.

Ralph slept on the floor in the kitchen for most of the morning. Thus, it was just before noon that, washed and refreshed; he came out of his refuge to seek news of his sisters. He knew the risk he was taking. He was a proscribed royalist, walking the streets of a town in daylight, a town where there were many who could recognise him and betray him. But there were also one or two old friends who, even now and for past times' sake, would help him and would not expect too much of a reward. One of these was a widowed, elderly woodcarver who lived but a short walk from the Desborough home in a neat cottage close by the gun fortifications that had guarded the North-east side of the town. Hurrying this short distance, Ralph found the woodcarver at home.

Once over his amazement at seeing Ralph, and reassured that Ralph was not staying but only seeking information that would speed him on his way, the woodcarver was friendly and not too unhappy to see him. In his small kitchen he sat Ralph down by the hearth and fed him with cheese and weak ale. While Ralph consumed this noon fare, he questioned the woodcarver concerning his sisters.

"Taken, I hear" replied the old man, gravely.

"One of Le Vaughn's officers marched them off to the Castle."

Ralph felt a deep sorrow for Mary and Martha. Northampton Castle was a grim, hard place, and his sisters were not strong in spirit. Could this mean that Le Vaugn had the letter - he tried to understand the implication of this. Le Vaugn was a Parliamentarian and, as such, an enemy of the King; but he had heard whispers that Le Vaugn was strong for a reconciliation with Charles Stuart. Ralph's mind was in turmoil. His success, his failure, his lost sisters, the consequences of someone like Le Vaugn having the letter continued to race round and round inside his

The loss of the letter, the fact that it was now gone and that he had no idea as to where to start any new quest, began slowly to impress itself upon Ralph, as he sat in the woodcarver's kitchen; and as his failure became plainer to see, the cost of his obsession began to press in upon him. The full measure of his treatment of his sisters began to stand uncomfortably before him. Now, in the woodcarver's kitchen, his conscience laid out before him the selfish and callous way he and his father had left them. How, in consequence, they had not only lost their home and their way of life, but had been forced to live spied upon and shunned by their neighbours. Ralph groaned in remorse. He part punished himself by telling the woodcarver his sorry tale of family neglect.

"Well, my Lord, that may well be how you sees it, but there are many as think the better of them who went to fight for the King rather than stopping quiet and doing well in trade" comforted the woodcarver.

"Can my sisters be rescued from that castle?" asked Ralph.

The woodcarver did not look very happy at Ralph's question. He could see possible involvement of a sort he wished to avoid.

"Now, Sir, you don't want to go into that place. It could cost you your life."

Ignoring the brake that the woodcarver was desperately placing on his ambitions, Ralph began to cross -question him about the life of the castle where his sisters were located; what visitors they had, who went in and out, what guards on which entries - and many other questions which he hoped the woodcarver could sensibly answer. It transpired that the woodcarver was a regular visitor to the castle selling his wood shavings and sawdust. The castle stables had an insatiable demand for soft flooring. This Ralph saw as a valuable part of a rescue sortie. The wood carver also informed him that, those incarcerated in the castle - and at this moment there was an assortment of thieves, poachers, suspected royalists - could have food taken into them as long as they had friends and money to arrange it. Ralph had no clear plan as to how he was to take his sisters from such a parliamentary bastion but knowledge of their exact location was vital. He knew he had to suborn the woodcarver to his will and make him an accomplice to his enterprise.

Although young in years, Ralph's time abroad in the more unpleasant parts of the Low Countries had taught him much about human nature. He therefore eschewed any appeal based on loyalty to kin or friendship to the Desborough family. Reaching inside his jacket, Ralph extracted a small gold pendant and, with a sigh, threw it to the woodcarver, who caught it instinctively.

"That" said Ralph "would feed you through the winter."

From the middle finger of his left hand he pulled a gold ring which carried the Desborough Coat of Arms. "As would that" he continued, holding up the ring to the woodcarver.

"Your help is what I require. I shall bear the danger of this enterprise. Take this ring - and you are my man."

The woodcarver hesitated but a second before reaching out for the ring.

"I've always been a friend of the Desborough family, my Lord. I shall be your man."

Ralph smiled somewhat cynically to himself, and swiftly gave orders to the woodcarver to take food to the castle for his two sisters. He was to say that his mission was paid for by the Capstick family, who were too frightened to come themselves. He was to find out as much as he could about where the sisters were imprisoned, and who had charge of them.

"You are to do this at once ", insisted Ralph.

"I will have no delay in this matter".

Partly regretting his greed, the woodcarver made up a basket of simple food and Ralph saw him to the door of his home. Before letting the woodcarver out into the street, Ralph looked steadily into his eyes.

"Do not betray me," he said.

"I shall always be close by, and should matters go badly because of treachery, it would go badly for you also."

The woodcarver nodded, and left to perform his mission. After waiting a few moments, Ralph followed him.

It was but an hour before the woodcarver returned flushed and excited. He was surprised to find the house empty, but relieved when Ralph followed him through the door.

"Well?" enquired Ralph.

"What news have you for me? How are Martha and Mary?"

The woodcarver was full of his excitement. Assuring Ralph first that his sisters were well and had good thoughts of him, he turned to those matters that had been particularly required of him.

"You have chosen well, my Lord," he said.

"The castle is full of bustle and excitement at the moment. All are full of the great Lord Le Vaugn's triumph in the town centre. Some say the King himself is coming to Northampton. Others say Cromwell is to be impeached by Parliament, but all this is set against much coming and going in the castle. All prisoners, apart from your sisters, my Lord - have been released, and preparations are being made for fresh troops to be accommodated within the castle. There is much jubilation about the place, and small insignificant visitors, if they keep out of the way, are hardly noticed."

"And where are my sisters? Where are they kept, are they closely observed?" demanded Ralph.

The woodcarver turned from Ralph and sat himself on a stool by the low table on which was left some of the ale and cheese that Ralph had eaten earlier.

"Master Ralph" he said.

"Let us eat and drink together, and as we so replenish ourselves, I can tell you all that I found in the castle. And if I tell it slowly and in my own way you shall, if you listen carefully, hear all there is to tell." Seeing the sense of careful considered debate, Ralph joined his co-conspirator at the table and ate and listened as the woodcarver slowly recounted the full details of the sisters' plight.

Chapter 14

The tale was a simple one. In the general movement within the castle, his sisters had been taken from the more pleasant but barred rooms of the castle to an old, now disused, privy room set in the walls of the castle. This room had no bars to the windows and was not uncomfortable in summer, but would be a cold, hard place in winter weather. Within the bare stone walls there was little comfort for the two women, a rough straw mattress being the only furnishing. Sixty feet below the narrow, high-set window was the rough growth of trees and bushes of the old castle midden. The guarding of the women was in the hands of the castle gaoler. He was a former blacksmith in the town who had lost his house in a fire some years before, but his skills had always been useful with keys and locks and so he had found his new employment. A strong, middle-aged man with now only two women to look after, he took his duties lightly.

Ralph had hoped for news of a frailer, less active warder, for a plan was beginning to form in his mind as to how he might release his sisters. After some further questioning of the woodcarver, Ralph was decided. There was hope if they moved at once, whilst the good humour of the garrison was still evident.

Pointing to two large, closely woven wicker baskets, Ralph asked the woodcarver

"It is those that you fill with shavings and sawdust when you visit the castle?"

"It is" affirmed the woodcarver.

"And no one would think twice if there was another with you carrying a second basket?" continued Ralph.

"I think not, my Lord. In fact," continued the woodcarver.

"That is an easy way to enter the castle quietly and with few casting looks your way but." and a certain anxiety now entered his voice, replacing his earlier enthusiasm.

"What then? There is the gaoler, and what part are you expecting of me?"

"Little more" reassured Ralph.

"Once you have me inside the castle you may depart. There will be one more task for you then, but it will not be so dangerous. Meanwhile, before all else, you must purchase some things for me from the market."

The woodcarver returned an hour later with the items required by Ralph. Although bought with gold, his excitement in their venture was increasingly his motivation in helping Ralph. The two conspirators sat at the old wooden table and talked over the details of the plan to rescue the sisters. They agreed that the feeling of well being in the castle due to the success and good humour of Lord Le Vaughn would aid their enterprise. The entrance to the castle, however, would continue to be guarded and control of entrance and exit would not be relaxed. Mary and Martha were located in a quiet, out of the way part of the castle and, although the gaoler's room was at the base of the stairs that led to their cell, it was a long winding staircase and he was in fact some distance from them. All this, they agreed, would help them. Central to their success was to be the strength of the sleeping draught purchased by the woodcarver, and Ralph's skill with mallet and chisel. In this latter, a precious hour was spent as the woodcarver instructed Ralph on the performance of a specific task.

It was about the sixth hour after noon when two working men, each carrying a large pannier on his back filled with a mixture of wood shavings and sawdust, approached the entrance to Northampton Castle. In bright evening sunlight, the elderly woodcarver and Ralph were waved through without challenge into the central courtyard. Ralph's heart was beating with an excited urgency as he followed the woodcarver with his heavy burden towards the castle stables. Halfway across the courtyard, a voice rang out.

"Hey, you there! Woodcarver! What's your business?"

It was the castle steward. Well-knowing the woodcarver's official purpose, for he had dealt with him often enough in the past, the steward had to assert his authority through questioning his presence. Nevertheless, he was an easy-going man, and the woodcarver speedily agreed with him a price for the sawdust and shavings to be spread on the stable floor. Paying the woodcarver the few coppers agreed, the steward turned away no longer interested in the two men. Ralph and his companion made their way to the stables.

Now came the most difficult part of Ralph's plan. Whilst distributing their load about the stable floor, a place had to be found for Ralph to hide. The stables were not empty, and a number of stable lads were either grooming horses or repairing tack. Luckily a blacksmith's forge was glowing brightly next to the stables, and the noise and bustle of horses being shod meant that no one paid much attention to two menials attending to the floor. But still no hiding place presented itself, and Ralph was becoming desperate. The hayloft above the horses' stalls seemed his last chance, but it would be a once only trip. Ralph could not risk being seen going up and down from the loft.

One quick dash up the ladder was all that could be risked, and once there he was committed. Thus, when two pairs of eyes confirmed that no one was looking their way, Ralph hoisted onto his shoulder the pannier - empty now of sawdust, but revealing in the bottom a coil of rope and a small canvas sack - and swiftly climbed the ladder into the hay loft.

There was no shout of challenge and, with a quick wave of farewell to the woodcarver; Ralph crept into the dark of the furthest corner of the loft. Below, the woodcarver released his held-in breath, wiped sweat and sawdust from his brow and, heaving his pannier onto his back, strode purposefully out of the stables, across the courtyard and out of the main gate of the castle. No one spoke to him or enquired as to his companion. His role was virtually complete; now he had to wait for darkness to perform his final task.

Ralph now had to remain undiscovered in the hayloft until dark; being so close to the summer solstice, he knew he had some hours to wait. He cautiously pulled hay all around and above him, and then lay quiet and still. The one thing he must not do, he reflected, was to move about. The hiding place was a good one, but wisps of hay floating down to the stables below would soon reveal his presence.

During his vigil several visits were paid to the loft to secure hay for the horses, but generally the lads kept close to the trap doors so they could see what they were doing. Eventually, darkness fell on the now deserted stables, and Ralph gingerly began to stretch limbs that had grown stiff through inaction. Rolling gently to his feet, he straightened up out of the hay and looked into the pitch blackness of the loft. He could see nothing, not even his hand in front of his face. Gradually inching his way forward on what was now a dangerous journey to find the opening with the head of the ladder, Ralph held the pannier close to his body. Silently, he found the ladder and made his way to the stable below. As his eyes accustomed themselves to the dark, he could vaguely make out the courtyard and the main gate to the castle. The horses in the stable had been disturbed by his movements and he could hear one in particular beginning to tap his hoof on the stable floor. much more, and one of the sleeping grooms would awaken and investigate the cause of the disturbance.

"For God's sake keep quite!"

He could feel panic welling up inside him.

"Wait, take a moment, breath Ralph."

He took his own advice and after a few minutes he felt calm enough to leave the protection of the stables. To avoid any who might see him he crouched down by the castle wall that adjoined the stable. He could now see that there was a guard at the main gate. Two soldiers sat next to a small brazier that glowed in the darkness. Fortunately, the pool of light it cast illuminated only a small area around the main gate and the central courtyard remained in darkness. The soldiers were clearly awake, and he could see that there would be no unseen exit that way. Ralph calculated that it was some two to three hours before dawn, and that now was the time to put his plan to the test.

Moving swiftly across the central courtyard, Ralph carried his pannier to the corner entrance to the stairs, which led to his incarcerated sisters. All was quiet, and he strained his hearing for any sound of movement. He knew he was now directly outside the gaoler's room and any confrontation now would be disastrous. Like the loft, the stairway was pitch black, and Ralph could not see where he should put his feet. Holding the pannier with his right hand, he gingerly felt for the wall with his left and, thus steadied, he climbed the stairs one by one, tentatively searching out each rise with his foot.

As he laboriously mounted the twisting stairway in the darkness, Ralph became totally disorientated. He lost all consciousness of space or location; his being became totally focused on the small piece of wall under his left hand and the feel of each new step. He felt another surge of panic rise within him.

Take a rest Ralph. You are doing this. Just keep calm and slowly climb these steps."

For a moment, he stopped his climb, and forced himself to relax. Then once more he started to feel and fumble his way up the stairs. After what seemed an endless time of stumbling and noisy shuffling, his searching foot told him that the steps had ended and he was now standing on a level, flat area. He slid down against the wall, his strength dissipated by the excitement and tension of the climb. After a moment of just sitting quietly in the dark, he summoned up the nerve to take from his pocket flint and tinder, he then struck a light first to a hand full of hay and then to a small candle. Shielding the light with his body and the pannier, he rapidly scanned the area now revealed. He breathed a sigh of relief as he saw that the landing was windowless, and that the only door was the one described by the woodcarver as leading to his sister's cell.

"Check the light Ralph."

He retraced his steps down the twisting staircase to see how far the light from his candle revealed itself. Confident that he would hear footsteps before the light was seen, he returned to the landing. From the pannier he took the items central to his sisters' escape, a small corked bottle, two chisels from the woodcarver, a mallet with the head covered in cloth, and a long length of rope. Off all the items, the rope had been the most difficult. In order to carry the required length, he had compromised on strength. He could only hope that it would hold.

Setting the candle close to the door, Ralph began cutting at the wood surrounding the lock. Remembering the instructions from the woodcarver, he started at the door's edge, gouging out the hard wood. Occasionally he risked a blow from the muffled mallet to speed the work.

He had been at his task only a few seconds when a voice called out from within the room.

"Who's there? What are you doing?"

"Hush, Martha" whispered Ralph, his mouth up against the door. "It's me, Ralph. Be quiet! I am trying to open the door."

He heard a scurrying, and some quiet, agitated talking between his sisters, and then resumed his task, stopping every few moments to listen out for footsteps; at one point, he went back down the stairway to confirm that all was well. Although the door was thick the wood was old and in parts suffered from a dampness that allowed Ralph quite quickly to fashion a hole just above the lock. Both his sisters knelt at the inside of the door to whisper encouragement to him. After enlarging the hole, he passed through the Mary the small stone bottle.

"Pay heed to me" he whispered, urgently.

"Take this draught equally between you. It is necessary for your escape."

"What is it?" hissed Martha. "Why must we do this?"

"Do not vex me now. Trust me, and do as I say, or we shall all be discovered."

The passion of Ralph's response quietened the sisters, and in the darkness of their room they drank the strong sleeping draught that the woodcarver had purchased from the apothecary. Satisfied that his instructions had been followed, he renewed his efforts to secure entry to the prison cell. He continued turning and twisting his chisels into the wood. After some twenty minutes, the final splinters broke away and the door swung open. Ralph knelt silently by the open door listening for any sound that might be a response to his presence, but the castle remained silent, the stairway remained silent, and Ralph noted that his sisters were silent also. Holding the candle high, he entered the room and saw them both gently sleeping, side by side on the floor, clasping each other's hand.

Ralph moved tools and pannier into the room and, using what blows he dare, drove the two chisels into the doorframe so that their handles kept the door closed. It was a poor defence, but should the gaoler check his prisoners he would at least see a closed door even though it would hardly satisfy a more than cursory glance.

"OK Ralph. Now for the hard part"

His emotional state was one of both fear and elation. He had reached the final part of his plan. The way out was not through the doorway, but through the open window of the former privy that had been made a cell. He was going to lower his drugged sisters one by one down the side of the castle into the thicket below, where the woodcarver should be waiting.

The sleeping draught had saved him from having to persuade his sisters to undertake such an horrific journey. Freed of this tension, Ralph resolved to treat his sisters with all gentleness, but essentially as sacks of grain. Taking the limp body of Mary, he tied one end of the rope around her waist and secured the other end around his own. Trying not to think of the danger, he gently placed Mary on the window ledge and eased her into the darkness, holding the rope tightly in his left hand. Bracing his body against the wall he slowly played out his rope inch by inch, hoping that Mary was similarly descending to the woodcarver below. The strain on his arms was tremendous but he was determined to make Mary's descent as easy as possible.

Just as the spare rope was close to being all used up, the weight on the end disappeared. Mary was down, and Ralph could rest.After a few moments, his waist felt the rope around it tighten as it was tugged hard from below.

"*Now for Martha*" thought Ralph, grimly.

Five stressful minutes passed, then Ralph had successfully delivered Martha Desborough from Northampton Castle in the same manner as her sister, and he found himself alone in the cell with the whole rope lying around him. He was exhausted and totally drained. His arms ached and his hands had been rubbed raw.

He gave himself a few minutes before he collected the bottle, retrieved the chisels and mallet and placed all in the pannier. The rope would be left hanging, but his enemies were to have nothing else.

Ralph cast around for somewhere to secure the rope for his own descent. To his horror, the light from his candle showed no safe anchorage; the smooth stone walls had no place for him to attach the rope and the small pieces of furniture were equally useless. After moment's frantic thought, Ralph retrieved a chisel and set to work grimly to make a further hole in the middle of the door. It took him longer than he wished, and he was sweating profusely as he fed the end of the rope through the hole and back round the door. The loop through and around the door would anchor the rope, but it meant that all his weight would be borne by the door's hinges.

"*So be it,*" thought Ralph.

Keeping the other end tied around his waist, he threw the rest of the rope out of the window. Pulling hard against the open door to test its holding power, he backed towards the window and gently eased himself out into a black void.

Ralph had been brave in the heat of battle, but the courage he found to go down the rope that night was of a level he was never to require again. He grimaced with pain as his arms took all his weight. Desperately, he tried to ease his arms by finding a purchase with his feet, but such relief was short and quickly lost. More than once he struck his head and scraped his hands against the castle wall. The pannier that he had tied to his belt caught at him and caused him to twist and catch against the stonework. Ralph resolved to close his eyes and concentrate all his strength on lowering himself to the ground below; he would ignore the hurt and the fear, and force his body to his will.

In such a mental state, Ralph succeeded in managing his descent until he ran out of rope and found himself still not on the ground but hanging from the castle. He was now terrified; the rope around his waist was cutting into him, and his arms were in agony and without any strength.

"Help Me," cried Ralph. "Help me."

A voice replied from below. It was the woodcarver.

"I can see you" he called quietly, You are near."

Ralph realised that the extra rope needed to anchor him to the door was responsible for the shortfall. Arms aching and now desperate, he felt he had to trust to luck, he had strength for nothing else. Taking one of his chisels he cut the taut rope and fell for what seemed an eternity, but was in fact a few feet onto the woodcarver, before hitting the ground below.

Chapter 15

Martha Desborough lay prone on the ground at the foot of the castle wall. She wanted to sleep but someone was shaking her and talking to her and she was so tired that she wanted him to go away.

"Please wake up" whispered the woodcarver.

"Oh, please for pity's sake Miss wake up," he begged as he continued to shake her.

The early dawn light was just beginning to rise over the horizon, and it was just possible for the human eye to see Mary and Martha Desborough lying on the ground with the woodcarver desperately trying to rouse them. It was less easy to see the huddled form Ralph Desborough sitting with his back to the castle wall with his hands clutching the thigh of his left leg which was stained rich with blood. In his final triumphant fall, Ralph had sustained a blow from his own hand and his blood had stained the earth below him. It was not a death cut, but the blood loss was growing

"Keep trying" he gasped to the woodcarver.

"They must be wakened before daylight"

The woodcarver redoubled his efforts and Martha slowly began to respond to his urgings. Her regaining consciousness was, however, a confusing episode. In the darkness, being shaken by a strange man at a place of which she knew nothing, Martha reacted violently and noisily towards the woodcarver. Removing himself from her and with soothing words he finally quietened her and established a remembrance of what she was doing and where she was.

"We are taking you from the castle, my lady" he said.

"You and your sister have been rescued by Master Ralph and you are both safe, but I have unhappy news and would wish to tell you with little hurt and at leisure but I cannot for time is pressing. Your brother, he who has delivered you from the castle in his final fall has injured himself. He does not wish us to stay here my lady but first he would speak with you".

The woodcarver was in a desperately anxious state. Daylight was now fast approaching and he was to be found with two escapees from the castle of Lord Le Vaughn and a wounded proscribed royalist. He wished to be away. He had almost run and left the Desboroughs to their own devices, but now the women were awakening, he felt he could not honourably fly the field.

"Oh, dear God " cried Martha, fearful of the woodcarver's words.

"Oh Ralph!" She wailed, and rushed to kneel beside her wounded brother.

"Hush Martha" sighed Ralph.

"listen to me with care for you must take Mary and leave me here. Let me tell you how I love you and Mary and how now too late I see the folly of pride and honour and unreal loyalties. I am sure too that father would feel this way. How mad we were to leave those we truly loved and should have cared for! I am sorry Martha, please forgive me."

"Oh, Ralph you and father were the most precious things in our lives we would bear anything for you " sobbed Martha.

"Aye" grimaced Ralph " and we let you and how you have suffered". "Martha, I have failed in my quest for the King's letter and it has gone, I know not where, but I don't think that I care any more. It is you and Mary that must be made safe."

"Hush Ralph" soothed Martha tenderly.

"We will take you away from here and care for you."

Ralph held tightly the flesh around his wound.

"In a moment I shall try and stand it may be that more blood will flow and I shall faint. You and Mary must go."

Martha felt her strength flooding back into her. Now her time had come; no more the poor woman to be protected. Ralph needed her. Only she and her strength could save them all. A strange elation settled on her; she would see it through.

The woodcarver, having exhausted his courage, sought to steal silently away to his own home.

"Hold!" hissed Martha.

"You will not desert us now. If we are taken your part in this will be known. Help us but an hour more, and in time, I swear, you will be rewarded."

Before the woodcarver could speak, she drove him on to action with her words.

"Quietly waken my sister, inform her gently of our hopes. I must now deal with my brother."

The woodcarver, too frightened to run, hesitantly approached the prone body of Mary, to do Martha's bidding. Martha turned to face her brother, with great exertion she carefully lifted him to his feet. Ralph did not faint, and slowly he gained a mastery over his pain and his body's responses to it

"I will not leave you, Ralph," said Martha.

"You will not die. Yes, you have lost much blood, but it flows softly, not with the massive spurts that herald death."

Tearing long strips from her under-dress, Martha bound the wound tightly. She worked quickly and urgently, for the full power of daylight was close at hand. She turned to see the woodcarver and Mary watching her.

"Come, my friend. Come, Mary. Between us, we must raise Ralph and see him safely away from this place."

Now the full urgency of movement and the danger of being discovered forced itself upon Martha's consciousness. They had to get away off the streets of Northampton. Though their uncle at Earls Barton was the ultimate destination, their need for food and mental rest required a closer haven.

" To return home is to surrender" she thought to herself.

"We shall go to clerk Hedlow's home. He is a decent man and may give us at least a temporary refuge. There is no one else".

Holding one side of a dazed Ralph, and with Mary and the woodcarver helping, Martha Desborough walked into the town. As she and her party shuffled along, they sought to establish a normality about the picture they offered to those that they might meet. It was, she knew, an open and hazardous journey across Northampton to reach the clerk's house close to the Eastern Derngate and there was no escape from drawing attention to themselves.

Lord Le Vaughn was not to be irritated, for he preferred to complete his noon meal without interruption. He sat at his table in his large turret room eating thick sheets of pork from a skewer, whilst listening to his gaoler sobbing and screaming as

Colonel Fell stripped flesh from his arm with his knife. Despite being held to the floor by three bulky pikemen, the gaoler was thrashing about and making it difficult for Fell to be accurate with his torture.

"Enough of this Fell" said Le Vaughn, tossing a now empty skewer onto the table in front of him.

"Take him away and kill him. The fool has neglected his duties and betrayed me and must now pay the price of his failings. Those women may have led me to a prize that would have bound Charles Stuart to my will for evermore. Now they are gone together with whoever plucked them from their cell. One day we may return to that part of the game and find who was responsible, but today we have other more pressing matters to effect."

In response to his master's change of thought, with a wave of his hand, Colonel Fell ordered his pikemen to take the now-whimpering gaoler away.

"My Lord" said Fell, with a triumphant smile on his face. T

"Today you will have Charles Stuart within your castle walls and all England at your feet. At this moment Lord Easton and his friends will be about to take the King to Towcester, where but in a short time you will meet him to escort him to the safety of Northampton, then you will be the master, and the army, Fairfax and Cromwell will be as nothing. Who can oppose the authority of the King and your power?"

"I have prepared two letters of impeachment," said Le Vaughn.

"One is for Fairfax who is weak and irresolute, yet remains the head of the army, the other is for the far more dangerous Oliver Cromwell. Once he is brought to trial and sentenced, we shall face no more opposition."

Le Vaughn paused to drink from his favourite silver goblet.

"When I have the King here, you will take these letters to London and wherever you find them you will personally arrest Fairfax and Cromwell."

Colonel Fell smiled and with a familiarity born of a successful venture he helped himself to a twin goblet to that held by Le Vaughn and filling it with red wine raised it in toast to his master.

"To Charles Stuart, to his new Chief Minister and to the death of two very foolish soldiers".

The two men of power looked each other full in the eye drunk their toast and laughed out loud. It was in just such a good mood that the castle steward found them when he ushered a grim-faced Lord Easton into the room.

Le Vaughn on seeing Lord Easton was alarmed and enraged.

"Why are you here Easton" he cried.

"You should be with the King; our plans require it.

"You fool" hissed Lord Easton in reply.

"Today two hundred Troopers of the army led by a Cornet Joyce came and forcibly took the King away from Holdenby to I know not where! What I do know is that the army has the King and our plans to save that sainted man are as nothing!Far worse, our plans, your scheming, Le Vaughn - has delivered our King to his enemies. You have been too late in this matter."

With a cry of fury Le Vaughn threw his goblet across the room. At the very last push, when he had the prize, he sought so close to hand, his enemies had outdone him. He sat down at the table and tried to concentrate his thoughts on the consequences of Lord Easton's news. Lord Easton was himself hot and tired for he had ridden in great haste to bring his news. He, too, sat himself down at the table and for the first time began to think through the new perils that his master, the King, might now have to face. Colonel Fell joined the two Lords in sitting but he had little real concern for this new turn of events. There would always be other great men with new opportunities who would have need of his skills and who would reward him well for them. He would rather avoid failures and by this latest turn of fortune, Le Vaughn, for all his great wealth and power was now facing dishonour, disgrace and possibly death.

"So, Fell" grunted Le Vaughn.

"What do we do now. All my plans to acquire powerful friends and allies were dependent upon securing the person of Charles Stuart, and on his freely working to my will. I needed him as my puppet."

Lord Easton's eyes narrowed in surprise as he heard Le Vaughn's words concerning his King, the King to whom he had pledged undying loyalty, a King for whom he and his family and many other noble families had lost everything. Easton did not like the disrespectful way in which Le Vaughn spoke, neither did he care for the substance of what he heard. He had not been part of this company to subjugate the King to this merchant prince. A deep anger, born of being deceived, began to well up within Lord Easton.

"Well, Fell" continued Le Vaughn.

"We are in a desperate position. Do we still try to use our influence on behalf of a rapprochement between King and Parliament, or is it now time to bow the knee to Cromwell and the army? If only for a short while until we have time to restore our position."

Before Fell could reply there was a knock on the door and an army messenger entered and handed Fell a message. This the Colonel read in silence and then turning his own dark eyes towards his master he said.

"Cromwell is with the army at Newmarket and is advancing on London to arrest your friends in Parliament and this Cornet Joyce has taken the person of the King to the army stronghold at Newport Pagnell. It would appear, my Lord, to be time to submit or flee."

Le Vaughn sat still for a number of seconds, his mind speedily addressing the options facing him. Eventually he spoke and as he did so Lord Easton held himself rigid with the concentration of listening.

"For myself, he said.

"I shall go to the low countries. I have wealth and friends there, and young Charles Stuart will need help and advice from one who sought to aid his father. Yes, Fell, I think our fortunes are with youth and the King's son. The father always lacked strength. Pah" snapped Le Vaughn with a derisory laugh, "taken by a Cornet".

This abuse of his beloved master proved too much for Lord Easton. He had never liked this arrogant upstart, his scheming and lack of honour. Snatching a dagger from his belt he strode up to Le Vaughn and plunged it deep into his chest

"You dog" he cried "you traitor to your King".

Le Vaughn's eyes widened with disbelief as the knife hit him, then his jaw dropped and his eyes bulged as pain and the realisation of his death faced him. In his final moments of life, he wrapped both his strong arms around Lord Easton and pushed his face up against him as if trying to meld with his murderer.

Colonel Fell rose from his seat and swiftly drawing his sword ran it into the back of Lord Easton who screamed in pain and writhed in the arms of Lord Le Vaughn. Fell paused and then with added strength pushed his sword on through the body of Lord Easton into that of Lord Le Vaughn. Both men locked and skewered together shared their final groans as they fell to the floor.

Turning to the messenger, who stood stunned by what he had observed, Colonel Fell said calmly.

"You have seen that I have just killed two men who openly plotted to restore Charles Stuart and subvert the hopes and needs of the army. You will immediately ride to Newmarket and tell General Cromwell what you have seen. I shall provide you with letters to inform him that Northampton is secure for the army and that it looks to its leaders to force Charles Stuart and Parliament to meet our rightful demands for liberty of conscience and peace."

The messenger, white faced and uncertain, nodded his assent and gratefully fled the room to prepare himself for the journey and to await Colonel Fell's letters. He had news for the whole castle, the whole of England.

Colonel Fell quietly surveyed the bodies of his master and his accomplice, picked up his empty goblet of wine, refilled it and silently drank a toast to his own health and success. Once the messenger was gone, it would be prudent also to leave England for the delights of France and the service of a King's son.

Chapter 16

The yard of the Peacock Inn was full of bustle and activity. Troopers were loading swords, bags of shot, small barrels of gunpowder, pieces of horse tack, blankets and a thousand and one other needs of war into the small handcart they had brought from London. There was a sense of excitement amongst the men. They were anticipating leaving a billet that, although comfortable, had not been pleasant. Now they were preparing to be back on to the road, riding their horses as cavalrymen should. So, they chatted and laughed with good humour although lashed by the tongue of their Corporal, who clearly did not share their sense of well being.

Tull could see that Ketch was in a dark mood and the west countryman did his best to see that the bubbling torrent of words associated with Trooper Holditch were kept well away from his Corporal. The three of them were old comrades, but that would not save them if they were the cause of exacerbating his current sourness.

Ketch's frown and sharp words were born of a number of forces. He was still feeling rejected by Major Blake and Thurloe, smarting inside at the ingratitude of those who had used him. However, this resentment of his treatment, although he would not admit this to himself, was still tinged with a hope of once more being involved in such exciting matters. Thus, his recent experiences were producing an emotional uncertainty within him. What ultimately had pushed his mood to the darker end of the spectrum were the rumours of a wounded cavalier about the town. He had no wish, at all, to find and arrest Ralph Desborough. He had also heard of Le Vaughn's market square triumph of the day before.

"Come on, you lazy dogs" he cried.

"Prepare yourselves for some real soldiering. You've had too fancy a time in this ale house."

"God's Host on Earth," he sarcastically exclaimed.

"You don't look like you're ready, to go about his work, Nathanial Larkin."

The Troopers scurried about in response to his orders. They knew that in reality this was pretty mild behaviour and that if Ketch had a serious dissatisfaction with them it would be far worse. Although spurred on by their Corporal to continue their preparations for London, they momentarily stopped to look as two of the inn's servants carried Cornet Marlowe out into the yard. A third servant hurried before them with a chair. Ketch was delighted to see his officer was on the mend.

"Gently there" he growled.

"Place him in the sunlight. Let's get some warmth onto the Cornet."

"Well Ketch" grunted Marlowe, as he gingerly moved in the chair making himself comfortable.

"I am out on parole. The apothecary says as long as I rest the leg I can sit outside and I might be fit to travel a few miles tomorrow. In the cart" he grimaced.

"Trussed up like a sack of potatoes."

Ketch smiled and then sighed. Cornet Marlowe travelling by cart might be a welcome sight, but he doubted he would retain his good humour on being bumped along the London road.

"Ketch" said Marlowe.

"Get me into that corner where it is quiet, keep the men at work, and then when you are ready come and have some words."

Ketch organised the moving of the Cornet to a quiet corner of the yard and after issuing a few more tasks, he rejoined the Cornet.

"You have had a dangerous time here in Northampton" said Marlowe "and I would not be surprised if your mysterious Major Blake did not once more seek to use your talents".

"To tell the truth", replied Ketch, with a strange remembrance in his eyes.

"I enjoyed the excitement of it all, for I found great pleasure in the test of mind and spirit that such duties bring; but as for any future opportunities for such matters, who is to tell? I would like to say goodbye to clerk Hedlow, 'though. Things have turned out badly for him now that Le Vaughn has Northampton and sent us all scurrying back to London. Whether the recovery of the King's letter will make any difference to all our fortunes only the future will tell us." Ketch stood to give, a final few orders to his troop, so that they would be fully prepared to leave on the morrow. Botterill the innkeeper came out of the back door of the Peacock and walked up to the sitting Cornet, and in a torrent of words said I don't know what this all means and I think you must now stay and we shall need you, sir, for you must help us now..."

"In God's name, stop babbling!" growled Marlowe. "What are you saying, man? What has happened? Speak slowly and to the point of it."

Botterill, stood before the Cornet shaking with fear and trepidation.

"The army have taken possession of the King's person at Holdenby House and taken him away. Two hundred Troopers have him, no one knows where. What will happen to him is now in God's hands, but he is the better off, for scarce did this news reach us than there was murder in the castle. Lord Le Vaughn, the richest man in England, is dead... and another

Lord as well, and Colonel Fell, the garrison commander has disappeared."

Botterill, looked a pitiable sight with his slumped shoulders and wheedling voice.

"What will happen now?" he whined fully warming to his tale.

"Who will protect us? Your men must now stay here! "

At this he fell to his knees before the Cornet.

Initially bemused, but rapidly gaining sense of the messages brought by the innkeeper, the Cornet kept Botterill on his knees as he began to carefully cross question him. Ketch could scarce take in all he had heard."I must see Hedlow, Cornet, he will make sense of this."

Ketch, although in a hurry, forced himself to walk slowly through the streets of Northampton. He could feel almost physically the news of the King's seizure and the events at the Castle being passed on from house to house, friend to friend, neighbour to neighbour. The atmosphere about the town was one of excitement and release. He could hear snatches of conversations between townsfolk; traders were giving out the news to attract passers-by to their stalls. The fear that he had felt on first arriving in the town was ebbing away. Cornet Marlowe and his troop were now the legitimate authority in the town.

As he made his way to Clerk Hedlow's house, he could see in the near distance becket's well. It seemed a long time since the murder of Preacher Hayack.

A bloody murder which had yet to be resolved.

For some time, he had been sure as to the person responsible for the deed but had not pursued the matter as a result of the urgency of recent events. He was also uncertain as to how to proceed. However, he could not leave Northampton without sharing this knowledge with someone who, whilst in authority, had a sympathy with those in despair. He would raise the matter with Hedlow in taking his leave.

He was welcomed into the house by a serious faced Robert, who gestured to him to remain quiet as he ushered him into the small parlour. Before him sitting on the small settle in Hedlow's parlour were Mary and Martha Desborough, deep in conversation with the old clerk. Seeing Ketch, the clerk welcomed him in. The two sisters were both alarmed and frightened at this sudden appearance of someone whom they thought of as an enemy. They sat together, both fearful and defiant at what this Roundhead Trooper would do with them

"Come in, come in, Ketch" said Hedlow.

"I believe you know these two ladies. They have released themselves from Lord Le Vaughn's custody and are resting preparatory to a long period of residence in a quiet and remote part of the county.

Their brother, Ralph, has disappeared, having secured their release. I am sure that the army will have little cause to detain them from their journey - do you not agree?"

"Their brother's disappearance is indeed a mystery," said Ketch.

"I had heard reports of a wounded royalist wandering the town seeking sanctuary. Such a potentially dangerous man should be apprehended.

Martha rose to her feet.

"My brother is a gallant and brave man, Corporal Ketch, who says he has failed his King and his family. He is weak and wounded, and a man who once did you a kind service when you had a knife at your throat. Martha turned her eyes upwards to the parlour ceiling - and the room above.

"You could take your man if you wish, Corporal!"

With her two hands clenched in front of her, Martha stood in front of Ketch, silent, waiting. Ketch, in turn, stood fair square in front of Martha and looked deep into her hard, determined brown eyes. He mused, stroked the nose of his pale face, and then smiled the sweet, slow smile that warmed his face into handsomeness.

"You shall have him, Martha. He is no threat to the Army, and Cornet Marlowe's troop is on its way to London. I have just called in to say goodbye to my friend, the Clerk."

Martha sank down on the settle by her sister, and the two women embraced tearfully. Discreetly, Ketch turned to Hedlow.

"Lord Le Vaughn is dead. Colonel Fell has flown the country, and the Army has Charles Stuart firmly in its own grasp. I do not think that these ladies are so dangerous that they must be detained by me. They have suffered a grievous loss."

Ketch addressed the two women.

"I do not know your full story," said Ketch.

"But I can see that you are both tired and completely exhausted, and have others to attend to. I have no doubt that you have been brave and resolute in defence of your cause and your family but now you would be well to be away from Northampton as is soonest possible."

"Thank you " said Martha in a low voice.

"We have sought the protection of the Clerk, and he has been an honourable man and a true friend to two women of no substance and many enemies. Before your news he was prepared to run the risk of Lord Le Vaughn's displeasure and the violence of Colonel Fell. He is a fine and brave man" and she smiled her thanks at Hedlow.

"You, sir," as she turned back to Ketch, "also have shown a kindness towards us,we, who opposed your hopes and sought to deceive you. On behalf of us both, I thank you."

All this proved too emotional for Mary who broke into sobs born of relief and a bone-weary tiredness.

"Come, come," cried Hedlow.

"Enough of this! You ladies require peace and rest before you undertake any journey. For the moment, this is a safe place for you. Robert shall take you upstairs where you may rest and sleep."

The order was given and, as the drooping sisters left the room, Hedlow beckoned Ketch to a chair.

"Well, Ketch, I am not only pleased to see you but the news you bring turns my world around and that's no mistake! Le Vaughn dead you say and Fell gone! That is handsome news indeed for Northampton. No doubt the army is pleased to have the King in their grasp, but for us, today means a new time - a better time - for Northampton. The yoke of a cruel garrison has been lifted; the town will be able once more to manage its own affairs, and I may have a position of Secretary to the Council once more. Indeed, my friend, you bring a message of deliverance."

"Unfortunately, I cannot stay in Northampton," said Ketch.

"The Cornet wishes to be away back to London and we shall leave today. I think your task would have been easier had we stayed, but there is already a feeling of release with the news that Le Vaughn and Fell no longer have this town in their grasp."

"You are of course quite correct, Ketch we shall manage well enough even without you. I expect at any moment to have Councillors Trussell, and Lugg knocking on my door with plans to restore their authority" and he smiled wryly.

"I shall have much to do, but I shall find time to look after the ladies above and make certain that they are got safely out of Northampton."Lowering his voice, a little he continued.

"Evidently you had some success with your quest, both you and our mysterious Major Blake have been busy."

"Yes" replied Ketch.

"The King's letter was found and delivered to the highest in the army, who finally was convinced that Charles Stuart was no longer to be trusted. Now the army have him - and no doubt the politics will go on."

Hedlow, laughed.

"You have become very cynical very quickly, Ketch. You must be careful not to lose your engaging innocence and honesty."

"Between ourselves, my friend", said Ketch.

"I must be careful not to lose my soul in the company I have signed up for!But," he continued.

His face became grave.

"There is another matter I would discuss with you."

"I wonder" he continued,

“If I could trouble your servant, Anne, to pour us two glasses of your excellent red wine."

But of course, replied Hedlow, looking somewhat surprised.

“It was remiss of me not to have offered you refreshment.”

He stopped sensing the serious mood. Once more he rang his silver bell and instructed the answering Anne to pour the wine

Anne moved without spirit, seeming devoid of interest in those about her. Her face was partly hidden by her heavy wings of hair. As she moved about the room performing her task, Ketch started to speak to Hedlow in a slightly raised and artificial tone. By this sudden change in his manner, he quickly grasped the Clerk's attention.

"There is the matter of the unresolved murder of preacher Hayeck," said Ketch.

“A nasty, bloody affair which must still deeply trouble the citizens of Northampton."

"Indeed" answered Hedlow, not quite understanding the purpose of the conversation.

"There are few who will go anywhere near that well after dark even when desperate for water. To think that such a monster still lurks amongst us is most distressing."

"Yes" continued Ketch.

"But I wonder if the murderer is necessarily a monster. There could perhaps be circumstances that might explain, if not excuse, such an act."

"I find that somewhat hard to accept, Ketch" interjected the Clerk.

"It was a most bloody affair."

"Yes" agreed Ketch.

"But let me just pursue these thoughts a little further. The blood you refer to was indeed much in evidence, but of course the preacher was a man who himself had drawn the blood of many others. He was well known for the savage way in which he dealt with many of the female royalist camp followers after Naseby."

Hedlow gave a warning look towards the now rigid form of Anne as she stood before Hedlow's dresser quietly staring intently into a glass held in her left hand. Ketch rose to his feet and stared out into Hedlow's garden as he continued his tale

"Blood there was on his forehead, the result of the blow dealt him by Ralph Desborough, blood at the back of his head, the result of Martha Desborough pushing him over against the well. That was the blow that left him unconscious on his left side. More blood there was from the fatal knife stroke to his stomach, dealt to him by his murderer, who departed leaving the Preacher lying on his right side. All this is agreed by you and your nephew, the Constable."

Ketch turned from the window, and his quiet voice filled the room.

"What we have not addressed is the name of this person who would plunge a knife deep into the stomach of an unconscious man and why they would undertake such a terrible task."

"Do you know who this person is?" asked Hedlow in a low quiet voice as he saw Ketch's eyes fixed on the immobile Anne.

In response to the Clerk's question, Ketch crossed the room and gently took the glass from Anne and set it down on the gleaming dresser. Still holding her by the wrist, he sat down once more in his chair. Anne stood next to him with her head bowed low.

"I ask you to consider, Hedlow," he continued, his voice now soft.

"Not as a learned clerk or man of law, but as a man, the following tale of unhappiness and despair. A young woman, perhaps following her lover, somehow becomes a part of the King's army before Naseby. She witnesses the sickening nature of men dying in pain and agony. Unable to escape, she herself is found, when the fighting is over, by the battlefield scavengers who come out to loot and steal from the dead, to rape and torture all the wounded and weak they can find. She is not spared, and is forced to endure bodily humiliation that you and I Hedlow could not even imagine. Worse even than that, those that have abused her have a final indignity to impose. They cut her face slowly and with pleasure so that in future the whole world will know of her humiliation and abuse. There will be no escape, ever, for her. No man will want her, she will be forever a pariah. They almost certainly laughed as they cut her, for they tried as much with me on a separate occasion."

As Ketch told his tale he continued to hold gently the wrist of Anne, who remained standing silently by his side but now with her head turned away and lowered. Hedlow sat forward in his chair his attention totally absorbed by what Ketch was saying

"She found safety in the house of a good man who took her in as a servant and treated her kindly. She slowly began to find some peace.But one day she sees the same group of men, who tortured her, still harassing people and searching for victims. One night, quite by chance, she goes to draw water from the well, a kind act to help a house look after a soldier who has experienced an attack, similar to that which she herself endured. Her own nightmare is brought forcibly back to her. Then, through some providence she finds her main torturer lying by the well apparently asleep or unconscious. She can save her peace, her new life or she can continue to live as a potential future victim dreading his eventual discovery of her. Perhaps that is too kind an explanation. It may well have been a burning desire for revenge that drove her to drive her knife deep into his bowels."

"May God save her soul" exclaimed Hedlow softly.

"He was a wicked man he should not have another victim. Such a woman would need forgiveness, care and understanding, a safe place to live, time to rediscover her dignity and her God."

"So, thought I, also" agreed Ketch and he stood to his feet and gently released Anne's hand.

"Go about your master's business Anne. We have no further business with you."

Without a word Anne turned her face first to Ketch, and then to Hedlow. Her lips trembled with the start of a smile, before the tears started to flow from her eyes and she ran from the room.

Ketch turned to the old clerk to see his face revealing an astonishment he had previously kept under control.

"So, Anne murdered Preacher Hayek," he exclaimed.

"Her motives are clear once explained, but how did you know that she had actually done it."

"I don't, and I never really will, not for certain" replied Ketch, and with something approaching a weary sigh he sat back into his chair."She has not denied it and that is sufficient confirmation for me. It was the pails of water that told of her movements in the night. Although dazed and battered that night from my own clash with the preacher and Titus. I remembered the free use of water you and Robert made when bathing my wound and making up some soup. Yet the next morning both pails were ,once more full of water. Robert had brought only one pail from the well and had looked after me through the night, and that only left Anne. And I remembered footsteps hurrying to this house in my delirium that night. It is strange that even after such a deadly knife stroke she still wished to fulfil her domestic duties and refill those pails."

"Pails which finally betrayed her to you " said Hedlow.

"But if I read your disposition aright, Ketch, this is where this matter of blood will end. You and I, and one other person, will know who killed Preacher Hayack."

Ketch nodded his assent, and the two men were quiet for some moments, each with his own thoughts. Then Ketch stirred, rose to his feet and took his leave from the kindly clerk.

As he turned from his final parting at the front door, he caught a glimpse of a graceful form, a smile and a pale hand raised in farewell. He was given no time to reflect for at that very moment two men of substance were bearing down upon Hedlow's home and calling his attention. Ketch gave a final salute and left Hedlow to the mercy of his council colleagues.

A troop of some twenty cavalrymen, in double line, steadily walked their horses up the hill past the monument to Eleanor of Castile. In a small cart behind travelled an injured officer who, from time to time, bellowed orders to a pale faced Trooper who seemed to be in charge. Ketch did not mind the Cornet's temper; he could in turn, if he so wished, chase his comrades Tull and Holditch. The troop was in good humour. They were out of a town that had not welcomed them, but had been sorry to see them leave. Their army and its leader, Cromwell, seemed to have a firm grip on England's affairs and they were on their way back to their regiment. Only Ketch had a feeling of loss, but he knew that even that was not real. Deep down inside himself he knew he had done well. And who knew but that Major Blake and Secretary Thurloe would have work again for him some day.